MURDER IN CHIANTI

T. A. WILLIAMS

Boldwood

First published in Great Britain in 2023 by Boldwood Books Ltd.

Copyright © T. A. Williams, 2023

Cover Design by CC Book Design

Cover Photography: Shutterstock

Every effort has been made to obtain the necessary permissions with reference to copyright material, both illustrative and quoted. We apologise for any omissions in this respect and will be pleased to make the appropriate acknowledgements in any future edition.

A CIP catalogue record for this book is available from the British Library.

Paperback ISBN 978-1-80483-228-8

Large Print ISBN 978-1-80483-227-1

Hardback ISBN 978-1-80483-229-5

Ebook ISBN 978-1-80483-226-4

Kindle ISBN 978-1-80483-225-7

Audio CD ISBN 978-1-80483-234-9

MP3 CD ISBN 978-1-80483-233-2

Digital audio download ISBN 978-1-80483-232-5

Boldwood Books Ltd
23 Bowerdean Street
London SW6 3TN
www.boldwoodbooks.com

To Mariangela and Christina, who both like a good whodunnit. With love, as ever.

PROLOGUE

TUESDAY MORNING

Beppe had always liked early mornings, and particularly in high summer as it was now. It had been a hot, clammy night and at this time of day, before the heat built up and settled over the countryside in a stifling pall, he felt refreshed. Although he had lived in this part of Tuscany for over sixty years, he knew he would happily swap the heat of July for a cold winter's day. Here in the shade of the trees it certainly wasn't cold by a long chalk, but the temperature was bearable. He stuck his hand out of the open window and directed the cooler morning air onto his face as the Land Rover bumped up the track alongside the golf course. It felt good to be alive.

He was shaken out of his contemplative mood by young Alfredo alongside him – for once without his nose buried in his phone.

'What's that, Beppe? Is it a wild boar?'

They had just come off the track past the woods and were moving out onto the eighth fairway, approaching the hole. Beppe followed the line of the pointing finger and saw a dark shape lying in the sand of the bunker to the right of the green.

'It'd better not be. We checked the fence only last week. Those damn things can do untold damage to the course in just a few hours,' Beppe grumbled in annoyance. 'And we haven't even brought the rifle.'

'Shall we go and scare it off?'

There was a degree of apprehension in Alfredo's voice and rightly so. An elderly farmer from the next village had been badly injured by a boar in his own vineyard only a few months back. But this morning they had solid protection in the shape of the Land Rover. Beppe didn't hesitate and he spun the wheel, heading straight for the bunker.

It was only as they drew closer that the realisation began to dawn on them that it wasn't a wild boar after all. The shape in the sand was unmistakably human.

'Do you think he's...?' Alfredo liked to give the impression of being a tough boy with his tattoos and his earring, but his tone now was that of a nervous teenager.

Beppe snorted. 'Drunk and passed out, more likely. Though why he had to come up here to one of my beautiful bunkers to sleep it off, I don't know.' He drew up a few yards short of the sand trap and climbed out. 'Well, he's going to get a rude awakening, that's for sure.'

He strode up to the lip of the bunker and stopped dead as he realised that this man would never have another awakening – rude or otherwise.

'Jesus!' He pulled off his cap and ran his fingers through his thinning hair. 'Would you look at that!'

'Oh God...'

Beside him, Beppe was vaguely aware of Alfredo's sharp intake of breath as they contemplated the figure sprawled in the bunker. The sand around his head had turned black as the blood from the catastrophic wounds had soaked away. They stood there, rooted to the spot, for a good long time before Beppe realised that there was something all too familiar about the clothes and the body. He hurried around the lip of the bunker until he could see the side of the man's face that wasn't buried in the sand. The grey moustache and the perfect teeth were unmistakable, as was the broad-brimmed, Australian leather sunhat lying over by the sand trap rake. There could be no doubt about it. Spinning around to the boy, who was as white as a sheet, he broke the news to him.

'It's Signor Hunter.' He couldn't believe what he was about to say. 'Somebody's killed Signor Hunter.'

'Are you sure he's dead? Shouldn't we check?' He started to head towards the body, but Beppe reached out and stopped him before he stepped into the sand.

'Don't go any closer. The police will need to come and investigate.'

'But what if he's still alive? Shouldn't we go for help?' Alfredo was still sounding shaky.

Beppe's eyes flicked back to the mangled corpse for a second or two. 'He's past help, Alfredo. Take the Land Rover and hurry back to the clubhouse. Tell them what's happened while I phone the police.'

'What *has* happened?'

'He's been killed, murdered, that's what's happened. Haven't you got eyes in your head?' Seeing the boy still staring vacantly at the crumpled heap in the sand, he clapped his hands to rouse him from his stunned state. 'Go, boy, go and tell everybody.'

By the time Alfredo had turned the vehicle and set off again, Beppe was already through to the emergency services.

1

TUESDAY NIGHT

'Are you as hot as I am, Oscar?'

Hearing his name, the dog opened one eye, but only for a second or two before lapsing back into a comatose state on the terracotta tiles. He was stretched out across the floor with his pink tongue hanging halfway out of his mouth. He looked as hot as I felt. Above him, the grainy black and white movie on *TV Toscana* was just finishing with a cacophony of discordant music. The soundtrack had been slightly out of sync all the way through, but that minor inconvenience had been eclipsed by the truly woeful dubbing into Italian. I had lost count of the number of times the scantily clad heroine had opened her mouth to scream a single syllable – unmistakably 'Help!' – and the middle-aged voiceover actress rendering her into Italian had produced '*aiuto*', no fewer than three syllables. Still, the movie had taught me a few more bits of Italian vocabulary so it hadn't been all bad, although I doubted just how many times in my life I was going to need to reproduce the word for 'werewolf'.

I gave my own pet werewolf an affectionate prod with my toe and continued my one-sided conversation with him; something

I'd been doing a lot of over the past year since he had entered my life.

'Well, even if *you're* comfortable, I'm boiling. How about a walk?'

As usual, the magic word galvanised the Labrador into action and he leapt to his feet, shook himself, and made a beeline for the door. Outside it was a little fresher than in the house, but still very warm even though the sun had set three hours earlier. The sky was clear and the stars were shining brightly enough to cast faint shadows of me and my dog against the white gravel track. Up here in the hills there was little light pollution apart from the distant orange glow of Florence to the north-east, and the only noise was the gentle sighing of the lightest of breezes in the branches above me. As my four-legged friend and I walked up the hill between the never-ending succession of cypress trees lining the track, I breathed deeply and reflected on how my life had changed so radically in less than a year. I was now retired, divorced, a budding writer, and living in a totally different country; and I didn't regret any of it apart from the divorce thing.

But that hadn't been my decision.

My reflections were interrupted by my phone. Unlike when I was DCI Armstrong of Scotland Yard, a phone call nowadays was something to be eagerly awaited and enjoyed. No longer was I being woken in the middle of the night to be told of yet another brutal murder in the big city. No more interrupted dinners or hasty departures at all hours, leaving an increasingly disillusioned wife all alone until she could take it no more. In the end, I had even left the force in the hope of winning her back, but it had been too little, too late. I was a free man now, but it had been a heavy price to pay.

This call turned out to be from Virgilio and it was more business than pleasure. Virgilio Pisano had become my best friend over here in Tuscany. He was in many ways what I used to be: a police inspector in the murder squad – in his case in the historic city of Florence – but he was lucky enough still to be happily married to his lovely wife, Lina. It came as no surprise to find that although it was almost midnight he was still in the office.

'*Ciao*, Dan. You weren't asleep, were you? Is it warm enough for you?' We always spoke Italian together these days.

'I thought I was going to melt this afternoon. I have a feeling I'm going to have to invest in aircon.' It was very unusual for him to call me so late so I had a feeling it might be work-related. 'What about you? How's business?'

'Booming as ever in the summer months. Why do people come all the way to Florence to strangle their wives or push somebody off the top of a tower? Anyway, look, the reason I'm calling is this: there's been a murder.'

'Now why doesn't that come as a surprise? Who, where, and when? And, come to think of it, why me?' I groaned theatrically. 'Don't you realise I've been retired now for over a year?'

Virgilio ignored the retirement remark. 'The who is a guy called Rex Hunter. The where is the Acquarossa Country Club, which is only a short drive from where you are, and the when is some time yesterday evening. I'll know more when I get the pathologist's report.'

'And the why me is because the guy had an English name?' Although Virgilio spoke good English, he called on me from time to time to help out. Although the official line was that when he was dealing with English speakers he called me in as an interpreter, we both knew that I quite enjoyed keeping my investigative hand in, and he appreciated my help.

'The victim was Australian and had been living here for seven years since buying the country club and golf course.'

'He *bought* it? No shortage of money there, then, by the sound of it.'

'Apparently he made a fortune in Australia before settling down over here. Although the staff at the country club are mostly local, his wife and family are over here and some of them speak little or no Italian, so I might need your help if you have time.'

'If I have time?' We both knew the answer to that one. Although I'd been filling my days writing my new book and reno-vating the little house I'd just bought, I had already discovered that retirement can sometimes get boring. 'No problem. When do you need me? Do you want me to come with you when you inter-view the family?'

'I've already spoken to most of them briefly in the course of today, but I'll need to speak to them again some time in more depth, and for that I'd like your help. But, first of all, what I was wondering was whether you might feel like going over to the club and signing up for a bit of tennis coaching. We both know your backhand needs work.'

He and I played tennis together most Saturdays, so he knew what he was talking about. 'Does that mean you want me to go under cover?'

'Sort of. At least at first. Give them your real name and don't make up stories, but just don't mention any connection with the police – over here or back in London. Maybe that way you can get people talking more freely and find out a bit more about the victim, the club, and his family than they're prepared to tell me. At the moment, I have a dead body but no apparent motive for murder, although I've already got the impression that the man wasn't universally liked. Anyway, how about it?'

I didn't hesitate. Like I said, Virgilio was my best friend over here. 'Of course I'll do it. I'll drive over there tomorrow and sign up for some lessons. How was the guy killed?'

'The back of his head was smashed in – and I mean smashed in, multiple blows. The murder weapon appears to have been one of his golf clubs found in the long grass near the scene of the crime.' There was a pause while he checked the file. 'A Callaway Mavrik driver, if that means anything to you. Golf's a mystery to me.'

'A driver's a big, hefty club with a long shaft, I know that much. If the person holding it managed to aim straight, even a kid could produce enough force to smash somebody's head in. Any prints on it?'

'No prints but the lab's still doing chemical and DNA analysis, but they say I shouldn't hold my breath. It looks as though it's been wiped clean.'

'Any clues on or around the body?'

'He was found lying in a sand trap, which had been meticulously raked all over to eliminate any footprints. Needless to say, even the handle of the rake had also been wiped clean. The murderer covered his tracks – literally.'

'And what about alibis for the people on site?'

'Assuming it happened yesterday evening, initial impression is that they all seem to be in the clear – to some extent. Like I say, I'll know more when the lab gives me a time of death.'

We chatted some more, and he asked me if I needed instructions on how to get to the club, but I told him there was no need. It was only a short drive away and I'd even been there for dinner the previous month when my daughter and her fiancé had been visiting. My future son-in-law was a keen squash player, so I'd taken him over there to give him a chance to beat me while Tricia lazed by the pool. The meal had been a bit pricey but pretty good. Otherwise, the inside of the place hadn't really made much of an impact on me, although the perfectly maintained grounds had been impressive. Most of our fellow diners had been golfers and it's not a game I've ever played, although colleagues on the force were always telling me it was a good way to get promotion – presumably by playing the boss and letting him win. As it was, my immediate superior had been a corpulent superintendent who was no doubt far happier with a round of toast, butter, and jam than anything as active as a round of golf.

After Virgilio had rung off, I sat down on a fallen tree trunk – a regular stopping point for Oscar and me – and pulled out my phone. A quick search revealed that tennis lessons could be booked online and three minutes later I had a two-hour session booked the following morning with somebody called Abigail. It wasn't going to be cheap, but Virgilio had told me his department would be picking up the bill. Before putting my phone away, I googled Rex Hunter and found him straight away.

There were numerous entries for the man, and it very swiftly became clear that he was a well-known figure back in his native Australia. He had made a fortune out of a series of 'heap leach' plants in Queensland. Further investigation revealed that these were a way of extracting fine particles of gold from old slag heaps and it appeared that he had cornered the market and come out with millions in the bank as a result. Why he had decided to emigrate to Europe, and to Tuscany in particular, was not revealed, but as far as I could see there was no question of him having left Australia under a cloud, so the chances of his death being the work of an Australian with a grudge were slim. It seemed likely that his killer was to be found here in Italy.

By this time, Oscar had tired of bringing me pine cones to kick so he could bring them back and drop them at my feet – he had definitely inherited the retriever gene – and had stretched out in the dry pine needles. He looked as if he would be more than happy to spend the night there. I, on the other hand, needed to get back to the house and get ready for tomorrow. I gave him a gentle nudge with the toe of my shoe and saw his eyes open, glowing an eerie green in the starlight.

'Come on, dog. Some of us have got work to do.'

Although Oscar didn't look too impressed, this sounded really rather good to me. The prospect of a brief return to my previous life was going to be welcome.

2

WEDNESDAY MORNING

The Acquarossa Country Club also looked welcoming as I drove in the following morning. The golf course, sports complex, and restaurant stretched over a pair of gently rolling hills to the south of Florence, the whole site dotted with the iconic Tuscan mix of umbrella pines and cypress trees. On my way there, I'd driven through acre after acre of the legendary Chianti vineyards, the rows of vines laid out with mathematical precision and punctuated by olive groves. The entrance to the club was through impressive stone gateposts and the drive to the clubhouse was flanked by an aromatic mixture of rosemary bushes covered in blue blossoms and a fine selection of colourful roses. It was easy to see that the ground staff here earned their keep. The clubhouse itself had probably once been a pair of large stone barns, now tastefully joined together into one unit by a complex network of glazed corridors leading to a main atrium. This was clearly the work of an architect and, equally clearly, it hadn't been cheap.

Virgilio had ordered that the golf course remain closed for now so there were very few people around. The only signs of life were a couple of young people in tennis gear heading back to the clubhouse after an early morning game and a fit-looking woman in a crop top and shorts who jogged past me. I gave her a little wave, but she was clearly 'in the zone' and gave no acknowledgement of my greeting. As she passed me, I saw that her cheeks were glistening with moisture. I wondered idly if this was just perspiration – it was already really warm – or if she had heard the news of the murder and was grieving. One thing was for sure: if young people like these were sweating, it didn't bode too well for a middle-aged man like me. Maybe I should have opted for just *one* hour of tennis coaching.

Although under normal circumstances I would have come ready changed and then driven home for a shower afterwards, I had brought my tennis gear in a bag as I thought it might be a good idea to use as many of the facilities as possible, so as to get an overall feel of the place. Leaving the car in the car park, I followed a path between lush shrubs and clumps of lavender swarming with bees. It was a charming spot and it seemed incredible that it could have been the scene of a brutal and gruesome murder only thirty-six hours previously.

I walked into the reception area through automatic glass doors that hissed closed behind me and the cool of the air-conditioned interior felt positively polar after the heat outside – but I wasn't complaining. After fifty-five years living in London, my first full summer in Tuscany was proving a challenge, although I kept telling myself that if a fur-clad Labrador could handle it, then so could I. Mind you, Oscar had been born here, so he was far better prepared for high temperatures than I was.

The entrance hall was a large open area, and the wall opposite the door was emblazoned with a tasteful, deep-green logo of a pair of cypress trees and the name of the club. On the right-hand wall was a polished wooden board with a list of names of winners of various golf tournaments picked out in gold. Below it was a glass-fronted cabinet containing a selection of trophies, ranging from gold plates to what looked like a silver Chianti flask. Photos of golf celebrities, some of whom I even recognised, decorated the rest of the wall, and all around the room were beautifully maintained plants in terracotta pots. There was no doubt about it: this place was definitely upmarket. A young man wearing a smart blue blazer and a tie bearing the same green logo gave me a smile from behind a marble-topped counter running along the opposite wall.

'Buongiorno. Benvenuto ad Acquarossa.' Hedging his bets, he also added in English, 'Good morning, sir. Welcome to Acquarossa Country Club.'

I walked over, dropped my bag at my feet, and answered him in Italian, even though his English sounded good. This wasn't just because I was secretly rather proud of the way my Italian fluency had improved over the course of my first full year here. I was going to be chatting to people here in Italian so there was no point in dissimulating. A badge on his lapel indicated that his name was Raffaello, and he was probably in his early twenties. 'Good morning. My name's Armstrong, Dan Armstrong, and I'm booked for some tennis lessons.'

He consulted a computer screen and confirmed that Abigail would be waiting for me at ten. He pointed out the entrance to the changing rooms and gave me directions to the courts. I thanked him and decided it wouldn't hurt to start my nosing about with him. I decided to plead ignorance.

'The car park's remarkably empty considering it's such a beautiful day. I would have thought you'd have lots of golfers here, or is it too hot for them?'

He shook his head. 'I'm afraid the course is closed. It's been closed since yesterday.'

'How's that?' I did my best to sound surprised. 'Isn't this a busy time for you?'

'Normally, yes.' I saw his eyes dart around before he lowered his voice to explain. 'I'm afraid there's been a death.'

'What, here? At the club?'

'I'm afraid so: on the golf course, by the eighth hole.' His voice dropped even lower. 'It was murder.'

'Wow. And who was murdered?'

'The owner of the club, Signor Hunter.'

'How terrible, and no doubt very sad.'

'Yes... yes, of course.' I could see him doing his best to look suitably sombre, but his tone gave him away and I tried giving him a gentle prod.

'But...? It maybe wasn't as sad as all that?'

Once again, he looked around furtively. Seeing nobody within earshot, he nodded. 'I'm sorry he was killed. Nobody deserves that, but he wasn't an easy man...'

At that moment, a door behind him opened and an attractive woman who looked as if she was in her forties walked in. She was wearing a blue skirt and an immaculate white blouse and, seeing me, she produced a welcoming smile that didn't quite hide the dark rings under her eyes.

'Good morning, welcome to Acquarossa.' Her badge indicated that her name was Elizabeth, and she was the assistant manager. Unlike the young man, her Italian accent revealed that she wasn't a native speaker, so I switched to English and saw that she understood.

'Good morning, my name's Dan. I'm here for some tennis coaching.'

The smile broadened. 'Good to see you, Dan. Are you here on holiday?' The accent was unmistakably Australian, and I wondered if she might be a member of the Hunter family.

'No, I live here now. I'm a writer.' That was a bit of a stretch. Okay, so my first book was currently being looked at by a small publisher in London, but I wasn't holding out too much hope of it being published any time soon.

'How interesting. Anything I might have read?'

'Afraid not. I should have said that I'm an *aspiring* author. I've only just finished writing my first book.'

'Well, good luck with it. Is this the first time you've been here to the club?'

I told her about the squash game and the meal the previous month, but then left them to it and headed off to the changing rooms. Two things were clear: Virgilio's suspicion that Rex Hunter hadn't been the most popular of men appeared to be dead right, and Elizabeth the assistant manager was either worried about something or maybe grieving for her dead boss more than her colleague on the front desk.

I changed into my tennis gear, stuffed my clothes into a locker, and made my way outside again. The heat hit me like a physical slap, and it occurred to me yet again that the idea of running about for two hours in the sun at my age probably wasn't that wise. I hoped there wasn't going to be a second unexpected death at the Acquarossa Country Club – in this case a fifty-six-year-old ex-copper who should have known better.

I walked past a row of parked golf buggies, looking for the tennis courts. These were about a hundred yards from the clubhouse, partially hidden from sight by a meticulously pruned laurel hedge and surrounded by a high wire fence. The good news was that the court where I was to be playing was partially shaded by three massive umbrella pines, each of them taller than the clubhouse itself. At this time of day, they provided welcome relief from the sun but I estimated the sun would have moved around by noon and we would be fully exposed. My coach was already waiting for me with a basket of tennis balls, and she came over to shake my hand.

'Hi, I'm Abigail. You okay with English?' Her accent was British. She was a good-looking woman, maybe in her late twenties, and with her blonde hair and long, golden-tanned legs I felt sure she would be popular over here in Italy. It hadn't taken me long to discover that Italians had a thing about blondes. And why not?

I introduced myself and we chatted a little before starting the lesson. I learnt that this was her second year here and that she lived in the nearby village of Acquarossa. There were no rings on her fingers, and she made no mention of a partner.

We knocked a ball about for ten minutes or so until she had got an idea of my level and my weaknesses. When we stopped and met at the net, she gave me her diagnosis and unsurprisingly it started with my backhand. For the next hour or so she instructed me until I could feel a definite improvement in my game, and this cheered me. Even if it turned out that I might not be able to help Virgilio solve the murder, I would at least be getting some positive benefit from my visit to the club.

By the time we stopped for a break and a welcome drink of water, I was sweating profusely and willingly accepted her suggestion of sitting down on a bench in the shade for a few minutes. After discussion of my tennis progress, I turned the conversation to recent events. This was what I was there for, after all.

'I gather from Raffaello at Reception that there's been a murder: the owner of this place, apparently.'

Abigail, too, took a surreptitious look around before responding. 'That's right: Rex Hunter. They say he was beaten to death with his own club.' Like Raffaello, she didn't sound too cut up about her boss's death. In fact, she didn't sound in the least bit distressed by his demise.

'Do the police have any suspects?' I tried to distance myself from the investigation, at least for now.

She shook her head but there was a flicker of something I couldn't immediately identify on her face – dislike, maybe? 'Not that I know of.'

'Any idea why he was killed? We are in Italy, after all; I don't suppose it could have been the mafia, could it?' Virgilio no doubt had people looking into this as a possibility but he hadn't so much as hinted at any involvement with organised crime. Still, I felt it was worth a shot as a conversation starter.

'I have no idea.' There was a long pause, which I didn't interrupt. Finally, she took another apprehensive look around before speaking. 'I really don't know, but I think the police would do well to concentrate their enquiries a bit closer to home.' Another pause. 'He wasn't a very nice man.' Her expression hardened and confirmed my suspicion that what I had spotted before had been distaste or more. 'In fact, he was a horrid man.' In spite of the heat, she actually shuddered.

'Is that the voice of experience speaking? Was he horrid to you?'

'If groping me and propositioning me is what you mean, then yes.' It was looking increasingly as though the murder victim had not endeared himself to many people around here.

'Ah, I see...' I gave it a few seconds. 'But surely he must have been way older than you.'

'About twice my age, but that didn't stop him. Just because he's got... he had money, he thought he could have whatever he wanted.' After another look around, she dropped her eyes to her hands. 'Do you know what he said to me? He said he'd give me "lots of gifts" if I had sex with him. Gifts! What did he think

I was: a common whore?' There was real anger in her voice now.

'And do you think he tried it on with other women here at the club?'

'I'm sure he did. He was a beast.' She shook herself and stood up. 'Anyway, enough about him. Come on, we still need to work on your serve.'

I followed her back onto the court, my thoughts still on Rex Hunter. It would appear that he had been a sex pest and there might be a number of women who would have been happy to see him out of the picture, starting with my tennis coach herself. Mind you, there's a big difference between wanting somebody out of the way and beating them to death with a blunt instrument.

By the time noon came, I was more than happy when the lesson came to an end. Not that I hadn't enjoyed it or found it useful, but my supposition that the sun would have cleared the trees by lunchtime had proved right and it was scorching hot. Even the metal bolt on the gate in the fence around the court was almost too hot to touch. I thanked Abigail and we arranged to have another session next morning at the earlier time of nine, in the hope of avoiding the worst of the heat. Back at the clubhouse, I took a tepid shower and gradually turned the water temperature right down towards the cold setting as my body slowly cooled down. I spared a thought for Oscar. I had left him at home with Maria, who came in on Wednesdays to clean, but she went off at noon so he would be left on his own. I decided to have a quick drink at the bar rather than a meal and head off home before he decided to chew through an electrical cable or raid the fridge, but I resolved to return to the club later on.

The bar ran along one side of the main central atrium. This was a spectacular piece of architecture and the curved glass panels in the roof reminded me of the Eden Project in Cornwall that I had visited with my wife back in happier times. Not unexpectedly, considering where the club was situated, I noticed that they had a terrific selection of different bottles of Chianti on the shelf behind the bar. It was far too hot for alcohol so I ordered two bottles of blissfully cold, alcohol-free beer, to which I was rapidly becoming addicted in the heat of summer. I drained the first one straight away but took my time over the second.

Instead of sitting down at a table, I perched on a barstool and chatted to the young woman behind the bar, who looked as if she was too young to be touching alcohol – but maybe that was just me showing my age. Her name badge indicated that her name was Annalisa, so I spoke to her in Italian. With so few customers she appeared happy to talk and, as with my tennis coach, I gradually brought the conversation around to Mr Hunter.

'I've been hearing about the murder. How awful. Presumably the police have been involved.' I did my best to sound like an interested outsider.

'They were here all day yesterday and I've just been told that they're coming back this afternoon to take statements from everybody.' She looked apprehensive. 'Do they think one of us did it? It's not nice being considered a suspect in a murder case.'

'I'm sure it's just routine.' Which it was. 'They probably need to establish who was where at the time of the murder. As for suspects, do *you* think it might have been somebody here?'

I saw her make as if to speak but then clam up and reach for a cloth to wipe the bar. A shadow fell across us, and I turned to see a man approach. He was a tall man with perfectly styled hair, wearing immaculately ironed blue chinos and a crisp white polo shirt. On his left breast was the logo of Acquarossa Country Club. He extended his hand and treated me to a broad smile. From the ease with which he produced it, I surmised that he had a lot of practice at greeting people.

'Good morning, welcome to the club. I'm Adam Hunter. Did I hear that you've been having tennis lessons?' His accent was faintly Aussie, and he made no attempt to address me in Italian.

He looked as if he was in his mid thirties, which would make him around about the right age to be a son of the victim. If this was the case, then it was interesting that he didn't look particularly overcome with grief at the demise of his father – although he might just be a good actor. He subjected my hand to a firm but thankfully not crunching handshake and I introduced myself in my turn, being careful not to mention my previous occupation or my real reason for being here today. He stayed with me, chatting about inconsequential trivia, ranging from the price of tennis racquets to the best Chianti producers in the area, before taking his leave. As he went off, presumably to schmooze other customers, I returned my attention to Annalisa behind the bar.

'Was that the manager?'

She nodded. 'That's Mr Hunter junior...' She stopped and corrected herself. 'Of course, now I suppose he's just plain Mr Hunter.'

'He seems a nice sort of guy.'

'A lot nicer than his father.' No sooner had she said it than she blushed. 'I'm sorry, I know we shouldn't speak badly of the dead.'

'You didn't like Mr Hunter senior?'

If anything, her blushes increased. 'I don't think many people here did – certainly not many of the women.'

This appeared to be a recurring theme. 'But his son's not like him?'

'Adam's very different from his father. He's okay.'

'Does he live locally?'

She nodded. 'He lives in the bungalow behind the villa.'

'The villa?'

'It's up at the top of the hill among the trees. That's where Mr Hunter lives... I mean, lived.'

'And is Mr Hunter senior's widow involved with the running of the club?'

'Oh no. They only got married a month or so ago and they didn't come back from honeymoon until recently. I've only seen her down here once.'

'Wow, only married a month and already a widow...' This struck me as one hell of a coincidence. I made no comment, but I made a mental note of the fact. Detectives don't like coincidences because, all too often, they turn out not to be coincidences at all.

I took a long swig of my beer and glanced at my watch before trying to sound as casual as I could. 'Can you think of anybody here who might have murdered Mr Hunter?' I drained the last of the beer and was already turning away as she replied.

'Not really. I don't think he had many friends, but that doesn't mean anybody would actually murder him, does it? I mean, who could bring themselves to kill somebody?'

That, of course, was what Virgilio had sent me here to find out. The fact of the matter was that the man had definitely been murdered so somebody, somewhere, had wanted him dead. The next step would be to establish motive for the killing; being a sex pest and not having many friends wasn't going to cut it.

3

WEDNESDAY AFTERNOON

After a light lunch at home of bread, cheese, and a couple of slices of cured ham from the leg I kept in the larder, followed by juicy figs from the gnarled old tree in the garden, I picked up my iPad and checked out the layout of the country club on Google Earth. To the left of the golf course were more Chianti vineyards while, on the right, there was a stretch of woodland sandwiched between the course and an olive grove, with more vineyards beyond. As I pored over the map, it occurred to me that I could probably kill two birds with one stone by giving Oscar a good walk and checking out the scene of the murder at the same time. Maybe I could also take a look at the Hunter family villa on the hilltop as I did so. Signs by the club entrance had made it clear that dogs and golf courses don't mix so I could hardly walk straight up the fairway with Oscar. Dogs – particularly black ones – also don't mix with bright sunshine, so the dense woods looked ideal for a refreshing stroll for both of us.

After giving the Labrador his lunch and both of us drinking a lot of cold water, I piled him into the car and drove back up past the club, stopping at the side of the road several hundred yards beyond the main entrance where a high wire fence indicated the point where the country club finished and the woods started. A decent path led into the trees, and it was pleasantly cool in there sheltered from the sun. Oscar had a fine old time sniffing out and marking what was brand-new territory to him while we climbed the gentle slope. I also did a lot of sniffing about, checking out anything of interest, but I left it to him to pee on the trees.

After about twenty minutes, I calculated that we had probably climbed far enough to be within reach of the bunker on the eighth hole where the body had been found. Sure enough, when I reached the edge of the trees, I could see the sand trap little more than a hundred yards away from me, cordoned off with tape. Between the course and me was the imposing barrier of that same wire fence a couple of metres high. A pair of bored-looking uniformed police officers were sitting on the perfectly cropped grass in the limited shade provided by their 4x4 but there was no sign of Virgilio or any of his murder squad detectives, some of whom I knew reasonably well by now. Not that it would have made any difference if I had seen somebody I knew, as the chain-link fence was taller than I was and there were no gates to be seen. I had to settle for perching on a tree stump while I checked out the location, with my dog scratching about in the dry leaves at my feet, as ever looking for something for me to throw for him to retrieve.

A track ran along the other side of the fence parallel to the course and carried on up the hill past the bunker. Presumably this continued around the course perimeter so as to allow maintenance of the fence, which was no doubt there to keep out any unwelcome guests, both animal and human. Certainly this formidable barrier made it all the more likely that the murderer had approached his prey from within the club grounds rather than from without. The clubhouse at the bottom of the hill looked small from here and I estimated it would have taken the murderer at least fifteen minutes to walk up to the scene of the crime. Although little clumps of trees dotted the course, the vast majority of the terrain was open grassland. Assuming Virgilio was right and the crime had taken place the previous evening when the victim had been playing golf, it would have still been daylight. It would have been hard for a would-be assassin to creep up on his victim without being seen by the man himself or anybody else who might have been out on the course. Did this therefore point to the killer being a member of the club – or at least a visiting player – and maybe known to the victim?

A dense clump of trees on the top of the hill indicated where the family's villa was situated and it looked as though the track provided access to it, although I imagined there also had to be a separate entrance. I decided to carry on up the hill to find out. In order to do this, Oscar and I had to abandon the trees and emerge into the full heat of the sun once more; I was bathed in sweat and Oscar was panting like a steam train by the time we reached a little bump in the ground from where I could see across to the hilltop. He had even given up bringing me sticks to throw for his favourite game of fetch and was padding along to heel unusually obediently for him, sticking in my shadow, and I knew we needed to get back into the shade asap.

The villa was an imposing building almost completely shaded and hidden by a dense plantation of trees, principally cypresses. Beyond it, a little lower down on the far side of the slope, was a more modern roof that probably belonged to Adam Hunter's bungalow. The views from up here were spectacular all the way across the valley of the River Arno and onward towards the deep green of the Apennines beyond. I imagined that from the villa, the Hunter family probably had a good view of Florence itself, although the city was hidden from my sight for now. The murder victim had certainly lived a life of privilege in a place like this; the sort of privilege that can lead to jealousy, envy, and maybe even hostility... but murder? Had the murderer come from here at the club or from elsewhere?

To the consternation of a couple of lizards, I sat down on a dry-stone wall and checked out the scene with a detective's eye. The track on the other side of the fence continued parallel to the wire before disappearing into the trees on the hilltop. Our killer could well have used it to approach the murder scene from above, rather than below, although this would have involved passing very close to the villa and the bungalow. Of course, if the killer had come down *from* one of these buildings, then it would have made things very easy for him or her. As far as I had learnt from Annalisa at the bar, the villa was home to the victim's new wife and the bungalow was where his son, Adam, lived but presumably other people like butlers, housekeepers and so on also lived up there and would need to be investigated.

The path I had been following had all but petered out by this time, so I decided it was far too hot to try and pick my way through the rough scrub of the hillside towards the villa. I turned around and started to return to the car. To be honest, this was also because I've always had a fear of snakes and this parched terrain looked like the perfect environment for a reptile or two. I'd heard that the Tuscan vipers were reputed to be able to kill a fully grown dog and I definitely didn't want to lose my best friend. Discretion seemed like the more sensible option, so I headed back.

On my way up to here, I'd spotted a decent track leading down the hill on the other side of the woods so I retraced my steps until I could pick this up. When we reached it, Oscar and I headed down it side by side, partially shaded from the sun by a line of cypress trees. The track led us between an olive grove on one side and an immaculately tended vineyard on the other, presumably belonging to the farm buildings I could see a couple of hundred yards off to my left. We had almost got back to the road when we came upon the farmer himself. And, from the look of it, he was in trouble.

The man was standing against the trunk of a very ancient olive tree and I immediately saw that he had been trapped there by a battered Ape. These ubiquitous little agricultural vehicles – pronounced 'ah-pay' rather than like the primate – popped up all over the countryside here in Tuscany and were a familiar work-horse among the members of the rural community. They were lightweight three-wheelers, which looked as though they had been created when somebody – probably after a good few litres of red wine – had had the crazy idea of grafting a pickup body onto a Vespa scooter. The result was no beauty, but they were very cheap to run and managed to go almost anywhere. This one, however, appeared to have rolled backwards, pinning the farmer against the tree. From the look of him, he was more annoyed than injured, but I hurried over to offer assistance. He looked up as he caught sight of me and I saw a smile of relief on his face.

'Damn thing. The brake doesn't work too well and it gave way.' He spoke Italian with a rich Tuscan accent. 'It's got me trapped.' Fortunately for him, the rear corner of the Ape had caught the tree rather than his leg, but I could see that his blue trousers were pinched between the vehicle and the trunk. 'My knife's in the cab otherwise I'd have cut my way out. I've been trying to tear the material, but my wife always insists on getting me heavy-duty trousers. I don't know what they're made of, but I reckon this stuff's bulletproof.' In spite of his annoyed tone, he had a friendly face, and he was probably a year or two older than me, just nudging sixty. His weather-beaten skin testified to the fact that, unlike me, he had spent most of his life outside.

I leant my back against the vehicle and braced my feet against the tree. With a hefty shove, the three-wheeler lurched an inch or two uphill and the farmer was able to make his escape. I let the Ape roll back against the tree again and turned to the man.

'You all right? Not injured?'

'I'm fine, just thirsty. I've been stuck here for over an hour and that sun's damn hot.'

He reached into the open-sided cab of the vehicle and pulled out a dusty two-litre bottle with a quick release wire top. He flicked it open and upended it into his mouth before handing it across to me. 'Thank you for helping out. That was good of you.'

I followed his example and took a couple of mouthfuls of the remarkably good wine. As a way to rehydrate it probably wasn't what the medical profession would have recommended, but it tasted good and it almost hissed as it slipped down my parched throat. From the look in Oscar's eyes, he wouldn't have minded a gulp or two of it as well but he would have to make do with the bottle of water I kept in the car for him.

'My name's Signese, Luigi Signese. That's my farm over there.' He set the heavy bottle down at his feet and held out a gnarled hand. 'Thanks again for your help. Much appreciated. I don't recognise your face. You from around here?'

As we shook hands, I introduced myself and explained where I lived, telling him that I was here doing a tennis course. As I mentioned the country club he looked up.

'I hear the Australian's been murdered.' He raised his eyes to the sky and crossed himself. 'Who says prayer doesn't work?'

'I take it you didn't like him.' It was fast becoming crystal clear that Rex Hunter really hadn't made too many friends around here. Had anybody liked him? In a murder inquiry, detectives always try to whittle down the list of suspects but in this case I just seemed to be adding more and more to the list.

'You could say that. He's cost me thousands of euros and God knows how many sleepless nights.'

At my prompting, he went on to explain that Hunter had laid claim to land that had belonged to the Signese family for generations, instructing a hotshot firm of lawyers in Florence to pursue the case. He shook his head ruefully. 'I've had to mortgage the farm to fight the case and I don't know how much longer I could have held out. He has powerful friends in high places.'

'Influential friends or do you think he's been bribing people?'

'Bribery - no doubt about it.'

'Have you any proof?'

He shook his head. 'They're too canny for that. No, I have no proof, but I know that's what he was doing. Did you know he deliberately demolished a ruined medieval chapel when he built his villa just because it blocked his view of Florence? If you or I tried to do something like that we'd be thrown in jail. Not him. Powerful friends and no moral compass – that's a dangerous combination.'

'And now that he's dead, does this mean your worries are over?' And, if so, did that provide a motive for murder?

He shrugged. 'Who knows? I can only hope that his wife or son or whoever inherits has a bit more moral fibre than the old man.'

I had been wondering about the terms of Hunter's will and who would inherit what was clearly a huge estate. Hunter had visibly been a very wealthy man and money, as I knew only too well, can be a powerful motive for murder. No doubt Virgilio was already working to establish who stood to gain from Rex Hunter's death. Presumably his wife, or maybe his children. Maybe Elizabeth, the assistant manager, if she was related to him. I hoped for the friendly farmer's sake that the beneficiaries would behave more reasonably towards him and his land. One thing was for sure: the list of people who disliked Rex Hunter was growing ever longer.

Luigi took a last mouthful of wine before handing the bottle across to me again. After taking a small sip – I was driving after all – an idea came to me.

'This is excellent wine. Is it yours? I mean, do you make it?'

'I do indeed, and it wins prizes every year in the best Chianti contests. Here, take it. I've got lots more.' He pushed the bottle at me, but I thanked him and refused, for now.

'Do you sell your wine? I'd actually like to buy a few litres if that might be possible?' I glanced around at the olive trees. 'And maybe some of your oil as well?'

'Of course I can sell you some. I'll be exhibiting at the Montevolpone fair in ten days' time, but I'd be happy to sell you some before that. Come around any evening and I'll give you a taste of my sparkling wine as well. Like I say, I'm just over there. The farm's called La Rosina.'

'I actually live close to Montevolpone and I'll be going to the fair, but I'm running short of oil so I'll call round to see you tomorrow if that's okay with you.' And while I was there, I would try to find out more about the genial farmer.

We arranged that I would drop in to see him the following evening and he thanked me once more before firing up the Ape and setting off in a cloud of blue smoke. I had hardly started down the track when my phone started ringing and I saw that it was Tricia. Either I phoned my daughter or she phoned me at least once a week, but we had spoken only a couple of days earlier and I wondered if something had happened. It soon turned out that it had.

'Hi, Dad, how're you?'

'I'm fine, sweetheart. You probably won't be surprised to hear that I'm helping Virgilio out on another murder case.'

'Oh, Dad...' We both knew that my job had been the main reason her mum had left me. Tricia's voice became more serious. 'Anyway, look, I've just been speaking to Mum and she and Timothy have just broken up. She's in a terrible state.'

This came as a surprise. I had never met the man for whom my wife had left me, but I'd got the impression from Tricia that things had been going very well between Helen and him. Wedding bells might even have been in the air. News that the relationship had ended filled me with mixed feelings. In spite of the hurt, I had wished Helen well for her life without me and it was shameful – if maybe understandable – to allow myself to wallow in *Schadenfreude*.

'I'm sorry to hear that.' And I was – at least for her sake.

'She's coming up to Birmingham to spend a few days with us.' Tricia and her fiancé, Shaun, had moved in together in January and that relationship at least appeared to be going well. 'Mum sounded terribly upset on the phone.'

'Give her my love.' It probably wasn't the appropriate choice of words for an ex-husband, but it just came out spontaneously.

'Oh, Dad...'

Tricia didn't say any more. She didn't need to. I knew the way she felt about her mum. I had felt the same way for thirty years, but had now accepted that things had changed, even if Tricia hankered for a return to the way things used to be. Instead, we changed the subject and I told her how beautiful the countryside was and how damn hot it was. She didn't ask me about the murder case, and I didn't tell her anything about it, but I did tell her about my meeting with Luigi and his Ape and how he had been embroiled in a legal battle to keep his farm. Tricia latched straight onto this. She had recently qualified as a solicitor and her field of particular interest was property development and territorial disputes.

'You should tell Virgilio, get him to look into it.' She and Shaun had met Virgilio and his wife last month and she knew he occupied a senior position in the Florence police. 'Just because somebody's got money, it doesn't mean they can buy justice.'

I agreed with her, but I had a feeling that the farmer's problems might not be over. It all depended on who would inherit from Rex Hunter.

No sooner had Tricia rung off than my phone started ringing again. This time it was Virgilio.

'*Ciao*, Dan. Where are you?' I told him that I had been nosing around the boundaries of the country club and he grunted approvingly. 'Feel like a coffee?'

'Something cold, more likely. Where shall we meet up?'

We met up in the little village of Acquarossa, only a couple of kilometres away. Although it wasn't that far from my home, I'd never been here before, and I found that it was a typical Chianti village and remarkably tranquil, in spite of being less than half an hour from the big city of Florence. It was almost entirely encircled by vineyards, the vine leaves shading the bunches of new grapes from the sun, and signs lined the sides of the road all along the way, indicating home-made Chianti on sale. There was an ancient church with a slim square tower, a hundred or so mainly stone houses, and what looked like the ruins of an old castle. Most of the houses had been renovated and many of these were probably owned by wealthy Florentines or foreigners as their weekend or holiday retreats. The majority looked as though they were currently being lived in, but it was the month of July after all. I wondered what the population of a place like this would drop to in the depths of winter.

There was a smart-looking bar/restaurant on the little central piazza with tables outside on the cobbles. This area was, of course, close to the heart of Chiantishire, and I had no doubt that many of the guests of the Ristorante Italia and at least some of the homeowners around here would be well-off Brits. I wondered idly how many of them were members of the country club. Tuscany had always been a favourite with the Brits and although new money had come in recently, some of the most beautiful villas perched on hilltops around Florence were still owned by old British families. I had come across a few of these families over the last twelve months and I wondered what the more snobbish of them had made of their new antipodean neighbour, particularly if he had gained a reputation as a womaniser.

A little stream – barely more than a trickle at this time of year – ran along the side of the road. This no doubt flowed down from here and into the River Arno heading westwards until it emerged into the Mediterranean just past Pisa. In spite of the name of the village translating as Red Water – I wondered if this might be something to do with mineral deposits below ground – there was so little water in the stream that it was hard to tell what colour it was. A duck was standing in the middle of one of the larger pools looking disgruntled as the water level barely reached up to the tops of its legs. Tuscany had been suffering from a prolonged drought this year and there was still no sign of the long-awaited rain.

A blue and white police Alfa Romeo was parked outside the bar and Virgilio and Sergeant Innocenti were sitting beneath a parasol. I went over to shake hands with them and Oscar made a beeline for Virgilio as soon as he recognised his good friend. By the time I reached their table, the dog was almost up on Virgilio's lap. I dragged him off and sat down with them. They both looked hot, and Virgilio took one of the paper napkins out of the distributor on the table and ran it over his shaved head.

'*Ciao*, Dan. Thirty-six degrees in Florence when we left and, if anything, it feels even hotter here in the hills. It's crazy.'

When their coffees and glasses of water arrived, I ordered a bowl of peach, strawberry, and white-chocolate ice cream and a bottle of cold mineral water. I asked the waitress if it was possible to have some water for Oscar, who was gazing lovingly at her. She nodded in agreement, ruffled his ears, and went off. I knew Marco Innocenti, the sergeant, pretty well by now and it didn't surprise me to see his eyes follow her as she walked away. That was something he had in common with my Labrador and I almost laughed as I saw both of them watching her until she disappeared inside again. Oscar had an eye for the ladies as well.

Marco was Virgilio's right-hand man with a good eye for detail – as well as for members of the opposite sex – and I felt sure he would go far. After the waitress had gone, I told the two detectives what I'd learnt in the course of the day, and both listened intently, scribbling notes from time to time. When I came to the end, after relating what Luigi Signese had told me about his land dispute, Virgilio gave a frustrated sigh.

'It's been pretty much the same with us. Rather than cutting down the number of people who might have had a grudge against Hunter, we just seem to be finding more and more of them. One thing's for sure, he wouldn't have won any popularity contests. When you get down to it, virtually everybody at the country club had reason to be glad he's dead. They just didn't like him one bit.'

'But enough to commit murder?' My ice cream arrived and as I savoured the first blissfully cold mouthful I heard my dog slurping up the contents of the bowl of water kindly brought by the waitress and placed at my feet. 'What about the family? Any suspects there?'

Virgilio answered first. 'The wife's an interesting one. They were only married a month ago and they only got back from honeymoon a short while ago.'

I looked across and caught his eye. 'So I gather. Are you thinking what I'm thinking?'

He grinned. 'You don't know the half of it. The new Mrs Hunter is only thirty years old.'

Sergeant Innocenti leant forward and pointed out the obvious. 'Half the victim's age.'

I thought I had better play devil's advocate. 'They say that age means nothing when you're in love...'

'Yeah, right...' After twenty-plus years in the murder squad, Virgilio sounded as cynical as I felt about such things. He checked his notebook. 'Hunter divorced his first wife only six months ago after thirty-something years. You won't be surprised to hear that it wasn't an amicable parting of the ways. She's now living in Perth, Australia, and Australian police confirm that she hasn't left the country, so we can count her out.'

'What about children? I met his son, Adam, earlier. Any others? What about Elizabeth, the assistant manager?'

I saw the two men exchange glances. 'No, she's just an employee, not part of the family, but Adam Hunter has a sister, Miss Jennifer Hunter, and she had a *lot* to say for herself.' Virgilio rolled his eyes at me. 'From the way she went on at us, you would have thought *we'd* beaten her father's head in.'

'So does that mean she loved her father? At least he had one friend.'

'It's hard to tell although, in fairness, we didn't talk for long. She was far too upset or irritable or whatever. We'll give her a day or two to cool down and then we'll sit down with her again. As for her brother, Adam, the one you met, I wouldn't think he was the sort to kill anybody. Very much a front-of-house man, used to shaking hands and smiling at customers. Mind you, his sister looks like a tough character. If she bullied him into it, who knows?'

I nodded in agreement. 'He certainly managed to turn on the charm with me, but how sincere he was underneath, I have no idea. So, what have we got? A much younger new wife who's possibly a gold-digger, an ex-wife with no love lost for the victim but a rock-solid alibi, a son and a daughter who might not be as sincere as they appear to be, at least one woman at the club who claims he pestered her, and a farmer next door who reckoned Hunter was trying to steal his land and hated his guts as a result. Add to them the suggestion from the receptionist and the barista that he was generally disliked, or at least wasn't easy to get on with – particularly if you were female – and that's quite a line-up. Who's your money on?'

'Too early to say. My men are looking into the finances of the place, the Australian police are checking on the rest of his family, and a call's been put through to Hunter's lawyer in Florence about the will. He's in court this afternoon, but he's calling back later today or first thing in the morning.'

'Anything of interest from Gianni?' I also knew Gianni, the pathologist, well by now.

'Not a thing. The murder weapon was wiped clean, as was the handle of the rake and the whole bunker had been raked smooth. Nothing suspicious was left lying around.'

'Would the murderer have been splattered with blood? It was a violent attack, after all.'

'Gianni says no. The shaft of the club's over a metre long so he reckons the killer wouldn't have had to worry about bloodstains.'

'What about time of death?'

'Monday evening between seven and ten. Hunter was playing golf with two other men that evening, but his two companions decided to pack up at eight-thirty and he carried on alone after they left. These were...' he consulted his notebook '... the club accountant, Peter Nelson, and a neighbour, William Roseland, both English... sorry, British. It was a regular thing and apparently they'd been playing together for years.' He looked up. 'I need to interview these two as they would appear to have been just about the last people to see him alive.'

'But surely on a fine summer evening, there must have been other golfers out on the course who would have seen him?'

Sergeant Innocenti shot us a grin. 'One of the perks of having your own golf course is that you can close it whenever you feel like it. Rex Hunter insisted on the course being closed from six o'clock every Monday and Thursday evening in summer, so that he could play without interruption: Mondays with his two friends and Thursdays with important clients or his son.'

'How the other half live!' I took another spoonful of my rapidly melting ice cream and looked across the table at the inspector. 'When you said Hunter's two playing partners were "just about" the last people to see him alive, is there somebody else who might have seen Hunter – apart from the murderer, of course? Presumably as the course was closed, there were no other players out there?'

'Jennifer Hunter claims to have seen her father standing near the crime scene on his own at...' he consulted his notebook '... eight forty-five.'

'Was she playing golf as well?'

'No, she says she was travelling back up the perimeter track. She didn't stop, but she says she recognised her father standing near the bunker and he waved.'

'And she didn't see anybody else?'

'Apparently not.'

'Not even his two playing partners?'

'No, seeing as they say they stopped playing at eight-thirty, they would have been almost back at the clubhouse by then.'

A thought occurred to me. 'By the way, what happened to his clubs?'

'Somebody – presumably the murderer – threw them into a nearby gorse bush at the same time as they threw the murder weapon into the long grass. I imagine the idea was that anybody passing by along the track wouldn't realise there was anybody still up there. Hunter's body was well hidden at the bottom of the fairly deep sand trap, so unless you went pretty close to it, you wouldn't know there was anything there.'

'That does, of course, put his daughter only a hundred metres or so from the crime scene around the time he was murdered, give or take a minute or two. I thought you said most of the people you interviewed had alibis.'

'She says she was travelling up the track at the time.'

'Presumably in a car. Was she driving or was there somebody with her?'

'Innocenti, check that, will you?'

The sergeant nodded, but then added an observation. 'Of course, if there was somebody with her, they both might have been in it together...'

Virgilio nodded grimly. 'Indeed.'

'And her brother? Does he have an alibi?'

'He claims he was at home with his partner.' I scooped up the last of my ice cream. 'What would you like me to do now? I've got another tennis session booked for nine tomorrow morning. I think Abigail, my coach, has told me all she knows, but I'll try pressing her a bit more just in case.' I glanced at my watch. 'Five o'clock. I suppose the ground staff will be going off about now. How about I go in a bit earlier tomorrow and check with them to see if they noticed anything?'

Virgilio nodded. 'Please do that. We've already taken statements from everybody, but you might be able to get a bit more information out of them. After your tennis lesson it's probably time for you to start getting involved with the investigation. Like I say, my men have taken statements from most people today, but I need to sit down with Hunter's two golf partners and the family again. We'll try and set up a meeting with them tomorrow. I don't know how much Italian they speak, so if you could join us that would be good.'

'Of course. There's always the possibility one or both of his playing companions could have had the opportunity to bash his head in. I imagine they could both have supplied alibis for each other if they had been in it together. The question is whether they had any motive. By tomorrow, hopefully, you'll know what Hunter's will says. It'll be interesting to find out who inherits.'

On the way home, Oscar and I stopped off in my hometown of Montevolpone to chat to Tommaso, the owner of the bar in the main square who had become a good friend over the past year. Apart from running the bar, he was also one of the moving spirits behind Montevolpone's *festa del paese*, the town fair – the very same fair where Luigi Signese would be exhibiting his wines. This festival took place in July every year and was in honour of the town's patron saint, James the Apostle. The fair was coming up on Saturday of the following week and planning was well under way. As it was evening by now, I ordered a cold beer and sat down alongside a group of other men who were discussing the programme for the day.

As ever, I was fascinated to see how the organisation and running of events like this naturally divided into two camps: the men and the women. The men did most of the heavy lifting, set up the stalls, led animals through the streets, and spent an inordinate amount of time over the preceding weeks drinking wine and talking. The women, on the other hand, did most of the work, including getting everything ready for the open-air dinner in the piazza, where lines of trestle tables would receive almost two hundred hungry diners. They also seemed to spend a lot of time drinking and talking, but their beverage of choice appeared to be coffee rather than alcohol.

I listened with interest as Tommaso took everybody through the programme, which started with a procession carrying the statue of the saint around the town. I noted that special attention had to be given to ensuring that the statue was firmly attached to its base in order to avoid the disaster that had happened in a neighbouring village some years back. Their saintly statue hadn't been properly fixed and had toppled off onto the cobbles, allegedly bringing drought and a terrible grape harvest as a result. Here in Chianti, everything revolved around wine and no chances could be taken with the all-important *vendemmia*.

The Montevolpone fair wasn't just a religious festival but also included all manner of things like a marching band, the most impressive fruit and vegetable competition, children's games, and stands where local wine and oil producers could sell their wares. There was also a 'best-looking pet' show. My own pet wandered around the tables sporting his 'he never feeds me' look although I'm sure nobody believed him, and I was talked into entering him for the pet show. He was still a young dog, and I had a horrible feeling he would cause chaos, but I knew it would all be in a good cause.

The arrangements made, the conversation changed to local news, and it soon emerged that the main talking point was the murder of *l'Australiano* at Acquarossa Country Club. Various ideas were put forward and I listened in silent fascination to theories ranging from a mafia hit – admittedly my first reaction to the news – to a crime of passion. Italy's mafia is a complex beast, made up of numerous different – and often competing – branches of organised crime, most of which originated in southern Italy or on the island of Sicily. A profitable business like the country club might have attracted mafia interest and Virgilio had people looking into possible connections but so far they had been unable to establish any links, so this was looking less likely.

It very soon emerged that the front runner was the crime-of-passion theory, which went something like this: Hunter had been well known and grudgingly admired by many as a Casanova. It was agreed that he had been a handsome man and, with all his wealth, he must have presented an appealing proposition to many ladies. Although none of the men present would have admitted it of their own wives, there were dire aspersions cast about his behaviour towards certain unnamed women – married and unmarried – in the area.

Considering we were at least ten kilometres from the club here, Rex Hunter must have been a very busy – and energetic – sixty-year-old indeed if even a tiny percentage of the stories were true. What was clear was that the impression Virgilio and I had already gained of him as a ladies' man appeared to be supported by independent witnesses – or at least a thriving bush telegraph. So did this mean a jealous husband or a scorned lover might be responsible for the murder?

And if so, who?

4

THURSDAY MORNING

Next morning, I left Oscar with one of my friendly neighbours and was at the country club by eight o'clock in the hope of chatting to the ground staff. My luck was in. No sooner had I parked in the nearly empty car park than I spotted a man and a woman working amid the roses, assiduously removing the weeds that had somehow survived the drought. Of course, I told myself, the flower beds here, like the golf course, no doubt benefited from some sort of irrigation system. In fact, as I wandered over to talk to them, I could see that the earth was damp.

I wasn't sure how to start up a conversation without revealing that I was part of the investigation and decided to take refuge in their special subject.

'Good morning, could I ask you experts a technical question? It's about plants.' They both looked up and returned my greeting. They appeared friendly, so I soldiered on. 'You see, I've just bought a little house a few kilometres away and I'm wondering which plants grow best in such dry conditions. I don't have the luxury of automatic irrigation like you have.'

They both stood up. The man was probably well over sixty,

but he looked active and moved well. The dark-haired woman beside him was probably less than half his age and good-looking in a tanned, outdoors sort of way. She was wearing shorts and stout boots, and her legs were almost chestnut in colour. She deferred to the man and let him do the talking.

'It depends how much water you've got. Have you got a well?' Seeing me shake my head, he went on. 'Water's expensive – you must have discovered that for yourself – so I'd advise you to go for low-maintenance plants, preferably the sort of thing you see growing wild around here.'

He went on to suggest all sorts of plants from oleanders to rosemary and I realised that he had just listed virtually every plant already growing in my little garden. His companion added a few more suggestions and I thanked them both before easing the conversation towards the events of Monday evening.

'I gather the golf course is still closed.'

'They say we should be able to reopen this lunchtime.' The man nodded a few times. 'Once the police have finished doing what they've been doing.'

'And what have they been doing?' I was becoming quite good at looking clueless by now, so I shot him a quizzical look and he took the bait.

'It was the owner, Signor Hunter; he was murdered.'

I affected a shocked expression and asked for more detail, which he appeared more than happy to provide.

'I was the one who found the body. I was up on the course first thing on Tuesday morning with young Alfredo and we found Signor Hunter lying in the bunker up by the eighth green with his head bashed in. It was horrible.' He went on to outline what I already knew, but then he added something I didn't know. 'It was the first time he'd played golf since he got back from Bali.'

The female gardener provided the explanation. 'He got

married, I mean remarried, a month or so ago and he'd just come back from his honeymoon.'

'I see. I assume he had other things on his mind. And so this was the first chance he'd had to play golf again?'

The groundsman shook his head. 'He came back over a week ago but although he normally plays with his son on a Thursday, they didn't play last week.'

'Pressure of work maybe? I imagine he had a lot to do after being away.'

The groundsman took a surreptitious look around and lowered his voice. 'That's as maybe, but I think the reason they didn't play was because they had a falling out.'

'What, father and son had an argument?'

'More than an argument.' He glanced across at the woman beside him. 'Ines heard them screaming at each other, didn't you?'

She nodded. 'It was just before lunch last Thursday.' She pointed towards the driveway. 'I was down there in among the rosemary bushes, and they came walking past. They weren't exactly screaming at each other, but they were making a lot of noise.'

'And what were they arguing about?'

She gave me an apologetic smile. 'It was all in English. I did English at school, but I'm afraid I hardly remember any these days, but they both sounded really angry about something.'

I filed away the fact that things didn't appear to have been peachy between father and son. And, of course, if Hunter's son had been the murderer, quite possibly his sister might have seen him in the act out on the course on Monday night but was protecting him out of sibling solidarity. As I stood with Ines the gardener, I decided to test out the Montevolpone men's theory about Rex Hunter and women. As delicately as possible I approached the question.

'Will Mr Hunter be missed? Was he a good boss?'

The groundsman gave a very Italian shrug. 'He wasn't the best, but we didn't see much of him.' He paused for effect. 'At least, I didn't.' And he looked pointedly at Ines, who blushed. In response to my questioning look, she explained.

'He had a bit of a thing for me.'

The groundsman snorted. 'He had a bit of a thing for anything in a skirt.'

I tried to sound casual. 'You mean he pestered you?'

'It was more than that. He cornered me in the greenhouse one time and if Beppe hadn't come in, I don't know what might have happened. He was all over me like an octopus.'

Beppe nodded. 'It was disgusting.'

'You should have reported him. Don't you have a Human Resources department?'

The expression on her face spoke volumes. 'No, all I could have done would have been to report him to the manager, but the manager's his son and we all knew he was scared stiff of his father.'

'Well, what about the assistant manager? She's a woman and she seems nice.'

The two of them exchanged glances, before Ines lowered her voice. 'Elizabeth would have scratched my eyes out. Everybody knows she'd been carrying on with Signor Hunter for ages. A friend of mine saw them out for dinner together just before he flew off to Bali to get married, and she told me they were all lovey-dovey.'

That appeared to explain the lines around the assistant manager's eyes. Presumably, unlike most of the other people around here, she had genuinely been grieving. I shook my head in disbelief. 'But didn't you just say that he's got married again and yet he was still fooling about with other women?'

Beppe extended his hands in front of him, palms upwards, in a gesture of helplessness. 'What can I say? That's the way he was.'

'Wow.' I thanked them and left them to their weeding.

On my way over to the tennis courts, I met another of the staff. His badge indicated that his name was Dario and that he was the golf pro, and the logos on his cap and polo shirt trumpeted his status. He gave me a friendly enough greeting and I took the opportunity to have a chat.

'I imagine you must be getting bored, seeing as the course is closed.'

'The driving range and the putting greens are still open, so I've got a fairly full schedule of tuition. Why, are you interested in a few lessons?'

'No, thanks, I'm just waiting for some tennis coaching with Abigail. I gather the golf course might reopen this afternoon.'

'That's what I'm hoping. In fact, I'm just on my way over to the clubhouse to see if there's any news.'

'Shame about Mr Hunter, wasn't it?'

'Was it?' His face was expressionless, but his tone said it all.

I raised my eyebrows. 'Not a fan?'

'You can say that again.' He gave the same apprehensive glance over his shoulder the others had given before he went on in a lower voice. 'I can stand people shouting at me, calling me names, or even telling lies about me, but cheating at golf! That, in my book, is totally beyond the pale.'

'He used to cheat?'

'And how! He just didn't like losing, so he'd go to any lengths to make sure he didn't.'

'Such as?'

'Such as having a pocketful of balls and making sure that any time he hit his ball into the rough, he miraculously "found" it again, suspiciously bright and shiny and lying in a perfect position.'

'Did he play for money? Was that it?'

'No, just for the hell of it. Do you know something? One of my predecessors – and there's been a regular turnover of golf pros here, for obvious reasons – made the mistake of beating him in a competition once and he got fired as a result.' He glanced at his watch. 'Sorry, I have to go but, in answer to your original question, no, as far as I'm concerned, it isn't a shame he's dead.'

This was becoming a familiar refrain. Rex Hunter hadn't enamoured himself to a whole crowd of people, but it was only now that they could speak out.

My tennis session with Abigail was fractionally cooler than the day before, but I was still glad when eleven o'clock came around. We chatted for a few minutes, but she didn't produce any more information about Hunter or his family, so I thanked her and headed for a cold shower and a change of clothes. I was just emerging from the changing rooms, feeling refreshed, when my phone rang. It was Virgilio.

'*Ciao*, Dan. Can you talk?'

'Hang on.' I strolled out through Reception towards the car park, giving a little wave to Raffaello behind the reception desk as I did so. Outside there was nobody within earshot. 'Okay, Virgilio, what's new?'

'Innocenti's spoken to Hunter's lawyer, Avvocato Pirandello, and he tells us the will was made years ago, and it leaves everything to his first wife and the two kids, to be divided equally between them. Interestingly, he received a call from Hunter's daughter, Jennifer, earlier asking the same thing.'

'Nothing for the new wife?'

'No mention of her, although the lawyer says Hunter had

been talking to him about wanting to make a change, presumably since getting divorced and married again, but as far as he knows Hunter hadn't done anything about it.'

I gave it some thought. 'What about life insurance? Does the widow pick up a million or two that way?'

'We're still sifting through his papers, but so far we haven't come across any life insurance.'

'So it looks as though she's been left out in the cold.' Considering that it was approaching midday and the sun was beating down relentlessly, this probably wasn't the best metaphor, but he got my meaning.

'Quite. At least that would seem to rule her out as a suspect. She had absolutely nothing to gain from his death, very much the opposite. It was definitely in her interests to keep him alive and happy.'

'Assuming she knew about the will. From what everybody's telling me, Hunter was a nasty piece of work so maybe he lied to her, saying he'd changed it even if he hadn't.'

'We need to find out. I want to sit down and have a serious talk to her. But she has just arrived here in Italy and doesn't speak a word of Italian. I've arranged to go up to the villa to see her at twelve. Feel like coming with me? I think it's time you slipped into your "interpreter" role.'

'Of course. I'll be there. How are you getting on with the club's finances?'

'According to the bank, the club's doing well, and the tax authorities confirm they're all up to date. I'm getting copies of the accounts sent through so we can check them. I have yet to interview the accountant, but hopefully that'll be this afternoon.'

After checking on Google Maps, I managed to find my way through the narrow lanes between even more vineyards to the widow's house at noon as instructed. Barely a minute after I had pulled up outside the fine old Tuscan villa, there was the crunch of gravel and the blue and white police car arrived, and Virgilio and Innocenti climbed out. We shook hands and walked up the stone steps to the front door together. It opened as we approached it, and we were greeted by a figure who could have come straight out of *Downton Abbey*. He was an imposing older gentleman wearing an impeccable morning suit in spite of the heat.

'Inspector Pisano, I presume. Good day, sir, please come in.' From his Tuscan accent he was from these parts, even though he looked as quintessentially English as Jeeves himself. He stepped aside and ushered us into the wonderfully cool air-conditioned hallway. 'If you would like to follow me, gentlemen.'

He led us along a corridor to a large and luxurious lounge, where we found a woman sitting on one of a pair of massive settees. She was a slim little thing and she looked frail and help-less. However, even the dark clothing she was wearing couldn't hide the fact that she was stunningly beautiful, and I'm sure if Oscar had been here, he would have started wagging his tail. I wondered what had convinced such a gorgeous woman to tie herself to a man twice her age. Rex Hunter either had had a magnetic personality or there had been some other attraction to lure her to an older man – like a few million in the bank, for instance. I could almost hear my ex-wife telling me off for being too cynical about human nature, but just like Virgilio, after decades in the murder squad, I had learnt to treat every relation-ship as potentially suspect until proved otherwise.

She stood up nervously as we entered. Virgilio glanced across at me, so I introduced him and Innocenti in English and intro-duced myself as simply 'Dan, the interpreter'. We all took seats and Virgilio began the interview while Innocenti listened to what was said. He was only there for show, really, as he didn't speak a word of English.

Virgilio started out in his pretty good English, only occasionally turning to me for translations of more technical terms, so I had time to take in the answers that the young widow produced. He began by asking her name and age.

'Natalie Angela Hunter. I'm thirty.' She had to clear her throat before answering, but the proximity of three investigating officers can have that effect on the most innocent of people.

'And you married your husband last month?'

'On the second of June. We were married in Bali.'

'Your maiden name, Mrs Hunter, if you please, and your place of birth.'

'Natalie Flynn and I was born in Sydney, Australia.'

After a few more general questions, Virgilio brought the conversation around to Monday night. 'When did you last see your husband alive?'

She blanched visibly but rallied. 'About five-thirty on Monday. He was just going out to play golf.'

'And you didn't see him again that night?' She shook her head, and he went on to ask the question that had been troubling me too. 'Weren't you surprised when he didn't come back home that night? There was no report of a missing person.'

Her eyes were on her hands, which were clasped together on her knees, the fingers trembling slightly. 'I was feeling tired, so I went to bed early.'

Call me paranoid, but I had a sudden feeling that she wasn't telling us the whole truth. 'So when did you first realise he was missing?'

'On Tuesday morning at about eight. Battista, the butler, brought me a coffee in bed and told me that Rex hadn't returned.'

'You slept in separate rooms?' Virgilio sounded as sceptical as I did. They had only been married for a matter of weeks, after all.

She flushed slightly and nodded. 'It was complicated.'

'Signora Hunter, this is a murder investigation. I'm sorry but you'll have to explain.'

'He was very set in his ways. He found it hard to sleep in a bed with somebody else, so he preferred to have his own room for sleeping.' She looked up shyly. 'He told me he'd been doing this for many years.'

Virgilio and I exchanged puzzled looks. No question that Rex Hunter had been a strange man.

'So were you worried when you heard he hadn't come home?'

'Yes, but not *terribly* worried. I thought maybe he'd gone off somewhere on Monday night and stayed over. He liked playing cards.'

'And with whom?'

'I honestly don't know. Maybe Will or Peter?'

'That's William Roseland or Peter Nelson, the two men he played golf with every Monday night?'

'That's correct.'

'Do you know them well?'

'Not at all, I'm afraid, I've just heard Rex mention them. You see, I've only just arrived here I've hardly met anybody.'

Virgilio went on to enquire how she had met her husband.

'I first met him nine months ago in a clinic in Sydney. I was working there in the hospital administration.'

'And he was there for treatment?'

'Yes, he came in for a procedure.'

'Of what nature?' Virgilio helped her. 'Now that he's passed away you don't need to worry about medical confidentiality.'

She nodded. 'The clinic specialised in cosmetic surgery. It was for a minor rhytidectomy.' Seeing the expressions on our faces, she translated. 'A facelift, to tighten the skin on his face.'

Now why didn't that come as a surprise to me? No doubt a dedicated ladies' man would seek to put off the ravages of time as long as possible.

'And did you see him often after that?'

'Every time he came to Australia.'

'And how many times was that?'

'Four, and on two occasions we went on holiday together: once to Thailand and then to Vietnam.'

'And this was while he was still married?'

'*Unhappily* married, very unhappily married. And it was only the Thailand trip. After that he divorced his first wife. ' Her tone was stronger now as she caught Virgilio's eye. 'I know what it sounds like; you probably think I went after him for his money, but it wasn't like that. I really loved him.'

She sounded sincere, but she was the first person I'd come across who had a good word for him so I had to ask. 'In spite of the fact that he was twice your age?'

'Age had nothing to do with it. I loved him.' If she was acting, she was damn good.

'And what about him? Did he feel the same way about you?'

'I know he did.' No hesitation.

I queried the relationship a bit more deeply. 'You met him nine months ago, and three months after meeting you he got divorced, and then you married him four weeks ago. But you were living on opposite sides of the world and over that time you'd probably only been together for, what, thirty or forty days total?'

'Thirty-two days.' She gave a little sigh. Again, if this was an act, it was masterful. 'I can remember every single one of them.'

'So you married a man you'd only known for a few months

and had only been with for a matter of a few weeks?' I couldn't keep the scepticism out of my voice.

'If you put it like that it sounds crazy, but I'm telling you I loved him, and he loved me.' She gave me an imploring look. 'That's just the way it was.'

I sensed that she wasn't telling us the whole truth but there seemed to be little more to be gained from proceeding along this line of inquiry for now. In fairness, I had to admit that I'd come here highly sceptical that a thirty-year-old could have married a sexagenarian for any other reason than money, so maybe I was being too cynical. But even so, deep down I remained to be fully convinced of her innocence. Although I didn't see her as a cold-blooded murderer, maybe she knew more than she was saying. Could it be that she knew the identity of the murderer, but was hiding it from us for whatever reason? Something here didn't stack up, even if Natalie Hunter was remarkably convincing, but I couldn't for the life of me put my finger on it. Virgilio took over again.

'Can I bring you to the subject of your husband's will?' We saw her look up at this. 'We've spoken to his lawyer this morning and he informs us that the will in his possession leaves your husband's entire estate to his former wife and his two children, Adam and Jennifer. As far as the lawyer's aware, no provision has been made for you at all.'

You didn't need to be the brightest of detectives to identify the expression that spread across her face. It started as bewilderment and very quickly turned to something akin to desperation. 'He left me nothing? But he told me...' Her voice tailed off helplessly.

'He told you what, Signora Hunter? Did he tell you about another will?'

'Yes, he told me he made a new one only a few days ago.' She looked up at him, almost pleading. 'You've got to find it.'

'A will needs to be witnessed. I don't suppose you know who the witness was, do you?'

She nodded immediately and reached for a little brass bell on the coffee table. Seconds after it rang, the lounge door opened, and the august figure of the butler appeared.

'You rang, *Signora*?' This time he was speaking English, albeit with a strong Italian accent.

'Battista, you witnessed my husband's new will, didn't you?'

As he looked unfamiliar with the vocabulary, I offered a translation, and he nodded his head. 'On Sunday evening.' He turned towards Virgilio and elaborated in Italian. 'Signor Hunter called me to his study after dinner on Sunday and asked me to witness a document. All I saw was the line where he signed, and the line below it where I signed as a witness to his signature. I have little experience of wills, but I imagine it was as you say, but I have no idea of the content.'

I glanced over at Natalie Hunter, who clearly had no clue what was being said, and I gave her a quick translation. 'He says he witnessed a document, presumably the new will. We're trying to find out where it is.'

Virgilio returned his attention to the butler. 'Where do you think the document you signed is now?'

The butler shook his head. 'I would imagine in his office, probably in the safe, but I really don't know.'

Although she couldn't understand the words, Natalie Hunter could tell from his expression that he hadn't been able to help. She looked across at Virgilio and beseeched him. 'Please can you find it? Please?'

'We'll do our best. The butler thinks it might be in his office. My main concern for now is to establish who might have had a motive for killing your husband. Can you think of anybody who might have wanted to see him dead?'

'Nobody at all.' She shook her head but, again, I got the feeling she maybe wasn't being completely open. Her fingers were twisting nervously and there was a hint of perspiration at her temples in spite of the blissfully cool air conditioning. 'I don't know much about his business dealings, so maybe it might have been something to do with that, but I've known him for such a short time and I've been over here in Italy for such a short time that I really can't help you.'

'Can my men and I have your permission to search the house? I'd like to get a forensic team in here as well, if that's all right with you, and I'd like to go through his personal effects in the hope of finding a clue to the identity of his killer.' We all knew that a search warrant could easily be obtained, if necessary, but there was no need.

'Yes, of course.'

Virgilio gave the order to Innocenti to organise a full search of the house. He pulled out his phone, stood up, and headed for the corner of the room to call the station. While he was doing this, Virgilio asked if he and I could be escorted to the dead man's office, and his widow jumped to her feet immediately. She led us to a room at the end of the corridor, looking down through the trees towards the golf course. A massive desk littered with paperwork stood below the window while a pair of upright chairs were stationed in front of it for visitors, with a pair of small sofas and a coffee table further over for more important guests or less formal meetings.

'Your butler mentioned a safe, Signora Hunter. Where is that, please?'

'I'm sorry, I have no idea... Battista!' She raised her voice and seconds later the butler appeared at the door. 'Do you know where my husband's safe is, please?'

I offered the translation, '*cassaforte*', and he walked across to what looked like a drinks cabinet in the corner and opened the polished wooden door to reveal a sturdy steel safe. It looked pretty ancient, and it was clear that it would need a key rather than a combination to open it. I caught his eye.

'I don't suppose you know where Signor Hunter kept the key?'

'I'm not completely sure, sir, but I believe he kept it upon his person.'

I shot an enquiring glance across at Virgilio, who was reaching for his phone. 'A bunch of keys was found on his body. I'll just check.'

He spoke to his office and received immediate confirmation.

'The key ring in his possession contained his house key, the key to a Range Rover, and an unidentified, old-fashioned key. That sounds like the one we need.' He returned his attention to the widow and switched back to English. 'We think he had the key on him. I'll get the forensic team to bring it up here. In the meantime, do you think he might have given a key to his son or daughter?'

She shook her head decisively. 'No way. He didn't trust either of them.'

'He didn't trust his own children?' Presumably in the eyes of Rex Hunter, blood was *not* thicker than water. This no doubt went some way towards explaining why his son had appeared far less distraught at his father's death than might have been expected.

'Well, maybe Adam, but definitely not Jennifer. He told me he wouldn't trust her as far as he could throw her.'

Clearly relations had been strained in the Hunter household, and the list of potential suspects was growing ever longer.

5

THURSDAY AFTERNOON

I went for lunch to the restaurant in Acquarossa with Virgilio while Sergeant Innocenti remained at the villa to supervise the team from Florence as they sifted through it room by room, looking for the new will or anything else of interest. The temperature was still high, but a hint of a breeze had sprung up and served to cool us down just enough as we sat under the parasol and ate. I opted for a mixed salad with smoked duck breast, rather hoping that it wasn't the same duck I had spotted in the stream the previous day. Lunch without wine was unthinkable to Virgilio – whether on duty or not – so we shared a carafe of the local red, accompanied by a lot of ice-cold mineral water. While we ate, we discussed the case, and the dysfunctional Hunter family. As we did so, I found myself thinking about love. Whether this had anything to do with the news I had received about my ex-wife and her man the previous day was not something I chose to debate. I glanced across at Virgilio.

'Do you buy into the whole both of them deeply in love thing? A thirty-year-old falling for a man twice her age?' I took a big swig of cold water and savoured the refreshing feel as it went down.

'Her, maybe. Him, unlikely. She certainly looked seriously upset at his death, a lot more upset than his kids did.'

'I agree; if she was acting, it was brilliantly done. Mind you, I've seen a few Oscar-winning performances from suspects in my time.'

'Me too, but let's assume for a minute that she really did marry a man she barely knew out of love, rather than for his riches. Stranger things have happened. If so, then we can exclude her from our list of suspects, because she wouldn't kill the person she loved, would she?'

'Try telling that to Othello, but in this case, yes, I agree. As for Hunter, there's no doubt his widow's a very beautiful woman, although the fact that she's younger than either of his children can't have been easy for the family to digest. Maybe it was a love match for him as well, but if we assume for a moment that his feelings for her were nothing like so strong, then why marry her? Lust, of course, but a man in his position could surely have satisfied his sexual appetite with any number of women. Maybe he deliberately married an unsuitable woman to spite his kids.'

'There doesn't appear to be much love lost between them, I agree, but why go to those lengths to spite your kids? All he had to do was change his will and tell them he was leaving everything to the local dogs' home.'

'Point taken. So maybe he really was madly in love with young Natalie. Do we think his kids were so angry that they decided to take the law into their own hands and kill their father? And don't let's forget his first wife. All right, she has a cast-iron alibi in the shape of God knows how many thousand kilometres between here and Australia, but she could have been pulling the strings.'

'Anything's possible, but wouldn't it have been more logical to kill the unsuitable new wife?'

'Ah, but what if they knew he was about to change his will in favour of his new wife? They knew they had to act quickly before he did that. Love's a powerful motive for murder, but so is hard cash. Maybe the argument between Hunter and his son overheard by Ines the gardener was because Hunter had just announced his intention of changing his will.'

Virgilio nodded. 'Adam Hunter is definitely a suspect, and we have to include his sister too, either because she was directly involved – she doesn't have an alibi – or at least by providing an alibi for Adam. To be honest, of the pair of them, I reckon she'd be more capable of committing murder than her brother. You haven't met her yet, but there's a treat in store for you when you do. She makes Darth Vader look like a pussycat. And then there's the ex-wife who, like you say, might have organised the whole thing from a distance.'

'With a hired killer, you mean?'

'It's been done before, or by getting her kids to do it. But the family aren't the only ones. Who else have we got? The farmer next door, unhappy staff members, particularly female ones?'

'And the golf pro had a very poor opinion of him – maybe not enough to kill him but still...'

I sipped my wine while I debated what we should do next. Of course, this wasn't my case, it was Virgilio's, but I already felt involved and, if I was honest with myself, I was enjoying the challenge. 'Do you think we should have a little chat to the assistant manager? According to what the gardener told me, Elizabeth McGregor had been carrying on an affair with Hunter while he was still married to his first wife and even after he'd already met Natalie – and that lends weight to our hypothesis that Hunter wasn't as infatuated with his new wife as she was with him. Jealousy's definitely a powerful motive for murder. What if Elizabeth was so outraged to see him come back with his new bride that she flipped and beat him to death?'

'Anything's possible but...' He flicked back through his note-book. 'She claims to have been on duty at the time and we've already been handed the CCTV footage for that night. I'll get Innocenti to double check to see if she could have slipped out at any point.'

At that moment Virgilio's phone started ringing. It was from his office in Florence, telling him that Peter Nelson, the club accountant, and William Roseland, the local industrialist, who had been playing golf with the victim immediately before the murder, would be at the club for interview at three o'clock and four o'clock respectively. I willingly agreed to Virgilio's request that I sit in on the questioning. Given that the course had been closed to all bar the three of them on Monday evening, it seemed highly likely that they might have seen somebody suspicious – assuming they hadn't been the perpetrators of the murder.

Peter Nelson arrived looking flustered. This, he explained, was because he had been in Rome on business and had only just got back. He was a tall, tanned man in his forties or early fifties, immaculately turned out in a stylish suit. As we shook hands, I distinctly felt his thumb press against the back of my hand and I recognised this immediately. A lot of my colleagues on the force had been Freemasons and, although I had steered clear, I knew one when I met one. Whether this might prove of interest in this case remained to be seen.

The interview was conducted in the accountant's office at the rear of the main building next to the changing rooms. It wasn't a large room, but it was light and airy with French windows opening onto a well-mown lawn. The interview was in Italian, which Mr Nelson spoke perfectly with a Tuscan accent. After confirming his name and contact details, he started on his account of the events of Monday night.

'We had a regular fixture, every Monday at six. That was me, Rex, and Will from Montespertoli. We've been friends for years.'

'When you say for years, how many years?' Virgilio had his notebook in his hands.

'I've been club accountant here for twelve years, ever since the course was first built, and I've known Rex for seven.'

'So you were already working here before Signor Hunter bought the place?'

'Yes, he bought the club seven years ago from the consortium that had put up the money to build it. I looked after the accounts for that consortium and Rex kept me on after he took over. I work three days a week for the club and two days a week for my private practice.'

'Who was in the consortium? Were you part of it?'

He shook his head ruefully. 'I didn't have that kind of money. It was made up of three local businessmen – one of them Will Roseland. They made a lot of money out of selling the club to Rex, although it was just a fairly basic golf course then. Rex was the one who transformed it into a country club with tennis, squash, the pools, and the restaurant and so on. He had plans to build a hotel as well.' He hesitated. 'I wonder if that'll go ahead now that he's dead.'

'Tell us, if you would, about Monday evening.'

'Like I say, it was a regular thing. It was a glorious evening, and it should have been very pleasant, but Rex was in one of his moods.' He glanced across the desk at us. 'I dare say you've heard that he could be a bit awkward on occasions.'

'We've heard he could be downright unpleasant.' Virgilio wasn't mincing his words. I saw Nelson nod in agreement.

'He wasn't an easy man to get on with.'

I'd heard that before. 'But you did get on with him? I assume if you were a regular golf partner you got on pretty well.'

'Rex was a bully and there are only two ways to react to bullies: stand up to them or kowtow to them. Business is business, so I chose the latter. I kept my head down and bit my tongue on occasions and, as a result, we managed to work well together.'

'Did you like him?'

We had to wait for an answer. 'I admired him as a businessman, even if I didn't always approve of his methods. He was a self-made man, and they can be difficult. Like I said, I kept my head down and acted as his friend when he demanded it.' He looked up helplessly. 'After all, my job depended on it.'

'By the way, Signor Nelson, how is it that an English accountant speaks better Italian than I do and ends up working over here? I've always thought that the Italian fiscal system was impenetrable.' Virgilio produced a little smile.

'I was born in Britain, but my mother's Italian. After my father died when I was just ten, she moved back here to Florence, and I was educated over here so it was natural for me to work in the Italian system. I soon discovered that being bilingual was a help to my career.'

'I see. Well, do carry on with your account of Monday's events.'

'Rex was late, and we didn't start playing until almost seven. He was like a bear with a sore head, and he snapped at both of us about the slightest thing – you know, accusing us of jingling coins in our pockets as he was trying to take a shot so as to put him off and so on.'

'Any idea why he was being so touchy that evening?'

'He didn't say much, but everybody at the club had been talking about him having had a row with Adam... and maybe Jennifer too. He was so grumpy that in the end Will and I invented an excuse and left him at eight-thirty. We left after the seventh and the last we saw of him, he was standing on the eighth tee, just about to drive off.'

'And when you walked back down to the clubhouse did you see anybody else?'

'No, there was nobody else about. The course is always closed for Rex's private use on Monday evenings. We didn't see a soul even though we took our time going back. We dawdled a bit as we had stuff to discuss.'

'What sort of stuff?'

'Financial stuff. Will has his own accountant, but he often bounces ideas off me.'

'You saw nobody, and nobody saw you?'

'I'm afraid not. When we got back down to the clubhouse we met up with a few other people, but out on the course there was just Rex... as far as I know.'

We shot a few more questions at him about Rex Hunter and about the club's finances but learnt nothing new. Finally, Virgilio stood up.

'That's about it for now, thank you. Tell me, as far as the club's concerned, is it profitable?'

Nelson answered immediately. 'It's *very* profitable. Of course, Rex put in a lot of money to develop it, but it's been paying that back better than I expected.'

'And what do you think will happen now?'

Nelson looked surprised. 'I assume Adam will carry on as manager as before.'

'And his sister?'

'Jennifer? I imagine she'll go back to Australia. She's only been here for a short while. She's not involved with the running of the club.' There was something in his tone that told me that he was glad about that.

We shook hands and Virgilio turned towards the door but

then turned back for a moment. 'Tell me, Signor Nelson, have you any idea of who might have wanted to kill your employer?'

Nelson spread his hands helplessly in a typically Italian gesture. 'Like I said to you, Inspector, he wasn't an easy man, and he had a knack for making enemies, but murder? I honestly don't know.'

Virgilio thanked him for his time, and the two of us went out into the gardens where we took a seat on a bench beneath an umbrella pine. Above us, a pair of red squirrels were playing, and I spared a thought for my dog. If Oscar had been here, he would have been barking the place down and trying to climb the tree.

'So what do we think of Mr Nelson and his story?' Virgilio sat back and stretched.

'Yet another person who didn't exactly love Rex Hunter. As he said, he just kept his head down and got on with it. As a person he seemed pleasant enough, but the fact remains that he was just about the last person to see Hunter alive, although we need a motive. Seeing as Hunter trusted him to do the club accounts, maybe he was stealing money, and when Hunter found out, Nelson killed him to shut him up.' I looked across towards the car park. At one end there were reserved parking spaces for senior staff and a very nice silver BMW was now sitting there. 'If that's Nelson's company car, it looks as though Hunter treated him well, at least financially. By the way, did you know that Adam's sister, Jennifer, has only just arrived here in Italy?'

He shook his head. 'I don't think it came up at preliminary interview. To be honest, she spent most of it having a go at us for police incompetence. We'll need to take a full statement from her later.'

'It's a quite a coincidence that she came over here only a matter of days after her father returned with his new bride and then, the next thing we know, he was murdered. Sound suspicious to you, too?'

'It does indeed.' We exchanged glances. Neither of us liked coincidences.

We interviewed the third member of the Monday night golf party in a quiet corner of the atrium. William Roseland was older than Peter Nelson, probably around the same age as the victim or maybe even in his mid-sixties. He was red-faced and seriously overweight, and I wondered what sort of golfer he was. Could he even see the ball below his imposing paunch? There was perspiration on his brow, but that might well have just been because of the heat outside. We shook hands but there was no hint of a Masonic handshake. He sat down and ordered a cold beer in execrable Italian. Considering he was reputed to own a ceramic factory nearby, I was surprised. As a result, the interview was carried out in English, and his strong Midlands accent made it necessary for me to step in quite frequently to interpret for Virgilio, who was clearly struggling. Roseland produced a carbon copy of Peter Nelson's account of Monday evening, but his answer to Virgilio's question about possible murderers was interesting.

'I don't like to point fingers but, for my money, I think you'd do well to look at his family.'

'When you say "family", are you referring to his wife or his children?'

Roseland produced a smile. 'You're the detective, Inspector, you tell me. For what it's worth, I know there's been bad blood between Rex and his children ever since he divorced his first wife and then it all flared up when he got married again. You know he didn't tell anybody about getting remarried until it was all over, don't you?'

'No, I didn't know that. How do you know there was bad feeling? Did Signor Hunter tell you?'

'Signor Hunter *junior*, Adam, told me. While his dad was away in Bali, I played golf a few times with him, and one day he told me all about it. He'd had a text message that morning saying something like *Just got married*. He was incandescent and when his sister came over, she looked positively homicidal. I was there, I saw her.'

Virgilio immediately pounced on Roseland's choice of word. 'Homicidal? Really?'

'Well, maybe that's too strong, but she was furious. She just about had smoke coming out of her ears.' He looked across at both of us. 'If you want to know what I think, I reckon she's mentally unstable. Rex hardly ever spoke about her, but just once he mentioned something about her receiving treatment. Peter and I knew better than to pry, but maybe that's what it was all about.'

'You think she had psychiatric problems?' This was interesting. I had come across countless murderers in my years on the force who had been adjudged mentally unstable. Of course, murder was a pretty insane act.

He nodded. 'You should have seen her last week.'

'Had she been planning to visit, or do you think she came over in response to the news of the wedding?'

'I'm pretty sure her brother called her and told her to come over. So they could put up a united front, I suppose.'

'But if the wedding had already taken place, what could they do?'

'What indeed?'

I could see where Mr Roseland's suspicions lay, and I couldn't blame him. We were going to have to interview Hunter's son and daughter very closely.

After the interview, Virgilio returned to Florence to sift through all the statements and to see if the accounts had produced anything of interest. Innocenti was also returning to the station with the contents of the safe, which had responded favourably to the key on Hunter's ring. The bad news, as far as the widow was concerned, was that there was no sign of the new will.

* * *

Now that I was no longer needed at the club, I decided to go and buy some wine and oil from Luigi Signese as agreed, but first I knew I had to pop back to pick up Oscar from my friendly neighbours. He loved going to them and they spoiled him rotten, but I couldn't expect them to keep on looking after him for hours on end.

Luigi Signese's farm was easy to find. Like so many farms around here, there was a sign by the entrance announcing that it offered home-made Chianti for sale, along with olive oil. I drove up a bumpy track between a meticulously kept vineyard and an olive grove, and through a pair of slightly wonky stone gateposts into an open courtyard. Here I found an ancient farmhouse with an adjoining barn. No sooner had I drawn up outside and turned off the engine than a huge shaggy dog appeared. It only barked once – a deep booming woof that sent half a dozen pigeons flying off the roof of the barn – and then it just stood and stared at us. I stared back in awe. I had no way of knowing its genetic origins, but as well as sheepdog and probably wolf, there could well have been a shot of brown bear in there. The thing was absolutely enormous.

Fortunately, the farmer appeared in response to the cavernous woof and beckoned for me to leave the safety of the vehicle. I climbed out and turned to point towards the back of the car.

'Good evening, Signor Signese. I've got my dog with me. Can I let him out? Your dog won't mind, will he?' By 'mind' I meant, will it eat him?

'Cesare won't mind. He's very friendly. Come in, come in.'

I wandered over to Cesare the wolfbear and let him sniff my hand. His tail started wagging and a second or two later I had his massive hairy front paws on my chest as he attempted to kiss me. I'm six foot tall and reasonably fit for my age, but he almost knocked me over, and I was extremely relieved that his intentions were amicable. Luigi hauled him off and I went over to let Oscar out of the car. My dog jumped out readily and turned towards the giant. For a moment I thought he might be thinking of making a run for it – and I wouldn't have blamed him – but he proved to be made of sterner stuff and was soon happily sniffing Cesare's hairy backside.

Together with the dogs, we went into Luigi's barn. It was a large space, almost entirely filled with big wooden barrels and heavy fifty-litre *damigiane* – bulbous glass containers sitting in straw bases like overgrown Chianti flasks. Some, he pointed out, contained wine, and some olive oil. He reached down and moved one of these with apparent ease in spite of his advancing years, so that he could offer me a seat on a straw bale. He produced a battered Chianti flask, from which he poured red wine into two glasses.

'This is last year's. It was a very good year. It's what we were drinking yesterday.'

I took a sip, and this confirmed the impression I had got the previous day. Luigi definitely knew how to make wine.

'Drink up and I'll give you a taste of the white.' We drained our glasses – it would have been rude not to, wouldn't it? – and he produced another old straw-covered bottle. The wine he poured out of this was a rich, golden colour and tasted as good as its red companion. But he hadn't finished yet.

'I promised I'd give you a taste of my sparkling wine.' He tapped the side of his nose conspiratorially. 'We've been making it the same way in this family for two centuries.'

'Your family's been here for so long?'

'This farm was built stone by stone by my great-great-great-grandfather back before the Risorgimento.'

The unification of Italy had taken place in the middle of the nineteenth century, so the Signese family certainly went back a long way. I could understand how the threat of losing some of this heritage to their Australian neighbour would have been a bitter pill to swallow. Bitter enough to commit murder?

'Want to see how I make the spumante?'

I nodded and he led me over to a corner of the well-compacted bare earth floor of the barn where all I could see were corks, several dozen of them, sticking out of the ground. He must have seen the bewilderment on my face as he grinned. 'Look, I'll show you.'

He scooped away several handfuls of damp earth until he could pull a bottle out of the ground. It was a champagne-style bottle, the cork secured by a wire cage. He held it up to the light and scrutinised it. 'Not quite clear yet but doing well. Another month or so.'

As he replaced the bottle in the ground and covered it with earth again, he explained his method. In essence what he did was to fill bottles with his white wine and then add a single grain of corn to each before sealing and burying it. The corn would cause secondary fermentation inside the bottles and the result would be a sparkling wine. The reason for burying the bottles was for security, as he went on to explain.

'The fermentation produces heat so that's why I keep the earth damp to cool the bottles down, but it also produces a lot of pressure in the bottles. Every now and then one of them explodes but as they're safely in the ground, nobody gets hurt. Now, why don't you come inside, and you can try my olive oil and I'll give you a glass of cold spumante to go with it?'

Inside Luigi's farmhouse I found myself in a vast, high-ceilinged kitchen with an old-fashioned, cast-iron, wood-fired range for cooking, but with an enormous and far from ancient television screen against one wall. Sitting in front of this was his wife, introduced to me as Dora, and three older ladies watching one of the innumerable Latin American soaps that flooded daytime TV here in Italy. Although I had never watched one in its entirety, I recognised the slick-haired heroes and the pneumatic heroines and the excruciating overacting. I was introduced to the three older ladies but failed to work out their exact positions in the family: maybe a grandmother, an aunt and a cousin, but I couldn't be sure. Cesare the dog wandered over to the television and flopped down on the floor in front of it with a thud, closely followed by Oscar. As they did so, a pair of black and white cats leapt athletically onto the top of the fridge and surveyed the dogs suspiciously.

The olive oil was the colour and consistency of engine oil after a hundred thousand miles, but I had got used to this by now. When Tuscans talk about real olive oil, this is what they mean. Luigi's wife prepared a couple of slices of toasted bread and poured the thick oil onto each of them, adding a pinch of salt. The result was fruity, it was tangy, it tasted of olives, and it tickled the throat as it went down. It was terrific.

'Here, try this.' There was a loud explosion that made both dogs look up from the floor as Luigi opened one of his champagne bottles. He filled two glasses with foaming white wine and passed one across to me. The ladies looked on indulgently but neither asked for, nor were offered any. 'Cin cin, and thanks again for your help yesterday.'

We clinked our glasses together and I took a sip of the wine. It was good in a seriously fizzy sort of way. To be honest, I would probably have preferred the original white wine without the addition of the grain of corn, but it was cold, it was refreshing, and once I had found the trick of drinking it without getting too much of it up my nose, it was enjoyable. In particular, drunk in these traditional surroundings with the man who had created it, it felt special, even if it was unlikely to have the Prosecco producers of northern Italy falling on their swords any time soon.

I left there half an hour later with a dozen bottles of red, a dozen white, two litres of oil, and a single bottle of fizz, which he had insisted I take as a present. I hoped it wouldn't explode on the journey home and wrapped it in an old jumper just in case. It had been a charming interlude and I came away highly sceptical that a man like this would have stooped to committing murder but, as Virgilio had so rightly said, anything was possible. And the sad fact was that of all our suspects so far, Luigi was one of the few with a concrete motive, easy opportunity, seeing as he lived so close by, and after the way he had lifted the huge *damigiana,* there was no doubt he had the means to batter somebody to death.

Before going home, I knew I owed Oscar a walk so I decided to kill two birds with one stone and navigated my way back up through the lanes to where Hunter's villa and his son's bungalow lay. I stopped at the side of the road a few hundred metres further on and set off with Oscar along a track between olive groves. The temperature had dropped considerably and it was a pleasure to be out in the open air.

Although it was past eight o'clock by now, the light was still good, and I could see players out on the reopened golf course below. Although it was a Thursday, it appeared that, with Rex Hunter's demise, the habit of closing the course that evening had been dropped. As far as I could see, assuming Hunter's murder had taken place just before nine o'clock, there would still have been more than enough light for him to see to play, and for any potential witnesses to see what happened to him. The track I was following dropped down towards the villa and I spotted a large, modern, clearly architect-designed bungalow a bit further along to one side. Like the villa, this had a private pool and what looked like a well-maintained garden. I couldn't see any signs of life in the grounds of either property, but I soon came across something of interest.

The track curved around to the left to avoid the wire fence surrounding the club and it was when I was probably no more than a hundred metres from the scene of the murder that I came upon a hole in the wire. Or, rather, it was Oscar who found it. One minute he was running through the scrubby bushes ahead of me looking for a stick and the next, I saw him on the other side of the fence, out on the fairway. Fortunately, there were no players close by and I was able to call him back to my side of the fence before he was noticed. He came back and it came as no surprise to me when my retriever proudly dropped a shiny white golf ball at my feet. I hastily found a stick and threw it into the woods to distract him while I picked up the golf ball and lobbed it back over the fence before anybody missed it.

I studied the hole at the base of the wire closely. It looked as though it had been made quite recently and the wire had been torn and pulled out of the ground, making a hole easily big enough for a Labrador or, indeed, a human being to crawl through. Had this been made by a wild boar – of which there were many in the area – or had it maybe been made by an intruder? I took a couple of photos and sent them over to Virgilio. The possibility of the murderer having come from outside once again reared its head.

But who could it be?

6

FRIDAY MORNING

I had another tennis lesson with Abigail at nine next morning and when I picked up my phone at eleven, I saw that I had missed a couple of calls from Virgilio, so I called him back.

'*Ciao*, Dan. I have some interesting news. Andrea Pirandello, Hunter's lawyer, has just called me to say that he received the revised will in this morning's post. It was posted on Monday afternoon and took its time getting to Florence. You know what the post can be like.'

'And does it make provision for his widow?'

'It leaves everything to her.'

'Everything?' And, of course, it immediately provided his widow with a powerful motive for murder.

'The club, the villa, his Range Rover, the contents of his bank account, and anything else you can think of. Hunter's son and daughter get nothing at all.'

'Wow, that's going to put the cat among the pigeons.'

'You can say that again. I'm glad for her sake that we found it. The contents of the safe were uninspiring: a few thousand euros in cash, passports, other documents but nothing that helps our enquiries. Anyway, I'm on my way to Acquarossa now to break the news to the widow first and then to Adam and Jennifer. Feel like joining me, even if it's just to see the two siblings go ballistic?'

I agreed immediately and hurried into the shower. By the time I got up to the villa, the police had already arrived and the front door was ajar. I ran up the steps and looked inside to see Virgilio and Innocenti standing at one side of the hall, accompanied by Battista the butler, and all three were listening intently to a shouting match echoing along the corridor from the lounge. Virgilio raised his finger to his lips and beckoned, so I tiptoed over and listened in.

'But you can't expect me just to pack up and leave overnight.' It sounded like a tearful Natalie.

'Who said anything about overnight?'

Virgilio caught my eye and mouthed the word 'Jennifer'. Certainly, Hunter's daughter didn't sound in the least bit sympathetic.

'This house doesn't belong to you, so I want you out pronto. And that means this afternoon.'

'But where shall I go...?' It sounded as though the tears had started again and Natalie was almost sobbing. 'I don't know anybody...'

'That's of no interest to me.' Jennifer was sounding more and more brutal. 'So go and start packing.'

'I'll give you a lift to Florence and we'll find you a hotel.' Adam's tone was far less confrontational, but his sister wasn't having any of it.

'Let the little gold-digger sort herself out. Go on, get on with it. I want you out of our house.'

It sounded as though the meeting was breaking up, and Virgilio caught the butler's eye.

'I think it's time you announced our presence, Battista, thank you.'

The butler led us down the corridor to the lounge door just as it was flung open by a red-faced woman with blonde hair. She was probably in her mid-thirties and her face was twisted in rage. She stopped when she saw the butler and snapped angrily at him.

'Yes, Battista, what is it?'

'Inspector Pisano and his colleagues are here to see you.'

Jennifer hissed like an angry snake. 'Well, they'll have to come back. Adam and I aren't seeing anybody at present.'

Virgilio stepped forward from behind the butler, blocking her path. 'I'm afraid you have no choice in the matter, we need to talk to you. Now, if you would just like to go back into the lounge...'

For a moment I even thought she might be about to lunge at him, but she must have thought better of it, spun around, and stomped back into the room. We followed. Battista remained outside, but I had no doubt he would be just around the corner, ears pricked.

We found Natalie sobbing on the sofa while Adam was just standing in the middle of the room looking helpless. He managed one of his PR smiles as he saw us. 'Gentlemen, do come in. How can we help?'

'I have some news that will interest all of you.' Virgilio walked over and laid his hand briefly on Natalie's shoulder. 'And you in particular, Signora Hunter.' He was speaking English. 'I've just had a phone call. You see, an envelope has arrived at your husband's lawyer's office containing the new will.' Seeing her look up, he proceeded to read from his phone, and I translated the terms of the will as he read them out. It didn't take long, but as the significance of the document registered, the faces of the three people were a picture.

Natalie's expression went from surprise to delight, but then she broke down in tears once again and slumped forward, her head in her hands.

Adam's smile disappeared in an instant to be replaced by a sickly expression. 'Are you sure, Inspector?' He could hardly get his words out. 'Surely there must be some mistake.'

'Of course there's a bloody mistake.' Jennifer's face that had been red before was now a livid purple colour and I wondered if she was going to explode like one of Luigi's bottles of spumante. Certainly, I could see how William Roseland had thought she might be unhinged. 'My father would never leave a penny to this little gold-digger. He was far too smart for that. I'm going to speak to the lawyer straight away. Come along, Adam.' She turned and headed for the door. Innocenti stepped in front of her and shook his head.

'You'll leave when the inspector tells you to leave.' He spoke in Italian, which she might or might not have understood, but his tone was uncompromising. I had a sudden flashback to my encounter with Cesare the wolfbear the previous day. If she had had hackles, they would have been raised. Yes, Innocenti was a brave man.

'It's all right, Innocenti, she can leave. They can both leave but...' Virgilio had been speaking in Italian in measured tones but now as he switched to English a grittier note entered his voice that even silenced Jennifer. 'But get it clear in your heads that this villa is not your property, and if I get reports of you coming back here uninvited or using that same tone of voice to Signora Hunter, I will see that you are arrested, charged with harassment and, if necessary, held in police custody. Is that quite clear?' There was no response from the siblings, so he asked again, this time with real force in his words. This drew a response from Adam first.

'We understand, Inspector.'

We all transferred our attention to his sister and waited. A nerve in her cheek was twitching ominously and for a moment I thought she might be about to have a stroke, but she finally nodded. 'I understand. Don't worry, Officer, I have no desire to set eyes on this little tramp ever again.'

'Good, I'm glad that's understood and, for the sake of clarity, if I hear you using words like that to describe Signora Hunter again, I will arrest you. I'm going to want to interview both of you in depth later today. We have your contact details and we'll be in touch. Do *not* leave the area. Is that clear? Now, you may go. Innocenti, *lasciali andare*.'

Innocenti stepped aside and Jennifer swept out of the room, followed by a far more subdued Adam. There was no doubt who called the shots in this relationship. Virgilio put his head around the door and called out to the butler.

'Battista, please see that Signor Hunter's son and daughter leave the building and then lock the front door behind them. Thank you.'

He walked back across the room and sat down opposite Natalie. He waited a full minute while she pulled herself together before he started speaking. 'Signora Hunter, you do understand the wording of your husband's will, don't you? You need have no financial worries. You're a rich woman. He did what he said he would do, and he has provided for you.'

Slowly she raised her face from her hands. When she spoke, it was so quietly that we all had to lean forward to hear clearly. 'Thank you, Inspector. Thank you all. It feels like waking up from a nightmare but, of course, the harsh reality is that, although I may no longer have money worries, I no longer have my beloved Rex.' If it was an act, it was a good one. Then she said something unexpected. 'I do so wish he hadn't done all this.'

'Done what, *Signora*?'

I thought I saw a momentary expression of something that might even have been guilt flash across her face, before it disappeared equally quickly. 'The will. He should have left them something. They are his kids, after all.'

'That's very magnanimous of you, considering the way they've just been treating you.'

'He told me what they were like. He told me his wife was the same sort.'

'What sort?'

'Devious, bitter, nasty people.'

It occurred to me that their father hadn't exactly been a saint, but I kept quiet and let Virgilio do the talking. I was still mulling over the significance of what had sounded like guilt in her voice. The last time we had spoken together, I had got the impression that she wasn't telling us the full story, and this just added to my conviction that all was not what it seemed. Although Natalie looked as if butter wouldn't melt in her mouth, something here still didn't ring true.

Virgilio was still giving her encouraging words. 'From what I've seen of the accounts, your husband has left you a lot of money, so there's nothing to stop you making provision for his children if that's what you want to do. Apart from anything else, Adam works here as manager, doesn't he? Will you keep him on?'

She nodded vaguely. 'I suppose so. That's if he wants to.' She looked up. 'I like Adam.'

'But not his sister?'

'No, although maybe it's not her fault. Rex told me she hasn't been well.'

'Physically or mentally?'

'He didn't say but, having met her, it looks to me like a mental problem.'

She was looking very forlorn, and a thought occurred to me.

'Natalie, who lives here apart from you? Battista, I imagine? Anybody else?'

'Mariarosa, Battista's wife. She's the cook and housekeeper.' Her voice was sounding a bit stronger.

'Do you have any close relatives who might like to come and join you, to provide a bit of support? Your parents, maybe?'

'My mum died nine months ago, and I'm an only child, but I could call Polly, my best friend, and ask her to come over. The thing is that she's in Australia.'

'Seeing as you've just come into a lot of money, why don't you offer to pay for her plane ticket to fly over and keep you company? I'm sure she'd enjoy a trip to Italy.'

She nodded a few times. 'Thank you. I'll do that. It'll be good to have a friendly face alongside me.'

Virgilio nodded approvingly, closed his notebook with a snap, and handed her his card. 'This is my direct line. Call me immediately if you have any trouble, but you shouldn't be bothered by Adam and Jennifer again. We're going to be speaking to them again this afternoon, and I'll reinforce the message that you and this villa are off limits.'

We shook hands and left the little figure sitting all alone on the settee. I felt sorry for what she had just been through, but I couldn't help reminding myself that the fact that she had now become the main beneficiary of her husband's estate automatically threw her name back onto our list of possible murderers. And near the top.

The three of us went for lunch at my place. Oscar welcomed us effusively and wandered around the table feigning starvation while we ate ham and melon, fresh goats' cheese, and raw broad beans – a local habit I had embraced – accompanied by slices of the wonderful Tuscan unsalted bread and some of my newly-acquired Chianti. This met with the approval of both detectives and I had a feeling Virgilio might well be making a trip to Luigi Signese's place one of these days to buy some for himself – as long as Luigi emerged from the murder investigation without a stain. We finished the meal off with fresh apricots from my tree. As we ate, we discussed the case in the light of the most recent developments and Virgilio went through the list of suspects again.

'Adam Hunter, his mother, and his sister have to stay near the top as they were under the impression they were going to inherit, even if it's now turned out that they didn't. The daughter is well capable of murder, I'm sure, and I get the impression that her brother's prepared to do what she tells him to do. I suppose it's even possible that the mother might have been directing things from the other side of the world, so she remains a suspect, but that's pretty tenuous. Natalie, the widow, now has a motive, although I can't really see her as a murderer but, as you keep telling me, Dan, stranger things have happened.'

I nodded. 'I also find it hard to believe, but who knows? I can't put my finger on it, but I get the feeling she isn't telling us the whole truth. Maybe it's just nerves after everything that's happened, but it's just a hunch I have.'

Virgilio nodded approvingly. 'Always trust your hunches.'

'We'll see. What about the mafia? Any chance they might have been involved?'

He shook his head. 'My people have done a lot of digging, but the word on the street is that there appear to be no links to organised crime. We're still checking but it looks very unlikely.'

'That leaves us with the farmer who made this wine that we're drinking. Luigi Signese comes across as a nice guy, but there's no concealing the very real hatred he bore towards Hunter, and now that we've found that hole in the fence, he had not only motive, but opportunity as well and, of course, a bag full of golf clubs supplied the means. He could have sneaked up through the woods, slipped through the opening and killed Hunter before disappearing back again. I like the man, but I'm afraid he needs to stay on the list.'

Innocenti joined in the conjecture. 'What about the accountant or the other guy who were playing golf with him on Monday night?' He checked his notebook. 'Nelson and Roseland. They could have had the opportunity, although there's no discernible motive.'

'Yet... there's no motive yet, but we need to keep looking. Those two have to stay on the list, that's for sure, but they're not the only ones.' Virgilio looked up from his food. 'The first person I want to interview this afternoon is the assistant manager, to find out if she really was having an affair with Hunter. After that we'll sit down with the two siblings. Let's start with Adam. Of the two, I get the feeling he's more likely to talk.' He corrected himself. 'When I say "talk," I mean answer our questions. I have no doubt his sister will be hard to shut up, but getting straight answers out of her to direct questions won't be so easy.'

7

FRIDAY AFTERNOON

It was an interesting afternoon. The interview with Elizabeth McGregor, the assistant manager, provided us with a fascinating insight into the sort of man Rex Hunter had been. At first, she tried to deny that anything had been happening between her and him, but she finally gave in and confessed.

'I first met Rex... Mr Hunter when I began working here just over two years ago. He was very nice to me, and I took to him from the start. I like men who know their own minds. Yes, I know he ruffled a lot of feathers around here, but the fact is that he turned a little local golf course into a major leisure complex in a matter of a few years. You don't do something like that without being assertive.'

'And at what stage did your relationship with Mr Hunter become more intimate? While he was still married or after the divorce?'

She had the decency to look a little uncomfortable. 'To be honest, it started soon after we first met. Our affair lasted for almost two years.' She looked up and offered some justification. 'He was very unhappy with June, his wife. She was Australian through and through, and he told me she never wanted to come over here in the first place. She hated every minute of it. She refused to try to learn Italian and he said she rapidly developed a drink problem. Living in the middle of a wine-growing region like Chianti offers a lot of temptation. As a result, Rex used to come to me for support and understanding.'

I couldn't help making reference to what so many people had been saying about Rex Hunter. 'You say he ruffled a few feathers. We've heard from a lot of people that in fact he could be objectionable. How could you fall in love with somebody like that?'

'That was on the outside. Yes, he could be tough, maybe rude on occasions, but with me, in private, he could be sweet.'

'But that's not what his first wife thought.'

She snorted dismissively. 'That was her fault, not his.'

'So how did you feel when he divorced her?'

'I felt happy for him. I could see the change in him after she went back to Australia. He was like a new man.'

'And how did you see your relationship developing with him after that? Did you think you would become the next Mrs Rex Hunter?'

We had to wait while she formulated her answer. 'I suppose, deep down, I hoped that would be the way it would pan out, but of course it didn't. We split up a few months back but we stayed friends, close friends.'

'And whose idea was it for you to split up?

'It wasn't mine. I loved him.' She suddenly looked up. 'But I didn't hate him for it, really I didn't. I certainly didn't feel bitter or angry enough to want to kill him. You have to believe that. I loved him with all my heart.' And she started crying.

Virgilio waited until she had wiped her eyes and blown her nose before continuing. 'Out of interest, do you happen to know on what grounds the divorce was granted? Presumably under Australian law, it's sufficient to show incompatibility.'

'He divorced her because she was unfaithful to him.'

The fact that he had repeatedly been unfaithful to his wife for at least two years was left unsaid.

'So she admitted she'd been unfaithful?'

Elizabeth nodded. 'Yes, and he was very happy about that because he ended up having to give her a lot less money than he'd feared.'

'And who was the man? Is he still with the ex-wife now?'

'Rex never found out. June made the mistake of boasting about it at a dinner party in front of a load of people, including Rex's lawyer. When she sobered up, she tried to deny it, but it was too late; the cat was out of the bag. But she never said who the man was. As far as I know, she's on her own back in Australia now. Whoever the man was, I presume they went their separate ways.'

'Tell me, Signora McGregor, did you expect to get anything from Signor Hunter after he died? Did he ever speak about leaving you anything in his will?'

She shook her head. 'Rex was very good to me. He bought me my apartment in Acquarossa a year ago, and he gave me other presents, like my car, for example. He was very generous, but I didn't expect for a moment that he'd leave me anything. Why, has he?'

Now it was Virgilio's turn to shake his head. 'I'm afraid not.'

I felt pretty sure I saw a look of disappointment flit across her face, but it was only momentary. 'Like I say, he gave me lots and I never expected more.'

'And you told us the other day that you were here on duty on Monday evening, isn't that so?' She nodded. 'And you say the CCTV footage proves that you never moved from here?'

'That's correct. I never went outside the building.'

'But of course, the cameras are out in the hall, not here in your office. That's a nice French window you have looking out onto the rear of the clubhouse. If you'd wanted to, couldn't you have slipped out that way?'

'I didn't kill Rex, Inspector, you have to believe that. I loved him.'

After the interview concluded, Virgilio and I went out to our usual bench and sat down in the shade until the time for our meeting with Adam Hunter. We both agreed that Elizabeth McGregor had looked and sounded distraught, and we both felt we believed her when she said she had loved Hunter and that his death had hit her hard. Her devotion to him appeared to indicate that he did after all contain a warmer, more human side just as Natalie had said, but there was no doubt that the crusty exterior was all that most people experienced. There was no way of knowing whether she had really been with him out of love, as she said, or whether she might have been in it for the free car and the apartment. If it had been love, then, of course, her grief might also be because the man she had loved had gone off and married another woman rather than her. And that sort of grief can easily turn into something more sinister.

At three o'clock, we went back inside and found Adam Hunter in his office. This was a pleasant room with windows looking onto the golf course and comfortable seating for visitors. There was a fridge in one corner of the room, presumably containing drinks for invited guests. We weren't offered any. He greeted us in Italian, which he spoke unexpectedly well. It very soon became apparent that he had checked with his father's lawyer, who had confirmed the news that he and his sister were to inherit nothing. He looked understandably shell-shocked. After warning him that the interview was being recorded, Virgilio tackled the matter head-on.

'Your name and age, please, Signor Hunter.'

'Adam James Hunter and I'm thirty-three.'

'Tell me, Signor Hunter, why do you think your father changed his will so as to cut you out? It seems a radical move.'

'It's a *very* radical move. Jennifer and I've been talking to our mother, and we can only conclude that he was losing his mind.' He looked straight across at us in a weak show of defiance. 'We plan to contest the will on the grounds of insanity.'

'I wish you luck. In my experience, proving insanity is very hard to do unless the person in question helpfully starts dancing naked through Piazza della Signoria or jumping off the Ponte Vecchio. Assuming, for a moment, that he wasn't going crazy, do you think he was trying to make a point? Was he trying to tell you and your sister something by excluding you?'

'If he was trying to prove that he'd lost his head over some random woman, he succeeded.' He was still trying to sound tough.

'Did he tell you or your sister that he might be planning to cut you out of his will? Think carefully before answering, as I have a witness who overheard the argument the two of you had outside in the gardens last Thursday morning.'

Adam's defiant stance didn't last. After a bit of prevarication, his shoulders slumped, and he admitted that his father had announced his intentions to him that day. I heaved a silent sigh of relief. Although Ines the gardener had overheard an argument, she hadn't understood a word of it, but Adam didn't need to know that.

Virgilio subjected him to close scrutiny as he continued. 'Here's what I've been wondering, Signor Hunter: could it be that you and your sister decided to kill your father before he could change his will, little knowing that it was already too late?'

To my surprise, Adam looked completely flabbergasted. I had expected bluster or anger, not complete and utter bewilderment.

'You think I killed my father? What do you think I am: a monster?' Rather like his father's young widow, if he was acting, it was a remarkable performance. Seeing him so obviously appalled at the suggestion rang true, and I found myself reviewing my suspicions. Meanwhile, Virgilio was still trying.

'You stood to lose a lot of money. You *have* lost a lot of money. People have been murdered for far less.'

Adam's reaction continued to be one of disgust and growing anger. 'I can't believe what I'm hearing. I'd never, ever, do something like that. If you're going to make those sorts of allegations, I think I need to have my lawyer here.'

'I'm only trying to get to the bottom of why your father was killed and by whom. Please can you confirm where you were on Monday evening between seven and ten? Don't be alarmed, Signor Hunter, we're asking everybody for their whereabouts.'

'I already told you the other day. I was at home having dinner.'

'And somebody can confirm that?'

'Yes: my partner, Emily. She was with me all evening, and all night, for that matter. She lives with me up at the bungalow.' He looked up, a spark of his earlier bluster returning. 'By the way, that house is in my name. I own it. My father's new wife... widow isn't getting her hands on it.'

Virgilio changed his tone to something less confrontational. 'Thank you for clarifying that. I just have one more sensitive question: do you think your sister might have killed your father?'

'Of course not. That's unthinkable.'

This time the expression that appeared on Adam's face was one of outrage but tempered with something else. Could it be that he secretly did think her capable of murder? I did my best to press him.

'We've been told that she may have had some psychiatric problems. Is that correct?'

'Yes, but nothing serious. She's always been highly strung but the medication she's on keeps her on an even keel.' His voice took on a more gentle note. 'She's my big sister and I love her, and all my life I've looked out for her. She's had her problems but she's not capable of murder, especially not our father. You have to believe me.'

This shed more light on the relationship between the two siblings. Clearly he thought of himself as his sister's guardian. Virgilio took over the questioning.

'Tell me, have you any idea who might have killed your father? It's clear he wasn't a very popular man.' Although Natalie and Elizabeth McGregor claimed to have seen a warmer, softer side to him.

Adam almost smiled. 'Popular? Most people disliked him, some probably hated him. He wasn't a man who endeared himself to others.'

'Including to his family?' I thought I'd just slip that in, and he nodded.

'My mother spent thirty-five years with him, and it almost killed her.'

'And did *you* hate him?'

'Maybe not hate, but I didn't like him, and I didn't respect him as a man. I despised him for his behaviour, particularly towards our mother. In answer to your question, Inspector, a lot of people disliked him, but I genuinely can't think of anybody who hated him enough and would have been crazy enough to resort to murder.'

When we came out of Adam's office, we headed for the atrium bar and ordered two coffees. We drank them at a table in the corner, far away from curious ears, and agreed that his reaction had appeared genuine and spontaneous. We weren't going to exclude him from our enquiries just yet, but he was looking a less likely candidate for our murderer. As we were talking, my phone rang, and I saw that it was Tricia. I shot Virgilio an apologetic glance and answered it.

'Hi, Tricia, all well?'

'Hi, Dad. I'm okay, thanks, but Mum's a wreck.'

'She's been staying with you?'

'Yes, since yesterday. It's painfully obvious that this break-up has hit her hard.' There was a brief pause before she continued. 'But it's not all bad.'

'In what way?'

'She says it's made her stop and re-evaluate the last few years. She's even been muttering to me that leaving you might have been the biggest mistake of her life.'

I had to make a conscious effort to stop my jaw from dropping. Never in a hundred years would I have expected to hear this. My wife had left me and divorced me, even though I'd given up the job she so hated so as to be able to spend more time with her. She had deserted me for another man, and it had hurt. Although I hadn't hooked up with anybody else since then, I had moved on with my life and had no intention of putting myself through all that again, so I responded cautiously.

'You said it yourself, Tricia, she's upset. Give her a bit of time and she'll get over it. As for us getting back together again, I'm afraid it's far too late for that now. What's done is done.' I glanced across at Virgilio, who was ostentatiously studying the laminated menu on the table so closely it looked as though he was committing it to memory. 'She doesn't really mean it. She's just feeling lonely.'

'I think it's more than that, Dad, at least I hope it is.'

'There, you've just said it: you *hope* it is. Listen, Trish, you've

90 T. A. WILLIAMS

got to be realistic. It isn't going to happen. Besides, I've got a new life in Tuscany now. She'd be lost over here.'

'About that... I've suggested that she and I go away together for a few days, to give her a break.' She paused again before delivering the *coup de grâce*. 'I thought we could take a two-day city break to Florence. I've explained to my boss, and she says I can have a bit of time off. And Mum's never been to Florence, as you know.'

My grandmother was Italian, and I've often had a sneaky suspicion that some convoluted thread of Machiavelli's DNA must have transferred itself through her line to my daughter. As a plan it was audacious, but hardly subtle.

'I really don't think that's such a good idea, Tricia. Where would you stay? I can hardly invite her to stay here with me.'

'I've found a nice little hotel not far from Florence main station. We can get a train direct from Pisa airport and be there in little more than an hour.'

'And when might this be?'

'There are seats still available on the morning flight this Sunday and back home again on Tuesday evening. That'll give us almost two full days of sightseeing.' Another pregnant pause. 'Anyway, she thinks it's a good idea, so I've gone ahead and booked everything.'

My mind was churning wildly. Today was Friday so this meant they were coming in less than forty-eight hours' time. I hadn't seen Helen for well over a year and in that time everything had changed for both of us. Doing my best not to appear too gobsmacked, I sounded another note of caution. 'Tricia, have you thought this through? Are you sure you're doing the right thing?'

'I have and I know I am. But listen, Dad: the decision's yours. I thought maybe we could meet up for dinner somewhere neutral on Sunday evening. No pressure on either of you. Sit down with her – don't worry, I'll be there as chaperone or umpire – and see how the evening goes. If it goes well, you can meet up with her again on Monday or Tuesday, and if it doesn't, at least you'll have seen her again.'

By the time the conversation ended, I had agreed to the Sunday dinner idea – as Tricia had known all along that I would – and had even let myself be bullied into maybe collecting them and bringing them out to my house the next day, depending on how the evening went. Tricia had insisted that it was only right that her mum should be able to see where I was living and meet my new best friend, Oscar.

The end of the call coincided with a small shot glass of clear liquid being deposited in front of me. As I dropped my phone onto the table, I caught Virgilio's eye, but before I could say a word he indicated with a movement of his hand that I should drink.

I did as instructed and, by the time I had regained control of my vocal cords after a throatful of grappa, I looked up to see that he was smiling.

'You look like that hit the spot.'

'It certainly hit a spot, but I'm not sure which.' I was pleasantly surprised to find I could still speak after the onslaught of the powerful spirit. 'But thanks. You probably gathered what's just happened.'

'I understand that you're hosting a dinner party for three on Sunday night. I wish you well with it.'

He knew the sad story of my separation and divorce and there was no need to remind him of it. All I could do was order another coffee to hide the grappa on my breath and brace myself for the forthcoming interview with Rex Hunter's daughter. I wasn't looking forward to it, but I felt sure that it was going to be a whole lot easier than the reunion with my ex-wife on Sunday.

* * *

We conducted the interview in the office of Peter Nelson, the accountant, who had gone to Florence for the rest of the afternoon. Jennifer Hunter was already there when we arrived, sitting ramrod-straight behind the desk, so that we had to sit before her. With my help from time to time, Virgilio conducted the interview in English, and he began as he had done with her brother by telling her the interview was being recorded and advising her to think carefully before answering any questions. She acknowledged his words with the slightest nod of the head. Whereas her brother had been looking stunned by the contents of the new will and his sudden change of circumstances, her expression was inscrutable – at first.

After getting her to give us her full name, date of birth – she was thirty-five – and current address in Australia, Virgilio started with the night of the murder.

'On Monday evening you told us you were on your way up the track to the villa at around eight forty-five. Is that correct?'

'The time's correct but I wasn't going to the villa. I refused to stay under the same roof as that little... as my father's new wife. I was going up to my brother's house where I've been staying.'

'And how were you travelling?'

'I was riding my brother's dirt bike.'

'You were riding a motorbike?'

Virgilio sounded as surprised as I was. Somehow, I hadn't associated this smartly dressed woman with anything so basic. I took a closer look at her as she replied. Beneath the supercilious expression on her face, I could see something else, something far more primitive. She positively exuded hatred – whether towards us or her new stepmother or life in general was uncertain – but there could be no doubt that she was only just about managing to keep a lid on it. It was like watching one of those Icelandic geysers as the first warning bubbles begin to appear shortly before a stream of scalding water explodes into the sky.

She gave us a challenging look. 'What's wrong with riding a motorbike? Adam and I used to ride to school on dirt bikes.' We could hear how hard she was struggling to keep control of her voice and her temper. 'Our family didn't always live in luxury villas. We were brought up in a wooden bungalow way out in the Outback. That's what we did.'

'I see. Tell me, please, exactly what you saw as you rode up the track past the eighth hole.'

'I saw my father standing near the sand trap where his body was subsequently found. He waved to me, but I didn't stop.'

'And you're sure it was your father?'

'Of course it was my father. You think I can't recognise my own father?' Her voice went up an octave, and I saw Virgilio do his best to ratchet down the tension in the room.

'Thank you. Tell me, would you say you got on well with your father? It seems clear to me that he wasn't a popular man. Even your brother agrees with me.'

'I hated my father.' The four words were delivered in a remarkably measured tone.

'Would you mind telling me why?'

'Because of the way he treated my mother. Can you imagine what it feels like, Inspector, when your school friends jeer at you because of your father's reputation?'

'And what sort of reputation was that?' Although we both knew the answer.

'He was a bully and a cheat, but above all he couldn't keep his hands off other women, some of them the mothers of my class-mates. He was like it all his life.'

'Even recently? He was getting on in years, after all.' Considering that Hunter had been only five or six years older than me, that was a bit close to home, but I said nothing. People had been telling me that fifty-six was the new forty-six, but there had been times over the winter when I had woken up feeling more like sixty-six.

'I said all his life, and I meant all his life. This latest woman...' We could see her making an effort not to explode into an outburst of invective. 'His latest wife was just the tip of the iceberg. Did you know, for instance, that he'd been carrying on a sordid affair with Elizabeth McGregor, the assistant manager here? And Adam says there have been others. The man was out of control.'

'And you hated him for it?'

'I already told you that.'

'Did you hate him enough to wish him dead?'

Without a fraction of a second's hesitation, she nodded. 'Many was the time I hoped he would die.'

'Did you hate him enough to kill him yourself?'

Once again she answered immediately. 'I don't know, maybe.' She wasn't looking at either of us. Her eyes were fixed on the middle distance, somewhere out of the window. I wondered if Virgilio was going to pounce on this extraordinary confession but his voice was expressionless as he asked, 'And did you kill him?'

'No, Inspector, I did not.' Her gaze returned to him now. 'I can't say I'm sorry he's dead, but I didn't do it.' And somehow, in spite of what she had just told us, I believed her.

'The fact is that by your own admission, you were almost certainly the last person to see him alive and you were in the very spot where the murder took place at the exact time of the killing. Am I right in assuming that you have no witness who could attest to your innocence?'

'No witness but, Inspector, the same applies to you.' She shot him a defiant glance. 'You have no proof that I did it, and I assume that here in Italy you still believe that a person is innocent until proved guilty. So you'll have to go ahead and prove that I'm guilty, but you can't, because I didn't do it. Besides, I wasn't the last person to see him alive. That would have been the murderer.'

Virgilio didn't acknowledge her taunt. Instead, he changed tack slightly.

'Your brother told us you've been having treatment for a psychiatric condition. Is that so?'

Her face darkened. 'That has nothing to do with you. If you want to look at my medical records you'll need to ask a judge. In Australia, these things are confidential.' She glared at him malevolently. 'But I can assure you that I had nothing to do with my father's death.'

Undeterred, Virgilio carried on. 'Why do you think your father decided to cut you and your brother out of his will?'

'I have absolutely no doubt that it was down to that... to his new wife. She made him do it.'

'And that made you very angry. I could see that myself this morning. Your father broke the news to your brother last Thursday that he was changing his will. Did Adam tell you?'

After a momentary hesitation, she nodded. 'Yes, he did. He was furious, as was I.'

'Furious enough to contemplate murder?'

'Contemplating murder is one thing. Doing something about it is another.' She paused for a second or two before continuing in a more level tone. 'Besides, Inspector, it wasn't in my interests to kill my father. Maybe if it had been, I might indeed have turned out to be his murderer.'

'And why was that?'

'I received a monthly allowance from him that meant that I was free to do what I wanted.'

'And that was?'

'I'm an artist, Inspector. I have a studio back home where I paint, and I sell my paintings when and where I can. I'm a realist and I know it's very unlikely I'll ever be able to make enough from selling my work, so five thousand dollars every month from my father meant that I could carry on. No, it made no sense for me to kill him.'

And, again, I tended to believe her.

8

SATURDAY

'What would you do, Oscar?'

I wasn't talking about the investigation, but it didn't matter to him. Ever since Tricia's phone call, I had been thinking about the impending arrival of my ex-wife. After a certain amount of reflection, I had booked a table for Sunday night at a little restaurant I knew in Borgo San Lorenzo, in the heart of Florence's *centro storico*. Virgilio had introduced me to it and he and I had eaten there many times and I knew the food would be good. But food was the least of my worries as I had been outlining to the dog as I drove back to the club on Saturday morning for my final lesson with Abigail. Today it was only for an hour, so I had brought Oscar with me. I would park in the shade, and he could snooze in the car and then I'd take him for a good long walk.

'What if Helen wants us to get back together? She has to realise that things have irrevocably changed between us. I'm going to have to spell it out to her, but I'm not looking forward to it. I have to tell her, don't I, Oscar?'

At the sound of his name, his furry face appeared over the back of the rear seat and for a moment I swear he shook his head at me in the rear-view mirror. Pretty clearly, he didn't know either. It didn't seem to bother him which language I was using, he was a good listener, but a bit of feedback every now and then would have been welcome.

'She doesn't speak a word of Italian. If she decided to move here, I'm afraid she might end up going the same way as Rex Hunter's first wife, getting all bitter and twisted. I couldn't face the prospect of her starting to hate me all over again. Better to just be brutally honest from the start.' Since our separation, relations between Helen and me hadn't exactly been warm, but there hadn't been any overt animosity. We had both accepted the situation and had done our best to get on with our lives. Now, Sunday's reunion risked stirring everything up again. Much as part of me was quite looking forward to seeing her again, the more rational part feared the worst.

I heard Oscar give a heartfelt sigh. I knew how he felt.

I parked in the shade of another of the huge umbrella pines, left all the windows half open and told Oscar to be a good boy. As I walked off to get changed, I saw him peering dolefully out of the side window, but by the time I came back out, he had decided to lie down again. He might not be too happy to be left on his own, but he would survive, and he would be rewarded with a good walk.

When I got to the tennis court, I came upon an interesting scene. Abigail was already there and she was standing by the gate, lovingly entwined with none other than Dario, the golf pro. Nobody had mentioned this relationship and I found myself wondering if it could have any relevance to the case. When they saw me, they broke up and he walked off, giving me a little wave and a smile as he passed.

The lesson finished at ten and I stood chatting to Abigail for a few minutes before heading back to the clubhouse. The conversation quite naturally came around to her relationship with Dario and she confirmed that the two of them were now very close.

'I think it's the Real Thing, Dan. He's a lovely man and we get on so well. He's just asked me to move in with him and I've said yes.' She caught my eye. 'It was looking as though he was going to lose his job here, so it's a big relief.'

'Lose his job? Why?'

Her expression hardened. 'Why do you think? Rex Hunter, of course.' She glanced around apprehensively, but we were alone. 'Just before Hunter went off to get married, there was a golf tournament here at the club. Dario was playing in a foursome containing Hunter and, instead of letting him win, Dario beat him. Hunter was so angry he told Dario to start looking for another job. I was really worried. I enjoy my job here, and tennis-coaching positions aren't easy to find, but now that Hunter's dead, it looks as though Dario and I can both stay here and, hopefully, settle down together.'

I wished her well and went off to change. All the time I couldn't help wondering why Dario hadn't told me about this and instead had pretended that the story of being fired had been about one of his predecessors. Had he realised that this would have made him a suspect for Hunter's murder? Did this even mean that he'd done it? Yes, it would have been an over-the-top solution to his problems, but there was no getting away from the fact that Hunter's death had done him a big favour.

When I got back to the car, I phoned Virgilio's office and spoke to Innocenti, who reminded me of what I had forgotten. Tomorrow was Virgilio and Lina's wedding anniversary and they had gone sailing around the island of Elba for the weekend. Innocenti was in charge of the investigation for now, so I passed on the latest news about the golf pro, and I heard him groan.

'The boss is going to go mad when he hears that: yet another name to be added to the list of suspects. You won't be surprised to hear that when I interviewed everybody at the club, the golf pro's alibi was provided by Abigail Whatsername, your tennis coach with the lovely legs. What this means is that if they're a couple, we have to treat the alibi with suspicion, just like Adam Hunter's alibi provided by *his* partner. We interviewed his partner, name of Emily – another stunner – and she confirms that he was at home all Monday night, but can we believe her? I'm beginning to realise that our original assumption that most of the main suspects had alibis isn't so solid after all. By the way, I interviewed your wine-making friend, Luigi Signese, and his alibi for Monday evening has been supplied by his wife and three ladies who live there with him, all of them related to him one way or another, so that's pretty worthless as well.'

'What about Nelson and Roseland? Does the CCTV footage back up their stories?'

'Yes, to a point. It shows them returning to the club at just before nine. It's normally a fifteen-minute walk – I did it yesterday – so I suppose it's just feasible that they followed Hunter up to the bunker, killed him straight after his daughter went past on the motorbike, and then ran back down the hill again.'

'Not that Roseland looks capable of doing much running.'

'I agree, it's possible but not probable. Besides, what motive could either of them have had?'

I drove out of the club and up to the same parking spot I had used on Thursday and retraced my steps. It was warm today, but not as stiflingly hot as the previous days and Oscar was running about happily. We walked down towards the hole in the wire to check if there might be any sign of footprints. Virgilio had told me his men had already looked but I've always felt happier checking this sort of thing myself. I immediately realised that it was a forlorn task as the ground was rock hard after no rain for weeks but something interesting popped up – or rather, was brought to me. While my back was turned, Oscar must have slipped through the hole in the fence again and I looked up to see his long black tail wagging contentedly as he sniffed about in the long grass at the edge of the fairway.

I called him and to my relief he obediently came back through to my side again, but I saw that he was carrying something in his mouth. This time it wasn't a stick for me to throw or a golf ball but a white leather glove. I persuaded him to give it to me and rewarded him by throwing a particularly large pine cone off into the trees for him to retrieve. As he crashed off into the undergrowth, I studied the glove carefully.

From where he'd been sniffing about, the glove must have been lying less than a hundred metres from the crime scene. I assumed it was a golf glove although I'd never set eyes on one before. There was of course no reason to believe that it might have anything to do with the murder, but it didn't look as though it had been lying on the ground for many days, so I slipped it into one of Oscar's poo bags – a clean one! – and decided to drop it down to Virgilio just in case. I remembered a case we had back in London a few years earlier where forensics had been able to get a partial fingerprint off the *inside* of a pair of Marigold gloves. This glove was soft leather, but it wasn't lined so maybe...

After our walk, I drove the half-hour down to Florence and managed to find a parking space near the station. Walking past a series of hotels towards the police headquarters, I couldn't help thinking about Helen's impending arrival the next day, and I wondered where she and Tricia would be staying. I was genuinely torn between pleasure at the thought of seeing her again and dread at having to tell her that I had no intention of finding myself on the slippery slope back to an unhappy relationship. Ours had been a happy marriage for the first twenty years, but it had soured more and more as the years went by and my job became ever more demanding. She had made what was probably the right decision two years ago to leave me, and I wasn't going through that again.

I found Innocenti in the office and I passed over the golf glove with a caveat that it might have nothing to do with the case. He promised to send it for analysis as soon as possible. We chatted some more about the case, but we both agreed that although we had no shortage of suspects, we would be hard pushed to build a case against any of them. While Oscar snoozed on the floor, clearly enjoying the air conditioning, I asked if I could sift through the items retrieved from Rex Hunter's safe. I spent several minutes making a close study of the collection of papers and documents but had to agree that there was nothing untoward in there. Unless there were further developments, we were stumped.

* * *

That afternoon, I walked from my house down to Montevolpone to check how plans for next Saturday's *festa del paese* were going. On the way there, I took Oscar down to the stream so he could have a swim. A month earlier, the water in one particular pool had been deep enough for me to go in for a swim as well, but now it was barely deep enough for Oscar to paddle about. Although a little cooler, it was increasingly humid today, but I thought I could see the first signs of grey clouds beginning to mass on the horizon. There was no doubt that the arrival of rain would be greeted with delight by all the farmers around here. On a more personal level, I had a sinking feeling that the grey clouds might prove to be an omen in advance of my meeting with my wife the following evening.

There was only one other person sitting outside Tommaso's café in the piazza and, to my surprise, I found that it was Beppe, the groundsman from the country club. He recognised me and gave me a wave.

'Good afternoon. Have there been any developments?'

I wandered over with Oscar. 'Nothing new. What's pretty clear is that Rex Hunter wasn't a popular man.'

'You can say that again.' He stroked Oscar's head. 'He's a hand-some dog. Are you showing him next Saturday?'

'I've said yes, but I've got a feeling it won't end well. He has a thing about other dogs.'

'Wants to fight them?'

'Very much the opposite. I'm afraid he's a bit like Rex Hunter used to be.'

Beppe grinned at me. 'Look out for Elizabeth McGregor's poodle in that case. That beast takes after her owner, if you know what I mean...' He gave me a wink and an unmistakable gesture with a clenched fist and a raised forearm.

I glanced down at my dog, who was now resting his head on Beppe's knee. 'Hear that, dog? No hanky-panky next Saturday, all right?' I returned my attention to Beppe. 'So what brings you to Montevolpone?'

'I'm waiting for my wife. She's at the hairdressers.' He glanced at his watch and stood up. 'Which reminds me, I said I'd pick her up about now. I'm from Acquarossa, but she's originally from Montevolpone and she always gets her hair done here. To be honest, she comes here more for the gossip than anything.'

'If she hears any gossip about Rex Hunter's murder, be sure to let me know and I'll pass it on to the Inspector.'

I went into the café and ordered a non-alcoholic beer. Tommaso and Oscar were old friends, and he brought the dog a bowl of water and a couple of breadsticks. We chatted and he told me that arrangements for the fair were going smoothly, although they were going to need all the help they could get for the feeding of the five thousand – or more precisely a couple of hundred – next Saturday night. I promised to lend a hand and he accepted my offer gratefully. Apart from my fears that Oscar might disgrace himself, I was looking forward to the event as I gradually settled more and more firmly into life here in Tuscany. This brought my mind back again to thoughts of Helen, and I was still thinking about our impending reunion as I made my way back up to the house.

Back home, I considered cleaning it in readiness for Monday's guests – depending on how tomorrow evening went – but Maria, my cleaner, had done such a good job that I soon gave it up as pointless. As it was late afternoon, I made myself a cup of tea and was just settling down to drink it in the shade of the loggia when my phone started ringing. It was Innocenti and he had big news.

'It's the widow, Natalie Hunter: she's been rushed to hospital. It looks like she's been poisoned. She's still alive but unconscious. As the boss is away, I don't suppose you could come down to the hospital with me to see what's what and help with interpreting? If she wakes up, we need to know whether she did this to herself or if somebody's tried to kill her.'

I immediately agreed and jumped in the car. I left Oscar in the kitchen with one of his big dog biscuits and orders to be good. Hospitals, like golf clubs, aren't too keen on dogs wandering about. Half an hour later, I met Innocenti and a uniformed officer in the main lobby of the Santa Maria Nuova hospital and we hurried along the corridor to the acute medicine department. When we got there, we were allowed to peek through a glass panel into a private room where Natalie Hunter was lying in a hospital bed linked up to all manner of monitors, machines, tubes, and drips. She was as white as the sheets on which she was lying. A doctor emerged from the room, removed his mask, and gave us an update.

'She'll live. We've pumped her stomach and done our best to flush as much of the Zancorepine out of her system as we can.'

'Zancorepine?' This sounded vaguely familiar to me, but Innocenti asked for clarification.

'It's a fast-acting tranquilliser. She's overdosed on it.'

'When you say "tranquilliser", what exactly do you mean?'

The doctor gave Innocenti a long-suffering look. 'I mean exactly that. It's a drug that's widely used for people suffering from acute anxiety, panic attacks, and so on. It has a calming effect on the brain. Taken regularly in the right dosage, it can be very effective. Taken to excess, it can be lethal. She's lucky the people who found her acted so promptly.'

'How did you know it was that drug?'

'In these cases, it's standard practice to do a blood test immediately after arrival and screen for a variety of pathogens. The results only came back a few minutes before you arrived, but we felt sure from the start it had to be something she'd ingested, so we'd already set about emptying her system as fast as possible.'

I checked with Innocenti, who told me that Battista had found Natalie lying unconscious on the floor of the lounge just after two o'clock. As she hadn't drunk alcohol with her lunch, he had realised straight away that all was not well and had called the emergency services.

After being informed that the patient was in an induced coma and would be in no fit state to talk to anybody for at least twenty-four hours, Innocenti and I decided we might as well leave the hospital. The doctor's parting words were that they hoped she should be able to go home on Monday or more probably Tuesday. At my suggestion, the uniformed officer was left outside the door to keep watch. If it *had* been attempted murder, I was afraid that

the perpetrator might well try again. When we got outside, Innocenti asked if I would mind going with him to the Hunter villa to
interview the butler and his wife, and I was happy to help. We
travelled up in two cars, but Innocenti was clearly in a hurry, and
he turned on his blue light and siren and put his foot down. I
settled into his slipstream, and we roared out through the
suburbs of Florence in no time. As a result, we got to the villa in
barely twenty minutes and found Battista comforting Mariarosa,
his wife, who was crying her eyes out. Through the sobs, the story
gradually emerged.

'Signora Natalie hasn't been eating very much, and so I said
I'd make her some soup today – you know, good hearty soup full
of vegetables – and she ate a decent-sized bowlful with some
bread. After the soup, I managed to get her to eat one of my
crème caramels and a small bunch of grapes. She was looking
quite cheerful by the time she left the table and went through to
the lounge.'

'What do you think happened?'

'Poison in the soup; it has to be.' Mariarosa sounded as if she
was in no doubt. 'It's not as if it was meat or fish that might have
gone off; it was just veg and a bit of Parmesan, followed by a
dessert. She must've been poisoned; it's the only explanation.'

'So she didn't look as if she intended committing suicide?'

'Not at all. In fact, she'd been looking and acting more relaxed
– still not happy by any means, but less agitated.'

Battista laid a comforting hand on his wife's shoulder. 'Tell
them what you think... about the window.'

Mariarosa wiped her eyes on her apron before continuing.
'We've been making sure we keep the doors locked at all times
just in case of unwelcome visitors.' She didn't name names, but
we all knew to whom she was referring. 'But as it was so sticky
today, I opened the kitchen window around mid-morning, and

without thinking, I left it open when I went upstairs to make up the *signora's* room.' She was sounding a bit calmer now. 'I think somebody must have climbed in the window. There was no way anybody could have done anything to the crème caramel. That was in the fridge, and it had already set. If anybody had tried to meddle with it, it would have been obvious. All I can assume is that somebody put poison in the soup.'

'Did either of you have the soup?'

Battista answered for both of them. 'Under normal circumstances I probably would have had some, but it's too humid today. The two of us just had a ham sandwich and some cheese.' He caught my eye. 'Thank God, or we'd be in hospital ourselves now... or worse'

Mariarosa looked up from her hands. 'Is the *signora* going to be all right? Do they know what sort of poison it was?'

Innocenti gave them the good news that it sounded as though Natalie would recover and that it looked as if she had been poisoned by some sort of chemical compound, but without specifying which. After that, we went through to the kitchen and Mariarosa pointed out the window in question. It was now closed. What's that old saying about the stable door and the horse? It had a low sill, and it was quite clearly big enough for anybody to have climbed through. We checked outside but found – just like with the hole in the fence – that the earth below the window was far too hard to show any footprints. We queried if they had CCTV here, but the answer was no. Just to be on the safe side, we went upstairs and searched for any sign of Zancorepine in Natalie's bedroom and bathroom, as well as in her husband's rooms, but to no avail. We even checked the waste baskets, but there was no trace of the drug or any container that might have held it.

When we came back downstairs, Innocenti and I accepted cups of coffee from Mariarosa, who was looking a bit more relaxed now that she had told us her tale, and we talked it over. It seemed indisputable that Natalie had been poisoned, but by whom? Neither Innocenti or I could see these fine old people as being involved so who did this leave? Innocenti pointed out the obvious anomaly.

'As far as I'm concerned, the finger of suspicion points firmly in one direction: Hunter's son and daughter, but why? If they killed Natalie, it's not as if their father's estate would pass back to them. That ship has sailed. So, if they did it, it could only have been out of spite. You know – if we can't have it, neither can she.'

'I agree. And if it was spite, I know who my money's on. I think we should go and pay a visit to Adam Hunter's bungalow so we can speak to him and his sister, particularly the sister. Of the two, I have no doubt she's the more dangerous, and I reckon she's easily capable of murder or at least attempted murder.'

Innocenti called the station and arranged for a forensic team to come and take the remains of the soup for analysis and to dust the kitchen and the windowsill in particular for fingerprints, but neither of us was very hopeful. With so much murder mystery on TV these days, even the dimmest criminals have realised that gloves are a good idea. While Innocenti was doing this, I had a word with Battista, who explained that there was a path linking the two properties. He told us there was a locked gate in the fence between the two and gave us the entry code. We walked out across the meticulously mowed lawn and through the ring of cypress trees until we reached a solid gate. Innocenti punched in the code, and we headed for the bungalow. This place could have come straight out of *Grand Designs* with its vast expanses of glass, teak, and marble, as well as its gorgeous infinity pool set into the hillside. Stretched out on a sun lounger next to the pool was a familiar figure in a bikini. She watched us through her sunglasses as she heard us approach.

'What do you want?' As greetings go, it was uncompromising.

'Good afternoon, we'd like to ask you a few questions.' Innocenti was trying to copy Virgilio's deceptively cordial interview technique, and I did my best to render this tone in my translation to her. Jennifer didn't reply in kind.

'Haven't you already asked me more than enough questions?' She sat up and draped a towel across her body. 'What now?'

'I'd like to know your movements today, particularly mid- to late-morning and around lunchtime.'

'Today? I've been here. Why, what's happened?'

'You haven't left the bungalow all day?'

'I just told you, no.'

'What about your brother and his partner? Are they here?'

She shook her head. 'They've gone into Florence shopping. So, tell me, what's happened?'

'Your father's widow, Signora Natalie Hunter, has been poisoned.'

She actually smiled, although it wasn't a friendly smile. I could see that she was still seething inside. 'Couldn't have happened to a nicer person. Thank you for bringing me the good news.'

'You're pleased she's been poisoned?'

'Don't sound so surprised, Officer. You know the way I felt about her. Well, at least now she can join my father wherever they both end up.' Her smile broadened. 'And I have no doubt where that will be: in the fires of hell.'

'Can anybody confirm that you've been here all the time today?'

The smile didn't leave her face. 'Not a soul, but there's no way you can pin this on me.'

'Because you were careful not to be seen when you went over to kill her?'

'Because I'm telling you I didn't go over there to kill anybody, and you can't prove that I did.' She settled back on her sunbed and gave a dismissive wave of the hand. 'And don't bother sending me an invite to the funeral.'

'There isn't going to be a funeral. The poisoner didn't do a very good job. Natalie's still alive in hospital. The doctors say she should be well enough to be discharged by Tuesday.'

Jennifer had put her sunglasses back on, but I got the distinct impression that Natalie's likely recovery came as unwelcome news. She quickly collected herself and when she spoke, it was still in her same abrasive style. 'A great shame. Well, better luck next time, whoever it was.'

We left her there and, as we made our way back out of the gate again, I was mulling over her reaction to the news. It was a pity she had been wearing dark glasses as I've always believed that one can read a lot from watching the eyes of a suspect, but from what I'd been able to see of her face, she hadn't appeared too surprised. Had she done it? Quite possibly. The problem would be to prove it. When we were firmly out of earshot of anybody in either of the two houses, we stopped. Innocenti voiced my feelings exactly.

'Not a nice person. She might well have done it.'

'I quite agree. She's a cool customer, smugly sure of herself, but did you see how she reacted to the news that Natalie's still alive?'

Innocenti nodded, his phone already in his hand. 'I'll call the station and get another officer sent over to the hospital to keep a close eye on Natalie Hunter. You're right: she's probably still in a lot of danger.'

9

SUNDAY

By the time Sunday evening arrived, I was as nervous as a teenager on a first date. Oscar must have sensed it, as he kept wandering over and giving me affectionate nudges with his nose. I had taken him for a long walk in the hills above my place that afternoon – and he had carried back no fewer than three sticks, which I added to his pile of retrieved items outside the door – so I felt sure he would sleep when I left for Florence, especially as I planned on feeding him just before I left. I couldn't take him with me as the restaurant didn't have outside seating and I knew I was going to miss his support.

But at least I would have my daughter there to help out.

Innocenti had called me at lunchtime to say that he'd interviewed Adam Hunter and his partner, who confirmed they had been in Florence the previous day but, in spite of listing the shops they had visited, they had been unable to produce conclusive proof that they hadn't sneaked back to the villa to poison the soup. Without embarking on a time-consuming check of CCTV footage in the city centre for any sightings of them, there was no way of excluding them from our suspicions for now, although I still felt the sister was the more likely of the siblings to be dabbling in murder.

The news from the hospital was more positive. Natalie had emerged from her coma in the course of the morning and was apparently now sleeping normally. She hadn't spoken more than a few words, but the signs were good, and I promised Innocenti I'd accompany him to the hospital on Monday to talk to her as soon as the doctors gave the word. A close police guard would be maintained on her until then.

I drove down to Florence for my dinner date, still feeling more apprehensive than happy at the prospect of meeting my ex-wife again. I found a parking space a few blocks from the restaurant and checked my watch. It was seven forty-five, so I took my time walking to the restaurant in order to arrive on the dot of eight as agreed. Rocco, the owner, greeted me warmly and pointed across the busy dining room to a round table in the far corner set for three people. Sitting there, facing me, was Tricia and in front of her, with her back to me, was Helen. I gave my daughter a little wave and made my way over to them with all the enthusiasm of a Christian being thrown into a ring containing a pride of hungry lions.

'Hi, Dad.' Tricia jumped up and ran the few paces towards me and flung her arms around my neck. As she kissed my cheek, I heard her whisper in my ear. 'You look terrified but wait till you see Mum. She's been like a cat on a hot tin roof all day.'

Slightly encouraged, I walked the last three steps to the table and looked down.

'Hello, Helen.'

'Hello, Dan.'

She turned her face towards me, and I was somehow relieved to see that she looked almost exactly the same as I remembered. Her hair was a bit longer but still the same style, and her face was instantly so very familiar. She was wearing a smart, red, print dress and matching lipstick and I found myself trying to remember the last time she had worn lipstick for my benefit. Of course, maybe this was just for her daughter's sake or because she was on holiday. It didn't prove anything. And even if it did signify something, so what? She had divorced me and that was that...

Or was it?

I stood there for a moment or two, wondering if I should shake her hand, or even bend down and give her a peck on the cheek, before deciding to do neither and taking a seat between the two of them.

'Didn't you bring Oscar?' Tricia sat down and launched herself into her role as talk-show host.

'No dogs in the restaurant. He's okay, I left him with an extra-large helping of food.' Although Helen had no doubt heard all about my dog from Tricia, I turned towards her and offered a few words of explanation, as much for the sake of having something to say as anything else. 'I'm the proud owner of a black Labrador nowadays. He's great company.' For a moment I regretted my choice of words. I hoped Helen wouldn't think I was trying to imply that the dog was better company than she'd been. To my relief, she smiled.

'Tricia's told me all about him. I look forward to meeting him.'

At that moment the proprietor came to ask if we'd like something to drink. I checked with my guests. 'Would a bottle of fizz be appropriate?'

Tricia was quick to answer. 'As far as I'm concerned, just seeing you two sitting down together feels like something to be celebrated. I say bring it on.'

Helen said nothing so, after a moment's deliberation, I ordered a bottle of sparkling rosé from the west of Tuscany, not far from the coast. Since settling over here, I had rapidly learnt that the Italians are fiercely proud of their regional differences, and although I knew that Rocco had bottles of French champagne and Venetian Prosecco in the fridge, I felt sure he would appreciate my choice of a local wine. A waiter arrived a minute later with the bottle and an ice bucket. He opened the bottle with just the slightest hiss and filled three glasses before settling it into the ice and leaving us. I was about to propose a toast when my daughter got there first, raising her glass and beaming at us.

'Cheers, Mum, cheers, Dad. It's wonderful to be here like a family again.'

Helen and I picked up our glasses and we all clinked them together before taking mouthfuls. I was relieved to find that the wine was as good as I remembered and, unlike Luigi Signese's fizz, it didn't assault the nasal passages.

We had a mixture of antipasti, starting with typical Tuscan bruschetta, some topped with chopped tomatoes and olive oil, and some spread with chicken liver pâté. Tricia's a vegetarian so she passed on these. She didn't know what she was missing. After these came freshly hand-carved Tuscan cured ham and succulent slices of orange-fleshed melon as well as a selection of olives of different colours and sizes.

Gradually, as we progressed from the antipasti to the main course – the two ladies declined the offer of a pasta course in-between – Helen and I started to talk. At first we directed most of our remarks to our daughter but, little by little, I found myself turning towards my ex-wife and speaking to her directly and vice versa. I told her about life here in Tuscany but scrupulously avoided any mention of the fact that I was currently helping out on a murder investigation. I told her about my book, although I played down my expectations of getting published any time soon, and she sounded pleased for me. In return she told me about the part-time job she had started with a local charity, which appeared to be very satisfying. She didn't say anything about the demise of her year-long relationship with Timothy Whateverhisnamewas and I didn't ask.

As we talked, I studied her surreptitiously, just as I felt sure she must be doing to me. There were a few lines around her eyes that hadn't been there a year or two ago but, compared to the last time I had seen her at the height of our divorce proceedings, she looked good and still as appealing as ever. The fact was that I suppose I'd never stopped loving her and had hoped against hope right up to the end that things might be able to return to what they had once been between us, but I'd been disappointed before. Now, once bitten twice shy, I knew I needed to keep my feet on the ground, but as the meal progressed I felt my resolve starting to weaken.

For our main course, Tricia had grilled pecorino cheese and grilled aubergine while Helen and I shared a *Bistecca alla Fiorentina*. This massive T-bone steak arrived on a platter, covered in rocket leaves and slivers of Parmesan, and was accompanied by a small mountain of fries. The waiter sliced the meat vertically and placed pieces on each of our plates, added spoonfuls of fries, and retired with a quiet, '*Buon appetito.*'

The meat was exquisite, but I was only partway through it when my phone rang. It wasn't a number I recognised, and I very nearly didn't answer, but something made me press the green button. I heard a man's voice. It took me a moment or two to recognise who it was, not least because he was obviously very upset and almost shouting.

'Dan Armstrong? Is that you? I got your number from the club database when you booked your tennis lessons. I've tried to call the number I got from Inspector Pisano but there's no answer. Listen, please, something's happened...' He paused and then corrected himself. 'Something terrible is going to happen...' As an afterthought, he added, 'It's Adam Hunter,' but I'd already worked that out.

'Hang on a moment, please.' I murmured a quick excuse to Helen and Tricia and took the phone outside onto the pavement. 'What's the problem, Mr Hunter?'

'My sister's gone crazy. She's taken my car and she's driving down to Florence to kill Natalie.'

I could hardly believe my ears. The brother was blowing the whistle on the sister? 'What makes you think she wants to kill her?'

'She's already tried once. She's just told me she was the one who put drugs in the soup yesterday. I didn't believe her at first – by doing that she could have killed not only Natalie but Battista and Mariarosa as well – but she says she really did it and she's gone off to "finish the job"– her words. Like I say, she's freaked out.'

I did a bit of quick thinking. There were two police officers guarding Natalie's room so she shouldn't come to any harm, but I realised that Jennifer had just given us an opportunity to catch her in the act. No amount of bluster or lies would get her out of that. A call to Innocenti and we should be able to set a trap. I did my best to keep my voice level as I replied, although I could feel the adrenalin coursing through my veins.

'Thanks for calling, Mr Hunter, we'll take it from here. Don't worry, we'll make sure your sister doesn't kill anybody.'

'She's not responsible for her actions...' Now he was sounding deflated. 'You see, she's had trouble in the past and that's why she's been on tranquillisers. It looks like they've stopped working.'

'We'll see that nothing happens to anybody, including her. Thanks again for doing the right thing, Mr Hunter.' Although it might have helped if he had told us more about this 'trouble' his sister had had when we had interviewed him before.

As soon as he rang off, I called Innocenti and was relieved to hear him answer almost immediately. I told him about Adam's call and heard him whistle in surprise. I then outlined my proposed plan to him.

'If I were you, I'd get the uniformed officers to conceal themselves while you go and hide somewhere in Natalie's room. Tell the medics on duty to let Jennifer slip in unchallenged. That way you can catch her in flagrante before she attacks Natalie, and you'll have all the proof you need to put her away.'

'Great plan, Dan, but there's just one problem: I'm out at Pontassieve on the other side of Florence at the moment. It'll take me twenty minutes or even half an hour to get to the hospital. I'll call the officers on duty there and get them to lay the trap. Hopefully they'll be up to it.'

I groaned. Apart from the threat to Natalie, this was a golden opportunity to catch our murderer. I took a deep breath and made a swift decision. 'Listen, Marco, I'm in Florence now, having dinner in Borgo San Lorenzo. I can be at the hospital in ten minutes. Call your men and tell them I'll come straight away, and then you come and relieve me just as fast as you can.'

I heard a sigh of relief at the other end. 'Thanks, Dan, that's amazing. I'll tell them to obey your every order as if you were the inspector himself. As for me, I'm on my way right now.'

I tucked the phone into my pocket and hurried back into the restaurant. Conscious that even now Jennifer was speeding towards the hospital with murder on her mind, I kept it brief.

'I'm very sorry. Something's happened, I have to go. If all goes well, I should be back within an hour.'

To my surprise, Helen reached up and caught hold of my forearm. 'Is something wrong? Are you all right?'

'I'm fine, thanks. It's not me.' I was touched by the caring expression on her face, but I had no time for personal feelings. 'I'll explain when I get back. I'm really sorry. *Ciao*.'

I went over to the bar and told Rocco that I would be back later and not to accept any offers of payment from my family. He gave me a reassuring smile.

'Your credit's good here, *Commissario*.' He had called me that ever since I first started coming here with Virgilio and he had worked out that we were both police officers.

I hurried out and set off for the hospital at a trot – after all the food I didn't feel like running – and I was there in less than ten minutes. I knew that time was of the essence. Adam would have wasted time trying to call Virgilio and then searching for my number after his sister had left, so Jennifer was probably well on her way here by now. I hoped I would have time to get everything ready. At the hospital, I found the two uniformed officers waiting outside Natalie's door and I hastily outlined what I wanted them to do. They had already been briefed by Innocenti and they had also been doing a bit of thinking. The room next to Natalie's was empty and the older officer suggested they wait in there while I hid in her room. They would be ready to pounce as soon as they got my signal. I nodded approvingly and looked around before spotting what I needed.

'See this.' I grabbed a little metal bowl from a trolley. 'When I drop this on the floor, you should easily be able to hear it. That'll be your signal. Have you spoken to the staff on duty?'

'Yes, sir, they know they're to ignore any visitors.'

I clapped them both on the back. 'That's great, guys. Well done. Okay, let's do this.'

While they went off to wait in the next room, I let myself into Natalie's room. It wasn't completely dark in there and a regular beep from a monitor recorded her heartbeat, which sounded reassuringly regular. The reading on the monitor was 63, which looked okay to me. I wasn't sure about the other numbers on the screen, but she seemed to be sleeping peacefully, so I left her alone and looked around for a hiding place. The other bed in the room was empty and for a moment I toyed with the idea of lying on it, covered by a blanket, but decided that it would take me too long to jump off and confront the would-be murderer. Instead, I took up station in the corner opposite Natalie's bed, reasonably well hidden from the door by a folded screen.

I had been waiting there for less than fifteen minutes when I heard a creak and saw the door begin to open. I braced myself and waited. A figure slipped into the room, scrupulously closing the door before looking around.

'Dan? Where are you?' The stage whisper came from Sergeant Innocenti.

'I'm here, come and join me. We'll be out of sight of the door here.'

He squeezed in behind the screen alongside me and made a very sensible suggestion. 'Didn't you say you were having dinner in a restaurant? Why don't you go back there? I can handle things now.'

Hindsight is a wonderful, if frustrating, thing. Looking back on it now, it's only too clear to me what I should have done. I should have taken his advice and headed back to my ex-wife and daughter, who were waiting for me.

But I didn't.

Maybe it was the thrill of the chase or some hang-back to my days on the force, or just the desire to see a very unpleasant human being brought to justice, but I told him I'd be happy to stay with him. We settled down behind the screen side by side, the only sound in the room the bleeping of the machines. We had to wait almost another half-hour, and I was beginning to think that Jennifer might have had a change of heart, when we heard a noise.

My watch had just told me that it was almost half past ten when we saw the door handle turn. A figure came in and headed resolutely straight for Natalie, stopping only to pick up a pillow from a nearby chair. Even in the half-light we could see that it was Jennifer. As she leant forward to press the pillow over Natalie's face, Innocenti and I leapt from cover and caught hold of her. I was glad to have Innocenti hanging onto her other arm because Jennifer fought like a lion, twisting and turning, hissing and spitting at us in fury. I was reaching for the metal dish to summon help when, like a light being switched off, she suddenly slumped in our grip, and we found ourselves almost having to hold her up.

Innocenti pulled out handcuffs and secured her hands behind her back while I went and called the two uniformed officers. From the look of Jennifer – she actually had foam running from the sides of her mouth – there would be no point in trying to reason with her tonight, so we let the two officers take her off to the station. Innocenti and I were just wiping ourselves down when a little voice from the bed captured our attention.

'What's happening? Who's there?' She sounded very frail.

'It's okay, Natalie. It's Dan Armstrong and Sergeant Innocenti. Everything's all right.'

'Was that Jennifer?' Her voice was still sounding ethereal. 'Was she attacking me, or did I dream it?'

I went over and caught hold of her hand. 'Yes, it was Jennifer, but we've got her. She can't harm you any more.'

'Was she the person who poisoned me?'

'I'm afraid so.'

'Do you think she killed my... Rex?'

'We think it's very likely, but we hope to find out tomorrow if she really did kill her father as well as trying to kill you. Anyway, don't you worry. Everything's all right now.'

She lay back and I could see her eyelids close. Then, just as Innocenti and I were making our way towards the door, I heard her voice once again, little more than a whisper.

'It's not how it seems.'

We listened for more, but that was all she said. We saw her eyes close and she relapsed into sleep.

10

LATE SUNDAY NIGHT AND MONDAY

'It's not how it seems.'

I kept repeating the words over and over in my head as I walked up the track in the starlight, absently kicking the pine cones that Oscar deposited at my feet as we climbed. He looked perfectly happy, which was more than could be said for me after the dinner debacle. At least if I kept my mind on the murder it stopped me thinking about the way I had screwed up what had been an unexpectedly pleasant evening with my ex-wife and daughter.

When I had got back to the restaurant shortly after eleven it had been to find the round table at the far end empty and a message on my phone saying:

Can't wait any longer. Have gone back to the hotel. Speak tomorrow. Oh, dad…!

Over at the bar where I went to pay the bill, I had received a sympathetic shake of the head from the owner.

'You guys never stop, do you? Must play havoc with your

private life.' Without asking, he put two glasses on the bar and filled them from a very expensive bottle of French cognac. 'Not so different from my life. My first marriage lasted twelve years and the last one didn't even make it to ten.' He held up his glass towards me. *'Cin cin, Commissario.'*

Out on the pitch-black hillside with my dog an hour later, I was still thinking hard. Why hadn't I taken Innocenti's advice and gone back to the restaurant? Things had been going better than I had expected with Helen earlier that evening after a shaky start. Had I deliberately been trying to sabotage any possibility of us ever getting back together again? I kicked a stone in frustration, but Oscar didn't even bother chasing it. He looked as subdued as I felt but maybe he was just tired. So was I, but I knew there was so much going on inside my head I would find it hard to sleep.

'It's not how it seems.'

What had Natalie meant by that? I sat down on the familiar fallen tree and racked my brains to find an explanation. Of course, it might just have been because she was half drugged and half asleep, and she hadn't meant anything by it. Or maybe, a thought occurred to me and gradually developed, maybe she hadn't been referring to the way Jennifer had almost killed her. What if she had been referring to something else? Maybe Jennifer wasn't really Adam's sister. Could it be that Natalie herself was somebody different? Might it even be that she and Rex Hunter had never got married at all? Maybe the whole thing had been a charade put on by Rex Hunter to punish his children that he considered worthless or ungrateful or worse. An image of the documents from his safe suddenly came into my head and I realised that one document that hadn't been there was a marriage certificate. Maybe there had been no wedding. But, if so, who was Natalie?

My mind returned to the restaurant as I sat there under the

trees in the middle of the night with my dog snoring at my feet. I could only imagine the scene at the dinner table after my departure a few hours earlier. I had a feeling that Tricia, sooner or later, would have told her mother that I was, in her words, 'playing detectives' again. I didn't need a printout of their conversation to know how Helen would have reacted to this news. Here she was, making a last-ditch attempt at some sort of rapprochement with her ex-husband, the man she had left because he had increasingly put his job before her – or so she had perceived it – and he had repaid her by doing just that. She must have been furious and probably bitterly hurt.

I owed her an explanation. I looked at my watch and stood up. I saw Oscar's eyes open but he made no attempt to move for now. He looked far too comfortable – which was very different from the way I was feeling. I pulled out my phone. It was far too late to call and explain so all I could do for now was to stall and hope I'd be able to put things right in the morning. In the end I just sent a one-word message to Tricia.

Sorry. x

'It's not how it seems.' Natalie's words kept coming back to me.

Could Rex Hunter have cooked up this whole thing just to see how his children would react when faced with the news that they had been disinherited in favour of his new young wife? It made little sense, but cheating at golf when just playing for fun, destroying a historic building because it spoilt his view, or sacking somebody for beating him in a game made little sense either. The more I learnt about this guy, the more I realised how bizarre he'd been – bizarre, self-centred, and ruthless, and with a cruel streak. As Virgilio had said before, surely instead of arranging such an elaborate charade, all he would have had to do would have been to tell them he was giving all his money to charity, but maybe he had wanted them to really suffer. He couldn't have anticipated that the result of this fake marriage would be his murder. Could he?

I resolved to get the police to double-check with the Australian authorities as far as the true identity of Natalie was concerned. There was one other possibility that occurred to me, and I found myself looking forward eagerly to interviewing her in the morning. Could I be right?

I went to bed at one o'clock, filled with mixed emotions. On the one hand there was satisfaction that we had been able to catch our killer – or at least a would-be killer – but on the other was the grim realisation that I had scuppered my last chance of getting back together with Helen. Although I had headed to the restaurant earlier that evening with the firm intention of explaining to her that I saw no future for us together, it still felt like a milestone reached. As I lay there sweating under just one sheet and with the window wide open, I gradually came around to asking myself a really tricky question: had it been easier for me to go off and leave her – just as she did to me – rather than have a grown-up conversation? I was still pondering my answer to this when I finally fell asleep.

I was woken a couple of hours later by a blinding flash and a thunderclap which sounded so close by, my ears were ringing for minutes afterwards. I sat bolt upright in bed as the rain began to pour down outside, and when I say 'pour down' I mean really bucket down. The noise was like being next to a waterfall. I heard a pathetic whine from downstairs and went down to comfort my brave guard dog, who was shivering in his basket. I sat on the terracotta tiles beside him and stroked his head as the storm gradually moved on. Or rather, the thunder moved on, but the rain didn't stop. In the end I went back up to bed, but when I woke up next morning, it was to find a black Labrador, who should have been downstairs in his basket, stretched out happily on the floor beside my bed.

Outside, it was still raining, and the track had turned into a river. Even Oscar showed little enthusiasm for his regular morning walk and just trotted out of the door for a quick pee before coming straight back in again. Even so, he got so wet in that very short time that I had to dry him with his towel, and the kitchen smelt of damp dog all morning as a result.

I checked my phone to see if there were any messages from Tricia but soon realised that there was no signal. The lightning must have damaged the transmitter. It looked as though I still had an Internet connection so I sent Tricia an email, asking if she thought I should speak to her mum to apologise, but it was almost lunchtime before I got a reply.

Hi dad. Hope everything worked out for you last night. As you can imagine, mum wasn't best pleased. She told me it brought back so many unhappy memories. The upshot of this is that she and I are about to take the train to Pisa where we'll spend the night. She's still very upset so it's probably for the best. I'll give you a call when we get back to the UK tomorrow. XX

Half an hour later, the phone started working again and a call came through from Virgilio, just back from his sailing weekend. He had news.

'*Ciao*, Dan. Thanks for holding Innocenti's hand last night. Great result. Sorry you got called, but there was no signal out at sea where we were. Now listen to this: Sydney police have been in touch to tell us that Jennifer Hunter has spent time in what they call a Closed Mental Health Facility after two separate acts of violence, fortunately not resulting in serious injury to anybody.

She was only released a few months ago. Guess what medication she's on.'

'Not Zancorepine by any chance?'

'Exactly. The forensic team have been searching her room at Adam Hunter's bungalow this morning and they've found two empty strips of Zancorepine in the waste basket. That was two weeks' supply, and the doctor says that that amount, crushed up and dropped in the soup, would have been enough to tranquillise an elephant or kill several human beings. Natalie Hunter's been very lucky.'

'How is she today? Have the medics said she's ready to talk? Has Innocenti told you what she said to us last night?'

'Yes, he did, and we've been doing a bit of checking. We've double checked with the Australian authorities, but Natalie's ID and that of Jennifer Hunter both seem to stack up. There's no sign of a marriage certificate here or at the villa, so it's looking as though there's more to this than meets the eye. The hospital say they want to keep her in for one more night, but that she should be okay to talk to us later on today. Innocenti said you'd offered to come along to help out. Is that okay?'

'Of course, assuming I can get down the hill. The track's turned into a river.' I glanced out of the window and was cheered to see that the rain had almost stopped, although the track was still a sea of mud.

'Don't worry, I'll ask the Carabinieri to send a Land Rover up to collect you. They love splashing about in the mud. Pick you up at two, okay?'

I managed to give Oscar a walk, followed by a swim in the now swollen stream to wash the mud off him, before the dark blue Carabinieri Land Rover came splashing up the hill to collect me and transport me to Florence. They delivered me to the hospital, where I met Virgilio in the lobby and, together, we made our way to Natalie's room. We found her sitting up in bed looking brighter although understandably far from relaxed. The first thing she did was to thank me most warmly for saving her life and then she went on to reveal that the attempted murder hadn't come as a total surprise.

'I told Rex he was making a big mistake. This sort of thing never ends well. I told him, but he didn't listen.' She looked across at us as we sat down. 'The more I got to know him, the more I came to realise that he could be very stubborn, even when some of his choices were obviously crazy.'

'When you say, "this sort of thing", just exactly what do you mean?' Virgilio kept his voice low and soothing.

'Playing brutal games with people, his own family. My mother told me he could be strange, but I hadn't realised how strange.'

'Your mother knew him well?' I pricked up my ears. Could it be my hunch was going to be proved correct?

'She knew him very well. You see, Rex was my father.'

Virgilio and I exchanged looks and I spotted satisfaction on his face as things slotted into place. Of course, that had to be it. I took over the questioning. 'You're telling us you are Rex Hunter's daughter?'

She nodded. 'Rex Hunter's *illegitimate* daughter. He turned his back on my mum thirty years ago when she told him she was pregnant, and I grew up hating this man I'd never seen who couldn't even be bothered to stay around to see his child.' She rubbed the back of one hand across her eyes.

'So how come you and he...?' Virgilio was using his soft, encouraging voice.

'I'm very sorry for misleading you, but Rex made me swear to keep the secret. After his death I've been so confused, especially with all the trouble about the will. I thought it easier just to stick to the marriage story until everything calmed down. When I told you that I only met him nine months ago that was the truth. And it's also true that I met him at the clinic, but he didn't come in as a patient. My mum died last autumn and, when he found out, he came to the clinic looking for me after all these years.'

'Your mother died in Australia?'

'Yes.'

'And he was living over here, so how did he know about her death?'

'The bank told him. You see, he paid my mother an allowance all my life and when she died, the bank contacted him.'

'And how much was the allowance?'

'Five thousand dollars a month.' She was quick to qualify her statement. 'That's Australian dollars. It wasn't a fortune, but it was enough for her to live on.'

'So he did at least try to behave properly in spite of abandoning your mum.' I was impressed. From what I'd heard about him this seemed out of character, but it just underlined what a strange and unpredictable man he'd been. After all, some people had liked him – not many but some, such as Elizabeth McGregor, for instance – so he must have been a Jekyll and Hyde character.

'I would have preferred a father. Still, like I say, he finally came to seek me out, and all that stuff I told you about him coming back and forth from Italy to Australia was also true, as were the two holidays he took me on. Although he waited almost thirty years to do it, he really bonded with me and I enjoyed having a father at long last, particularly since my mum had just died. Since I've been here I've been hearing more and more about the bad things he did but I never really saw that side of his nature. With me he was charming and loving, even if you find that hard to believe.'

'So when did he come up with this plan for the two of you to pretend you'd got married? And why?'

'A few months ago, while we were on holiday in Vietnam. He'd convinced himself that his kids were a waste of space – his words – and he said he wanted to put them to the test. By turning up with a wife half his age and saying he meant to change his will, he felt sure they would show their true colours. If they welcomed me, or at least didn't object too loudly, this would be the proof that they weren't as bad as he thought. As it turned out, he was right about them, or at least about Jennifer. Adam was fairly neutral towards me, but Jennifer was frosty in the extreme.' She sighed. 'And then, of course, they killed him and tried to kill me. I still can't get my head around that.'

Virgilio was quick to point out the facts. 'There's no proof yet that either Jennifer or Adam was responsible for your father's death. Hopefully we'll find out more when we interview Jennifer later today. Be that as it may, the fact is that you probably owe your life to Adam. He phoned Dan last night to warn us that Jennifer had confessed to him that she tried to poison you, and that she was on her way here, intent on finishing the job.'

Natalie looked pleasantly surprised. 'I didn't know...' Her voice tailed off but then she rallied. 'That's good, that's really good. I always thought he was very different from his sister.' She nodded decisively. 'I meant what I said the other day, you know. I didn't think it was right for my father to cut them off like that, and I intend to make provision for them both. After all, they are my brother and sister.' She nodded emphatically. 'Even Jennifer, in spite of what she tried to do to me. It sounds as though she's got big problems. Hopefully she'll get treatment rather than punishment.'

'She certainly needs help. Apparently she's had psychiatric trouble for years.'

'How awful. Rex shouldn't have tried to provoke her like this, knowing that she had that sort of background. I remember pleading with him not to go ahead with his little charade but, like I said, he could be very stubborn.'

When we emerged from the hospital, Virgilio and I headed for a bar. After the rain it was noticeably cooler – not cold, but much less oppressive than before – and we sat outside on the pavement to drink our coffees. Both of us were still digesting what Natalie had told us.

'He was a weird guy with a nasty streak, all right.' Virgilio looked across at me. 'I can see where Jennifer got it from.'

'And yet Natalie sounds remarkably balanced. Different mother, of course. I was impressed at what she was saying about making provision for the other two.' I took a sip of coffee. 'Tell me something: do you think she's right? Do you think Hunter was killed by his kids, or at least one of them?'

'Let's see what we get out of Jennifer, but who knows? The way I see it, they're the only people with a clear motive and shaky or non-existent alibis.'

'But Adam called last night to save Natalie's life.' I knew that this version of events didn't necessarily clear Adam of responsibility and when Virgilio replied, it was clear that he felt the same way.

'I grant you that looks like a point in his favour, but it might be a double bluff. He couldn't stop his sister going on the rampage, so he was trying to distance himself from her.'

I went back to police headquarters with him, where Jennifer Hunter was waiting in an interview room with a uniformed officer standing silently in the corner behind her. Jennifer didn't look up from her hands as we entered and said nothing while Virgilio turned on the recording equipment. He started by giving her name, the time and date, before addressing her directly.

'Jennifer Diana Hunter, you have been charged with the attempted murder of Natalie Hunter. This took place last night at

Santa Maria Nuova hospital here in Florence. What do you have to say for yourself?'

At last she looked up. 'Ask your friend. He was there.' She shot me an acid look.

'I'm asking you, Jennifer. Do you deny attempted murder?'

'I'm just sorry I was prevented from doing it.' Her tone was uncompromising.

'So your intention was to commit murder?'

'She deserved to die.'

'I'll take that as a yes.' She made no attempt to deny it, so Virgilio went on. 'And did you poison the soup that she ate on Saturday?'

'Yes, but obviously I didn't do a good enough job.' There was no hint of remorse, just annoyance that her plan hadn't succeeded. Virgilio's next comment shook her out of her apparent indifference.

'It might interest you to learn that if you had succeeded in killing Natalie Hunter, you would have been killing your sister, your half-sister.'

It took a second or two for the news to sink in before Jennifer looked up, an expression of disbelief on her face. 'Half-sister? What rubbish is this?'

Briefly, Virgilio recounted what Natalie had told us, and we both saw Jennifer's expression change as the full implications of the facts sank in. By the time he had finished talking, she was looking pasty-faced and uncertain, a far cry from her aggressively scornful attitude of a few minutes earlier.

'She's my sister? I have a sister?'

'And you almost killed her, just like you killed your father.'

Her head jerked up sharply. 'I did not kill my father. I'm glad he's dead – even more so now that I've heard what a sick trick he was playing on Adam and me – but I didn't do it. I told you that before. Yes, I saw him out on the course, yes, he even waved to me. Needless to say, I didn't wave back, I just rode on by. The last time I saw him, he was alive.'

And that remained her story and she stuck to it – and I, for one, believed her. We both tried for over half an hour to get her to admit to the murder, but she remained adamant that she hadn't done it. At one point I asked her if her brother had done it and she actually laughed – that same scary laugh of hers that had nothing of humour to it.

'Adam? Never in a thousand years. He hasn't got the guts. He still gets me to kill spiders for him.'

'You don't think he's capable of murder?'

'You've got to be joking.'

Finally, Virgilio wound up the interview and Jennifer was led off to the cells. He looked across at me with a weary sigh.

'I don't know about you, Dan, but I need a drink.'

We went out and found that the sky had cleared sufficiently by now for the sun to be breaking through the clouds. We found a table outside a café not far from the police station and ordered two cold beers. Around us the crowds of tourists came and went, unaware that we were on the tracks of a killer. Neither of us said much at first, both lost in our thoughts, until Virgilio put into words what I'd been thinking.

'I tend to believe her but if she didn't kill Hunter, then who did?'

'I know, I feel the same way and I've been running through the other suspects in my head. If we set aside Jennifer and Adam for the moment, that leaves Natalie herself. Neither of us see her as a club-wielding killer, but she might have seen the new will, realised she stood to inherit everything and killed Hunter so as to get her hands on the money straight away. What's more, she might have killed him not only for the money, but to repay him for walking out on her mother. Now that we know that Natalie was his illegitimate daughter, it actually increases the likelihood that she's our killer, however improbable that might sound.'

Virgilio nodded slowly. 'She has no real alibi for the time of the murder. The butler and his wife told us they were in the villa with her all evening, but it's a big place. From there to the scene of the crime is little more than ten minutes on foot. She could easily have slipped out, killed him, and slipped back again without them being any the wiser. And don't forget her first reaction after Jennifer's attack on her was to try to blame her father's death on her siblings.'

'So Natalie has to be a serious suspect, but who else is there? The accountant and the English guy who were playing with him had opportunity, but we haven't been able to dig up any substantial motive. Any chance the accountant was cooking the books, creaming off the profits?'

'Nothing so far. My people are still checking, but it's all looking above board at the moment. I've asked for a detailed report of the accounts. The other guy, Roseland, doesn't appear to have had much contact with Hunter apart from the weekly golf session, so nothing suspicious there. Then there's the golf pro who stood to lose his job. Innocenti's grilling him to find out why he didn't tell us that himself and asking him why he invented the story of it happening to somebody else. Add to that the fact that Hunter had been propositioning his girlfriend and that gives him even more motive. His alibi was provided by his partner so we can't rule him out either.'

'And of course there's Luigi Signese, the farmer who hated his guts. I like the guy, but the hole in the fence would have provided him with a safe and easy way of getting to Hunter and away again without being seen, so he's still in the mix. And we mustn't forget the assistant manager. I believed her when she said she was in love with Hunter, but love can lead to crimes of passion. Maybe she slipped out of the French window of her office and killed him in a fit of jealous rage after he turned up with another, younger woman, unaware that Natalie was Rex's daughter.'

Virgilio nodded slowly and gave me a rueful look. 'In spite of all the fun and games last night at the hospital, we still aren't much further forward. I need to speak to all these people all over again, don't I?'

'Afraid so. Let me know if you need my help.' I drained my beer and stood up. 'I need to get home to my dog before he starts chewing the place up. Any chance of a lift back home? I'll get these.' I headed in to the cash desk.

By the time I came back from paying for the beers, Virgilio was just coming off the phone. 'The Carabinieri taxi service will be here in five minutes. Thanks a lot for all your help, Dan. Sorry you got disturbed last night. I hope it didn't interrupt anything.'

'I'm not really sure if there was anything to interrupt. It was a weird evening all round.'

We knew each other very well by now, so I gave him a quick rundown of what had happened. His reaction was predictably sympathetic. 'Innocenti's call couldn't have come at a worse time, could it? I'm so sorry. So does this mean you're giving up on your ex-wife?'

'To be honest, that's been my intention all along and now it certainly sounds as if she's giving up on me.' I shrugged my shoulders. 'I don't like the way it happened, but I know it's for the best.'

'And it all fell apart because of the same old story: which comes first, work or family?'

'You and Lina manage to make it work.'

Virgilio nodded. 'So far, but I can't say she's too happy about me being called out at all hours. That's why I took her away for our anniversary weekend to somewhere we both knew it couldn't happen. But, Dan, as far as you and your ex are concerned, you're probably right that the best thing was to cut the cord. The fact is that you've got detective work in your blood. You know I value your help a lot, but it's not as if you're getting paid for it – apart from some much-needed coaching on your backhand.' A smile appeared on his face as an idea came to him. 'You know what you should do: why don't you set yourself up as a private detective? There must be loads of English speakers over here who need help from a pro like you.'

'You're saying your advice is for me to forget about Helen and concentrate on detective work?' I spotted the same Carabinieri Land Rover approaching, once again gleaming, the mud already washed clean from its flanks.

'That's something you've got to work out for yourself, my friend.'

11

MONDAY NIGHT AND TUESDAY MORNING

Oscar and I spent a lot of time that night discussing what I should do – well, all right, I did the discussing while he lay there and listened. At the very least I knew I owed Helen an apology for going off like that, but I couldn't get Virgilio's suggestion out of my head. Dan Armstrong, Private Detective, sounded like something out of a Raymond Chandler crime noir paperback from the thirties, but I had to admit that it had a certain ring to it.

'I can see us now, Oscar, solving crimes like a modern-day Sherlock Holmes. You can be Doctor Watson.' I glanced down at him, lying stretched out on the floor at my feet. 'Or would you rather be the Hound of the Baskervilles? Are you listening, Oscar? Sometimes I wonder why I waste my breath telling you things. What do you think of that?' Hearing his name mentioned, he opened one eye, checked that no food was on offer and subsided again with a heartfelt sigh. Undeterred by his lack of interest, I carried on fantasising. 'Me in my trench coat and one of those fedora hats, you with a little barrel hanging from your collar like a St Bernard. Only *your* barrel would be full of crime-solving gadgets, rather than brandy. Ah, yes, I can see us now...'

My fantasy was interrupted by my phone. As I answered, I saw that the time was almost midnight and I was surprised – and immediately concerned – to see that it was Tricia, not Virgilio, calling at this hour.

'Hi, sweetheart, everything all right?'

'I'm fine, thanks, Dad. I've left Mum in the room. She was feeling tired after all the sightseeing so she's already in bed. I told her I wanted a drink so I could get away to call you.'

'How's she doing? I feel terrible about having had to rush off like I did. If I tell you that it was to prevent a young woman your age from being murdered, would that make things better?'

'Oh, Dad, we both know you wouldn't have gone off if it hadn't been important. Mum was saying exactly the same thing over dinner. It's not what you had to do, it's the fact that you had to do it that's the problem. She told me she's always known she took second place in your life and last night was the proof.' Before I could say anything, she adopted a more positive tone. 'But it's not all bad, Dad. She came over here feeling seriously confused. Had she made the biggest mistake of her life when she left you? Should she try again? Well, she now knows she was right – for her, not necessarily for you and me – and it's sort of given her some closure.'

I couldn't blame Helen. Hadn't I just been dreaming of being a Philip Marlowe character or something out of a Conan Doyle mystery, when I should have been trying to decide on the correct wording for an apology to my ex-wife? She was right. I had loved my job – although I had moaned about it often enough – and I had loved my wife, but maybe it was time I admitted to myself, if not to her, that I had loved the job more.

* * *

On Tuesday morning, I received a call from Virgilio asking me to help with the second interview of William Roseland, the corpulent industrialist from Stoke-on-Trent, whose impenetrable accent often stumped the Florentine inspector. This time we would visit him at his house, rather than have him come to the club. At just after two, I packed Oscar into the car with the promise of a walk later on and set off. Roseland lived less than ten minutes further on from the club in a gorgeous old villa set in a fine garden filled with beautiful shrubs and bushes. Although the garden was extensive, the drive leading up to the house between two old cottages was narrow and there was barely room for us to park at the top alongside a gleaming Mercedes saloon, a smart red Alfa Romeo convertible, and Virgilio's car.

I left Oscar in the car with the windows open and walked over to meet Virgilio. Together we went across to the front door, which was opened by the man himself, today dressed in his golfing gear. Presumably, now that Hunter had been killed, he hadn't been able to have his free round of golf the previous night and he was making up for it today. His already florid face was flushed and there was perspiration on his brow again, but that might have been down to the heat rather than a guilty conscience.

'Come in, gentlemen.' Roseland led us through a large high-ceilinged lounge to a modern conservatory tacked onto the back of the building. This plastic monstrosity looked incongruous attached to a villa that had to be at least a couple of centuries old, and I wondered how he had managed to get planning permission – or maybe he just hadn't told anybody. Alternatively, he was from the same school as Rex Hunter when it came to planning regulations. Still, I had to admit that although it was undoubtedly an eyesore, an air-conditioning unit was whirring in the background, and it was pleasantly cool in there. He invited us to sit down and offered us drinks. He was still looking uncomfortable but being interviewed by the police can do that to people.

Virgilio shook his head and kept it formal. 'Thank you for the offer, Signor Roseland, but we're here on business and we don't have much time. I'd like to ask you a few more questions about Rex Hunter's murder.'

Roseland sat down opposite us and the wicker of the armchair creaked under his weight. 'Of course, Inspector, fire away. I'm not playing golf until six, so I've lots of time.'

'I'd like you to tell us a bit about the history of the country club. I believe you were part of the original consortium that developed the land as a golf course.'

'Yes, I was. There were three of us: Pietro Grosseto, Alessandro Mercurio, and me.'

'And who did you buy the land from?'

'Pietro Grosseto owned the lion's share of the land and he sold it to the consortium, making himself a pretty penny in the process.' From the expression on Virgilio's face, he hadn't understood much of what Roseland had said, so I translated and saw him nod.

'And the rest of the land?'

'Was bought from a handful of local farmers.'

This gave me an idea. 'Was one of the farmers Luigi Signese?'

His expression soured. 'Yes, and he did very well out of the deal. He didn't want to sell at first and he held out until we had to pay him the astronomical sum he wanted. Without his piece of land, we wouldn't have had the full access we needed. He was sitting on a ransom strip, and he knew it.'

This was news. I found myself wondering why Luigi hadn't mentioned that he had been well paid for the original sale of his strip of land. A guilty conscience, maybe? 'And did you bear a grudge against him as a result?'

He shrugged and shook his head. 'Not really. It was business. If I'd been in his position, I'd have done the same.'

'What about the other two in the consortium? What did they think of Signese?'

'Like me, it was just business. No real grudge, although I have to admit that when we heard that Rex was trying to steal a chunk of his land, we all had a little laugh.'

'You believe Hunter was trying to get the land by underhand means?'

He shrugged. 'That's the kind of man he was.' Clearly, any scruples Roseland might have had about his erstwhile playing partner hadn't been enough to stop him accepting the offer of free rounds of golf. I mentally filed Roseland into the *People I Don't Like* category inside my head.

'And you and your partners sold the finished golf course to Rex Hunter seven years ago?'

'That's right.'

'I believe your friend Peter Nelson was working for your consortium back then. Is he a good accountant?'

'Yes, he's a good accountant.' He hesitated for a couple of seconds. 'But, put it this way, when he decided to stay and work for Rex at the club, we were all pleased.'

'Why was that? I thought you said he was a good accountant.'

'He was good at his job, but there were a few unresolved questions. You know, accounts a bit cloudy, some sums of money going missing, nothing we could pin on him, but I wouldn't employ him again.'

'And yet you play golf with him each week. You're maybe even planning on playing with him this evening?'

'We get on fine on the golf course. Besides, I wasn't going to turn down the chance of having the course to ourselves once a week.' This only served to underline what I already knew about

Roseland. He sounded positively irked as he continued, 'Of course that's all stopped now.'

'Will you be playing with Peter Nelson tonight?'

'Yes, and Adam Hunter. Pity we'll no longer have the course to ourselves.' He gave a little sigh and sounded wistful. 'Do either of you play?' Seeing us shake our heads, he explained. 'It was like having a suite at a hotel with your own private bath, Jacuzzi, and chambermaids. There's nothing like it.'

'Talking of chambermaids, were you aware of Rex Hunter's interest in the opposite sex?'

Roseland's amiable smile left him. 'I think the word you're looking for is "obsession". Women were to Rex like drugs are to other people. He was addicted.' An expression of distaste appeared on his face. 'I found that side of him quite disgusting.'

At that moment a tall, good-looking woman walked past outside in the garden, without sparing us a glance. Incongruously, she was wearing the scruffiest pair of dirty overalls. She looked familiar and it took me a moment or two to remember how I recognised her. This was the woman I'd seen jogging past me on Wednesday morning when I'd gone to the club for my first session of tennis coaching with Abigail. Presumably this was Roseland's daughter and it looked as though, as well as keeping herself fit, she also had a hobby of some sort – maybe painting like Jennifer Hunter. I shot another glance across at the fat man. It never ceased to amaze me how singularly unattractive people could produce the most beautiful children. Of course, I reminded myself, my Tricia was a whole lot better-looking than her dad.

By the end of the interview, we hadn't learnt much more from Roseland. His description of Nelson as potentially a bit dodgy was interesting, particularly seeing as Nelson had indicated that he and Roseland had stopped to talk about financial matters on the evening of the murder. If Nelson really was a bit dodgy, why had Roseland bothered to listen to his advice?

The first thing Virgilio did when we got outside was to phone the office and tell Innocenti to instruct the team to go back through the club's accounts in even greater depth, just in case the accountant had been helping himself to some of the profits. If he had, and his boss had found out, that could well provide the motive for murder we had been missing. While in contact with Innocenti, Virgilio received two interesting, if frustrating, pieces of news. When the call ended, he told me what his sergeant had said.

'Apparently you handed in a glove that you found on the golf course.'

'Credit where credit's due; it was my dog who found it.'

'Well, the bad news is that forensics have been unable to lift any prints off it, but they did discover minute traces of blood on it, and the blood matches Rex Hunter's.'

I took a moment or two to consider the ramifications of this discovery. It now looked likely that this had been the glove worn by the killer, but did it offer any help in identifying him or her? Beside me, Virgilio's mind was running along the same lines.

'This could point the finger of suspicion at his two golfing companions...'

'Yes, but don't forget Dario, the golf pro... or Adam Hunter, for that matter. They would both have had golf gloves, and it would be logical for any murderer to wear a glove. I wonder...' I did my best to remember. 'Was it a left- or a right-hand glove?'

'Left, and according to Innocenti that means that the killer must have been right-handed. Apparently golfers only use one. Don't ask me why. The bad news is that he's been checking, and it appears that all of our suspects are right-handed, so no joy there.'

'And as far as gloves are concerned, Natalie could have taken one from her father's bag and, for that matter, Elizabeth McGregor, the assistant manager, would have had easy access to golf gloves as she worked there.'

We looked at each other and I said rather helplessly, 'Doesn't really help very much, does it?'

Virgilio shook his head in annoyance. 'I'll get Innocenti to do a search of each of the suspects' golf bags, but if our killer has any sense, he or she will have already replaced the missing glove.'

'So, where to now?'

'I'm going to head for the club and have another go at the golf pro and the assistant manager. I'm particularly interested to learn what it was that attracted her to a man who was more or less universally hated by all and sundry. Didn't you say you wanted to take Oscar for a walk? Why don't you head in the direction of Luigi Signese's farm? If you happen to bump into him, try asking him a few questions about the original land deal. Get chapter and verse about exactly which land Hunter was trying to steal from him and see if you can provoke him into admitting how deeply he hated the man.'

'I'll give it a try and I'll see what his reaction is when I mention that we know about the hole in the fence. If he made it or used it, he might give himself away.'

Oscar found Luigi Signese for me or, to be precise, he found Cesare, the wolfbear, and the giant led me to his master, who was in one of his vineyards, crouching down doing something to the vines. If the monster dog hadn't put in an appearance, I wouldn't have spotted the farmer. To my suspicious mind, this just highlighted how easy it would have been for him to sneak up through the vines, slip through the hole in the wire, batter Hunter to death, and then make his escape unnoticed. When he saw me, he straightened up and gave me a little wave with his left hand. His right hand was holding a pair of secateurs.

'Good afternoon. Out for a walk with your dog?'

I waved back and he kindly walked along the row to the gravel track I'd been following so we could talk. Although the tracks were drying out fast, the earth in the field beneath his feet was still very wet and his boots were thick with viscous mud. My trainers would have turned a not so charming umber colour in seconds if I'd tried to go to him.

'Good afternoon, Luigi, are you pruning?'

'Not really, we do that in winter. I spotted some blight on one of the vines and I'm making sure I cut it all away before it spreads.' He extended his hands behind him and straightened his back theatrically. 'I'm getting too old for all this bending. Farming's a young man's job.'

'Don't you have a son or daughter who could help out, maybe take over from you when the time comes?'

'I have two sons, but neither of them is interested in farming. One's in the police, based over in Prato, and the other one's at university in Florence. Guess what he's studying? History!' His tone made clear how he felt about that. 'He wants to be a teacher.'

'I used to be in the police – not here, back in London. In fact I've been helping out with a bit of interpreting for the investigation into Rex Hunter's murder.' I watched for any reaction but all I saw was curiosity.

'Have they got their eyes on anybody?'

'A number of suspects, I think.' I decided to go for it. 'You'll probably find you're on the list as well.'

He gave me a cheeky grin, a far cry from Jennifer's sinister sneers. 'Fame at last. Antonio, my son, told me they'd suspect me because the only alibi I've got is from my family. How do they think I did it? Did I hear that he had his head smashed in?'

I nodded. 'With one of his own golf clubs.' An idea occurred to me. 'I can't see how you could have done it without scaling a two-metre fence.'

His smile broadened. 'Ah, but that's where you're wrong. There's a hole in the fence just up there.' He raised his arm and pointed with the secateurs in the direction of the eighth green. 'I saw it yesterday and I was going to seal it up, but then I thought it might be evidence, so I left it alone.'

I was impressed. Of course, this canny countryman might be bluffing, knowing that we would already have found the hole in the fence but hoping by this display of openness to gain a bit of credibility. I liked the guy, but I'd met enough credible-sounding villains in my time to know that I shouldn't take anything at face value. For now, I feigned ignorance.

'So who made the hole?' It occurred to me as I asked the question that his monster dog was probably strong enough not only to make the hole but probably to chew up several metres of wire and a few fenceposts as well if he felt like it.

'I think it's a question of *what* made the hole. If you look closely, you'll see the wire's been ripped out of the ground. The only animal around here that's strong enough to do that is a wild boar. There's a real problem with them in this area. They don't just eat stuff; they dig up whole plants with their tusks and do a tremendous amount of damage. I've had some of my vines ruined by them, and I make a point of checking the fences regularly.'

'Thanks for telling me that. I'll pass it on to the inspector. By the way, he asked me to ask you which piece of land it was that Hunter has been trying to get from you?'

'Trying to *steal* from me, you mean.' There was real bitterness in the farmer's voice. 'As for which bit it was, you're standing on it – well, alongside it. It runs from here to the fence and down to the road – almost one hectare of prime agricultural land.'

'And that would include the woods and this olive grove?'

'That's right. There are olive trees here that are over two hundred years old. You know what Hunter wanted to do? He wanted to build a hotel, so that would have meant that all the trees would have gone.'

'But surely there are laws, conservation laws, that should prohibit that?' It was a deliberately leading question and Luigi's response was immediate.

'For you or me, definitely, but the Hunters of this world don't worry about laws when they've got the right friends.' He gave an ironic smile.

'Talking of friends, we've just come from interviewing a man called William Roseland. I believe you know him.'

The smile disappeared. 'No friend of mine. The fat Englishman who speaks terrible Italian. Did you know? He's been living here for almost twenty years, and yet he can hardly speak a word of the language.'

'I heard he was part of the consortium that developed the golf course and that you sold them a piece of your land back then.'

'That's right, and I stung them for as much as I could get.' He looked up. 'And then they sold out to Hunter, but he and Hunter stayed close. I've seen them playing golf together.'

Had he been spying on them from the obscurity of the woods, maybe? I looked him straight in the eye. 'The problem the inspector has with you, Luigi, is that you not only had the opportunity to kill Hunter, but you also had a powerful motive. Are you sure there isn't something you wish to tell me?'

'Well, I can only repeat that I didn't kill him. I'd never kill another man, not even a detestable human being like Hunter.'

The fact was that I believed him.

12

TUESDAY AFTERNOON

I drove up to the villa that afternoon to have another chat with Natalie who, while still weak, had been discharged from hospital. I took Oscar with me so he could have a walk afterwards and I let him jump out when he spotted his pal, Virgilio, waiting outside the villa by his car. While my dog licked his hand he filled me in on developments since we had last spoken.

'Elizabeth McGregor, the assistant manager, still denies any involvement in Hunter's murder. She actually broke down in tears when I suggested it, so if she was acting, she was doing very well.'

'And do you think she really was in love with Hunter?'

He nodded slowly. 'I do. She told me how much she had loved him and how caring, generous, and affectionate he'd been in return. It seems he really could turn on the charm when it suited him, even if most people never saw that side of him.'

'And the golf pro?'

'Innocenti's already questioned Dario Rossi, but I went looking for him and asked him a few questions of my own. He still continues to deny any involvement, and I tend to believe him. I asked him why he invented that story about it being another golf pro who got fired rather than himself and he said it was like you thought: he didn't want word of it to get out in case the new owner did just that. But he did give me a bit of interesting information. Over the past week since the murder, he's sold half a dozen golf gloves, and two of them were sold to people on our list of suspects.'

'I'm guessing Nelson and Roseland.'

'Half right; one was bought by Nelson, but the other by Adam Hunter. And of course there's no way of knowing if the golf pro helped himself to a replacement glove off the shelf in his own shop. I'm afraid the glove doesn't help very much.'

I told him what Luigi Signese had told me about the piece of land and how he had volunteered the information about the hole in the fence. Virgilio nodded, but we both knew we were going to need a whole lot more proof if we were to make a murder charge stick against any of our suspects.

I was just about to put Oscar back in the car again when the front door opened and Battista, impeccable and impassive as ever, appeared and gave us a little bow.

'Gentlemen, do come in. The *signora* asks if you'd like to bring your dog with you. She likes dogs. She's waiting in the lounge.'

I'd been wondering if Natalie had revealed her real identity to them, but Battista's choice of vocabulary didn't tell me anything. In Italian these days, women are most commonly addressed as '*signora*', rather than '*signorina*', even if they aren't married.

Natalie was waiting in the lounge and when she saw Oscar, she crouched down to make a fuss of him. He was a naturally friendly dog – particularly as far as women were concerned – and he nuzzled happily against her, tail wagging. As she looked at him, her careworn face even managed a hint of a smile.

'Do sit down.' She indicated the other sofa. 'Is this your lovely dog, Dan? I saw him through the window, and I wanted to meet him.'

'This is Oscar, and I'm sure he's happy to meet you too.' I've always thought Oscar was a good judge of character, so his very friendly reaction was definitely a good sign as far as I was concerned, although it was unlikely to stand up in a court of law. For a moment, I had a vision of a jury composed of dogs, and a bloodhound with a wig as a judge, but hastily dismissed the thought. Presumably the scales of justice would have been tipped in favour of the suspect holding the most dog food. It occurred to me that I had moved on somewhat and mellowed since giving up my position as Armstrong of the Yard. No doubt Helen would have viewed this as progress, although what my old super would have made of it was a different matter entirely. The only dogs he liked were the hot ones, preferably with lots of mustard.

Natalie rose to her feet and went across to close the door. When she returned to the sofa, she addressed herself to Virgilio. 'There's something I've been wanting to ask you, Inspector. Should I tell people my real status, rather than continue with the fiction that I was married to Rex? What do you think I should do? I like Battista and Mariarosa a lot and they've been terribly kind to me. I think it only fair if I tell them the truth, but only if you're agreeable.'

'It's your decision entirely. The people at the hospital know, Jennifer knows – although as far as I'm aware, she hasn't had any visitors to tell – and the police know. If I were in your shoes, I'd tell everybody. It'll be interesting to see the reaction of your half-brother to the news.'

As Virgilio spoke, I had an idea and put it to Natalie. 'How would you feel about calling a meeting tomorrow and announcing who you really are? That would give you the opportunity to explain that the whole thing was your dad playing some sort of convoluted game, and you can specify that it wasn't your idea. Make it quite clear that you were an unwilling accomplice in his scheming. I'd be happy to help with interpreting for you.' I glanced at Virgilio and saw him give a little nod. He could see where I was going with this.

'If you think it's a good idea.' Natalie sounded understandably hesitant at the prospect. 'I suppose it does make sense to tell everybody all at once, rather than drip-feed the information bit by bit. Who should I invite?'

I was quick to offer a few suggestions. 'Invite people around here who knew your dad. If you like, we can make a few calls and make the invitations for you. Certainly your half-brother and his partner, along with some of the staff of the club, but we could ask a few neighbours too, if you agree.'

Natalie looked relieved. 'If you could issue the invitations, that would be very kind. Should I give them food and drink? I don't know what you do over here.'

Virgilio stepped in with a suggestion. 'Why don't we invite people to come here to the villa for a drink tomorrow evening, say at six o'clock? That way people who work can come after they finish and then they can go off home for dinner afterwards. As for drinks, I suggest you get Battista to have a look in your father's cellar. I'm sure he must have had a few bottles of prosecco or champagne hidden away. If not, then I'm sure Battista will be able to rise to the occasion.'

With that decided, Virgilio went on to the serious stuff. 'You've probably realised by now that the fact that you inherit all your father's money makes you a prime suspect for his murder.' Natalie looked up sharply, but Virgilio raised a calming hand to reassure her. 'Dan and I've been talking and neither of us believes you to be a murderer, but we have to follow all leads and try to eliminate you from our enquiries.'

She slumped back and nodded her head. 'Of course, you have to do your job. I'll give you all the help I can, but I still think that if Jennifer was crazy enough to try to kill me, she's crazy enough to have killed my father.' My dog's canine radar must have registered the troubled note in her voice, and I was pleased to see him get up from my feet and wander over to rest a supportive head on her lap. She stroked him gratefully as the inspector carried on.

'Indeed, but Jennifer's not the only suspect.' Virgilio didn't go on to name the others. 'As far as you're concerned, it would help me a lot if somebody could corroborate your story that you were here in the villa at the time your father was killed. We know that Battista and Mariarosa were also here in the villa, but they say they were in the kitchen while you were in here.' He pointed to the French windows leading out to the garden. 'You see, it's feasible that you could have sneaked out, killed your father, and sneaked back again without them noticing. Was there anybody working in the garden who might have seen you? Were you making any phone calls, attending a Zoom meeting, anything like that?'

She shook her head. 'I was reading my book.' She indicated a paperback on the table. 'But I suppose you'll say I could have been doing that any time.' She stopped as she remembered something. 'But I did watch Sky News at nine o'clock, if that helps. They were talking about flooding in Queensland.'

Virgilio thanked her and made a note of it, although we both knew that in these days of catch-up TV this proved nothing. The questions continued but we got nowhere. In the end Virgilio thanked her and stood up, followed by Oscar and me. 'We'll get onto the invitations for tomorrow evening, and I'll get one of my men to call Battista with a headcount in the morning, so he and his wife know how many guests to expect.'

When we got outside, Virgilio and I stood in the shade for a few minutes, and I told him what had been going through my mind when I had suggested a get-together. 'I thought it might be good to get all the suspects – apart from Jennifer, of course – together in one place so you could put the cat among the pigeons with a fictitious announcement about getting close to solving the mystery or having new evidence or some such. That might just flush our murderer out.'

'It's a good idea. How about I make a formal-sounding announcement – you can translate it into English – saying that we're expecting to have new evidence in the next twenty-four hours that should lead us to our killer? You know, the usual: we think we should be able to make an arrest or arrests very soon.' He gave me a little shrug of the shoulders. 'Although if that doesn't spark some activity, we'll be back to square one.'

'Let me issue the invitations to Adam, Nelson, and Roseland in person. Roseland said the three of them will be playing golf at six so I could take Oscar for a walk then deliver the invite so I can see how they react.'

Working on the basis that it had taken roughly an hour and a half for Rex Hunter and his two companions to reach the eighth green on the night of the murder, my dog and I returned just after seven and walked up through the disputed strip of woodland until we were close to the scene of the crime. Sure enough, just coming up the fairway in the distance were Roseland, Nelson, and Adam Hunter. Roseland even managed to hook his ball into the rough barely twenty metres from where I was waiting, and I was easily able to attract his attention as he came over to hit it. I asked him to call his companions over so we could talk through the fence and they left their golf bags and came across, clearly puzzled to find me here.

'Good evening, gentlemen. I'm glad I spotted you.' Keeping an eye on Oscar to see that he didn't slip through the hole in the fence again, I went on to issue the invitation to them to a 'meeting' to take place at the villa at six the following day. I noticed hesitation on Adam's face in particular and added an ominous codicil: 'The inspector hopes to have an announcement which will impact all of you.'

Without giving them a chance to question the nature of the forthcoming announcement, I gave them a cheery wave and headed back into the trees with Oscar. As they disappeared from view, I was turning over in my head the reactions of the men. All three to some extent had demonstrated not only surprise, but a degree of apprehension. Tomorrow evening promised to be interesting.

13

WEDNESDAY EVENING

The meeting the next day was very interesting.

Virgilio and I arrived half an hour before the start time of six o'clock and went through with Natalie what we wanted her to say. She declared herself happy to do as instructed and repeated the all-important final sentence a few times so she would be sure to get it right. As the guests began to arrive, Virgilio and I studied them closely. Many looked as though this was the first time they'd been inside Hunter's villa, while to others it was clearly more familiar. Battista and Mariarosa had set up a table by the door into the lounge from where they dispensed drinks. From the display of bottles on the table, Rex Hunter's cellar had produced rich pickings. Determined to keep a clear head, I grabbed a glass of ice-cold sparkling water for myself and took up station by the window in a good position to survey the whole room.

First to arrive were the posse from the club consisting of Dario, the golf pro, and his girlfriend, my tennis coach Abigail. Along with them came the assistant manager, Elizabeth McGregor, and her face was a picture. It wasn't hard to read what must have been going through her head as she stared at the sumptuous furnishings, the gleaming marble floors, and the ostentatious collection of modern art on the walls. Although she had played down any expectations when speaking to us, there surely must have been a part of her that had secretly aspired to becoming the mistress of this house. At my suggestion, Virgilio's men had also invited Raffaello, the receptionist, and Annalisa, the barista, along with the groundsmen, Beppe and Alfredo, and Ines, the gardener.

Next to arrive was Luigi Signese. The farmer was almost unrecognisable in a smart suit, collar, and tie. Along with him was a young man with short dark hair and a neatly trimmed moustache. His facial features revealed instantly that he was unmistakably one of Luigi's sons. From the deferential way he greeted Virgilio, I reckoned that this had to be the son who was in the police. Seeing the two of them looking a bit out of their depth, I went over to greet them and introduced them to Natalie. For now, I just told them her name and the fact that she had become the owner of the villa and country club. They would discover her exact identity in a few minutes' time. Luigi's son, it transpired, spoke quite good English and I left them chatting amicably. Hopefully this would help them to bury the hatchet after the trouble her father's attempt to steal Luigi's land had caused.

After them came Nelson and Roseland, looking slightly apprehensive, but they both managed to hide it well, although I couldn't help noticing that Roseland's first glass of Rex Hunter's expensive-looking malt Scotch disappeared down his throat in an instant and was immediately replaced. Last, but not least, was Adam Hunter, his expression hard to read. Clearly he was familiar with the villa but seeing Natalie as the lady of the house couldn't have been easy for him.

Natalie did very well. Considering that this was her first sight of many of these people, she did her best to sound welcoming. With me translating into Italian as she went along, she thanked everybody for coming and told them how she looked forward to getting to know them all. Then she moved on to the nitty gritty.

'You're probably wondering why I've asked you all to come here so soon after the death of Rex Hunter. The fact is that I need to set the record straight.' I saw everybody snap to attention. You couldn't have heard a pin drop in the room as all eyes were on the little figure in the dark dress. 'You see, Rex Hunter wasn't my husband. He was my father.'

If I'd been expecting a universal intake of breath from the guests, I was to be disappointed. Predictably the only person whose reaction was vocal was Adam. He stepped forward until he was facing his half-sister, sufficiently far from her not to appear threatening, but I saw Sergeant Innocenti brace himself all the same. But Adam's reaction was anything but aggressive.

'That explains so much. You even look like the old man. It's been bothering me ever since I first saw you. Now it all fits into place. But why the charade?'

Natalie even managed a little smile for him as she went on to outline how she and her father had been reunited over in Australia after the death of her mother and how he had dreamt up what she referred to as 'this whole crazy game'. She didn't go into detail about why Rex had decided to play this macabre trick on everybody, and it was interesting to see how little astonishment there was to be seen on the faces of the guests. It was clear that crazy, irrational behaviour had been the norm for Rex Hunter.

The other person whose face I studied carefully was Elizabeth, the assistant manager and former lover of the dead man. As the realisation sank in that he had not, after all, gone off and married a younger woman, an expression of awe spread across her face. I rather wished I could have filmed it, as it would need repeated viewing to be sure, but it looked to me like a mixture of relief and regret. Was the regret because she had killed Hunter for the wrong reason?

Towards the end of her little speech, Natalie reassured all the country-club staff that there would be no changes, and I distinctly saw her glance at her half-brother as she said this. For his part, he was looking much more cheerful, and I hoped that boded well for their relationship going forward – assuming it didn't turn out that one of them was our murderer. Finally, she delivered the sentence supplied to her by Virgilio and me. 'I can't tell you how relieved I am that the police have told me they've made a breakthrough, and that my father's murderer is about to be brought to justice.' She turned towards Virgilio and thanked him before asking if he would like to say a few words.

If the anticipation in the room had been palpable before, now it was almost overwhelming. Virgilio deliberately took his time before stepping forward and my eyes scanned the faces before me for any hints of culpability. We had already worked out that our murderer was a very good actor, and it came as no surprise to see that nobody immediately stood out.

Adam was still looking gobsmacked after his half-sister's revelation, so his expression was particularly hard to judge. I thought I might have glimpsed a flash of apprehension on the chubby cheeks of Roseland, but Nelson beside him looked untroubled and, of course, they had been out on the course together and so provided alibis for each other. Elizabeth McGregor's expression didn't change, but she had already been looking stunned, so that proved nothing. As for Dario, the golf pro, and Luigi Signese, they looked positively intrigued but, as I said, our killer was a good actor.

Virgilio kept it short and sweet. 'I'm pleased to report that we have vital new information that should prove significant for our investigation. I'm afraid I have to ask all of you not to leave the area. Hopefully by tomorrow night we should have reached a satisfactory conclusion to our enquiries. Thank you.'

After this the guests started to leave, and I kept a close eye on the body language of each of them as they filed out. Of all of them, the most emotionally overcome was Elizabeth, while the least affected appeared to be Luigi and his son. The group of staff from the club were all looking slightly overawed, but not even the golf pro looked in the least bit guilty. If I had had to put money on the person most disturbed by either Natalie's or Virgilio's remarks it would have been Roseland. The question was what possible motive could he have had to murder Hunter? It looked unlikely that he stood to gain from the Australian's death, he didn't seem the type to have been involved in a love triangle, and he didn't appear to have any reason to be seeking revenge. As I watched his receding back I reflected that maybe he always looked like that after a couple of stiff drinks.

14

WEDNESDAY LATE EVENING

When I got home later that evening after having dinner with Virgilio and Oscar in a little restaurant with a patio overlooking the last range of hills before the valley of the River Arno and Florence itself, I took Oscar for a long walk to clear my head, and when I returned home it was to find two emails waiting for me. The first was from Helen, the second from somebody whose name meant nothing to me. I opened the one from my ex-wife first. Predictably, it related to our abortive meeting at the weekend.

Hi Dan

It was good to see you again in Florence. I mean that. It was.

Thank you for the meal, which I thoroughly enjoyed. I'm sorry you had to rush off but I'm glad to hear from Tricia that you're enjoying what you're doing. You need to live your life your way and I know that it will always be different from mine.

I thoroughly enjoyed my few days in Tuscany, and I can understand why you have decided to settle there. Wishing you a very happy life

Helen x

I reached for one of Luigi's bottles of red wine and poured myself a glass. After a hefty mouthful I read the email again and reflected on what Helen had said. Thinking back on the events of the past few days, I knew that she was right to blow the whistle on our relationship. One of us had had to do it and she had got there before me. She deserved somebody better than me – or at least somebody who could honestly say she was the most important thing in his life. Although this made perfect sense, it didn't help lift the sense of disappointment that settled on me as a result of the realisation that Helen and I were now irrevocably split up.

Fortunately, the other email did.

It was from a lady called Suzanne and it turned out she was one of the commissioning editors at the publishers in London who had been reading my whodunnit. The upshot of the email was that they liked the book very much and were offering me a two-book contract with an option to publish more of my work 'depending on sales'. As I came to the end of the email, I jumped to my feet and startled my dog by dancing around the kitchen like a mad thing, repeating over and over again, 'She liked it, she liked it.'

I was going to become a published author.

Oscar jumped to his feet and joined me in my dance. Such was my excitement, I almost didn't hear my phone until the discordant ringing of the bell finally cut through my euphoria and I picked it up. It was Virgilio and, by the sound of it, he was in a car.

'Hi Dan, news: Roseland's been found dead.'

'Jesus! We were hoping for some sort of reaction to tonight's meeting but I certainly wasn't expecting that. What happened? Was it suicide, murder, a heart attack?'

'A road traffic accident, apparently. His car's been found

upside down in a dried-up stream bed not far from his home. He was still wearing his seat belt.'

'Are we sure it was an accident?'

'That's what I want to see for myself. Want to come along?'

I met Virgilio at the scene of the accident, just past the country club, barely fifteen minutes away from my house. I knew this bit of road quite well by now. It was narrow and winding, and I found it hard to see how Roseland could have been going fast enough to lose control. The smart Mercedes – now considerably less smart after ending up nose first in the rocky riverbed – was upside down, and the pathologist's team were already there, waiting for Virgilio to take a look before they removed the body. The familiar figure of Gianni, the pathologist, came over to give us his initial findings.

'*Ciao*, Virgilio, *ciao*, Dan. He died between two and four hours ago, say between six and eight. Looks like death was by asphyxiation.' Seeing the expressions on our faces, he pointed into the vehicle where the bulky body of Roseland was hanging limply upside down from what had to be a very strong safety belt. 'There's bruising to his forehead, presumably where he made contact with something, maybe the steering wheel, and that must have knocked him out. The way the car ended up, his seat belt was across his throat and his weight did the rest.'

Virgilio and I bent down to peer inside the car, and I immediately smelt alcohol. I remembered seeing Roseland consume at least two whiskies at the meeting and felt sure this must have contributed to, if not caused the accident. The forensic team had rigged up lights and the interior of the vehicle was well illuminated. The window on the driver's side was open and it looked as though no fewer than four airbags had gone off, but they hadn't been able to prevent Roseland's death. The bruising across his forehead formed a neat horizontal line and must have knocked him unconscious instantly. The expression on his face was surprisingly calm and it looked as though he had died almost peacefully.

I went back up to the road where the police were already busy, taping off the area where a flattened 'No Hunting' sign showed where the car had slipped down the steep slope into the ravine. There were no skid marks on the tarmac or grass, and it looked almost as though the accident had happened in slow motion. As I was still ferreting around, Virgilio came up alongside me.

'Funny how all those airbags didn't manage to prevent him knocking himself out on the steering wheel.' The disbelief in his voice echoed the way I felt about it.

'And funny how the car wasn't going at any great speed when the accident happened or there would have been skid marks, if not on the tarmac, at least in the grass at the roadside as he went off, and nobody appears to have been coming around the corner towards him at any speed either.' I walked back in the opposite direction for fifty yards or so, but the only skid marks I came across were so old they had horse manure plastered onto them. Virgilio joined me.

'What's your take on what happened, Dan?'

I'd had time to consider this by now. 'Call me suspicious, but I have a feeling the accident wasn't an accident at all. How about this as a scenario? Roseland leaves Natalie's party at the villa at half past six, gives a lift to somebody who asks to be dropped off here. He opens his window to say goodbye and they knock him unconscious with a blunt instrument they just happen to be carrying, before pushing the car off the road.' I saw his eyes roll. 'Yes, I know, it's tenuous. Maybe CCTV as he left the club will show if he did have a passenger.'

'And if he didn't?'

'What might be more realistic is that he was driving sedately home after a bit too much to drink when he saw somebody he knew. He came to a halt, opened the window and leant out, only for that somebody to hit him in the face with a heavy object. From the shape of the wound, I'd say something straight like a cricket bat or an iron bar and it could easily have been wielded by a man or a woman. Seeing as we're in Italy, my money's on the iron bar rather than the cricket bat. The attacker then turned the steering wheel – which I wouldn't mind betting has since been wiped clean – and lifted Roseland's foot off the brake. It's an automatic so, assuming the engine was still running, the car would have driven itself down the slope and dropped into the stream bed.'

Virgilio nodded in agreement. 'Sounds about right. Just one thing: the engine was turned off. Forensics say it didn't just stall; somebody must have turned it off. There's a button that needs to be pressed.'

'I imagine the killer followed the car down the slope to check if Roseland was still alive. He or she then turned off the engine to prevent the noise attracting the attention of any passers-by, although I wouldn't think many people would have been walking along this road in the evening. The killer probably just sat and watched as Roseland strangled himself.' It wasn't a pleasant thought. 'They maybe even rearranged the seatbelt in such a way as to cause the asphyxiation. A pretty cold-blooded killing all right.'

Virgilio called up the slope towards the pathologist. 'Gianni, did you find a wallet? Phone?'

'A wallet with four hundred euros in it along with a selection of bank cards. No sign of a phone, though.'

'Did you check the steering wheel for fingerprints?'

'Wiped clean. Not even the victim's on there.'

Virgilio looked back at me. 'Well, if the victim's prints aren't on there, then it's definitely not an accident, and robbery doesn't appear to have been the motive. I'll organise a search of the surroundings in the hope of finding the iron bar or the baseball bat or whatever it was. We might even find his phone. The problem we have is that out here in the wilds, there are no security cameras, so there's no way of knowing who the assailant might have been.'

'I reckon he must have known his attacker. I can't see a man like Roseland stopping out here in the middle of nowhere on a quiet country lane for somebody unknown to him.'

'I agree. I'll get the team to search the verges for a couple of hundred metres each way in the hope of finding the tyre tracks of another vehicle. Fortunately, since the rain the other day, the ground's still soft enough to get prints. We'll also check for footprints near the vehicle, but a lot of people have been down the slope since the accident was reported.'

An unwelcome thought occurred to me, but it had to be voiced. 'Of course, there is one person that Roseland knew who lives close to here: the friendly farmer, Luigi Signese. If he had been waiting at the side of the road and waved the car down, I imagine Roseland would have stopped for him. I still don't see Luigi as a killer but it's a consideration.'

'You're right, it is.'

'Who reported the car off the road?'

He glanced at his notebook. 'A woman called Teresa Marchi. She lives in one of the houses near Roseland's, which is barely four or five minutes along the road, and she was cycling home from her friend's house around a quarter to eight. She saw something glinting, spotted the car in the gulley, and scrambled down to see if anybody had been hurt. That's when she discovered the body and called 112. She's back home now in a state of shock with one of my female officers keeping an eye on her until her daughter gets there to look after her.'

'And Roseland's wife? Has she been notified?'

'Innocenti and another female officer are with her and I'm on my way there now. She's called Silvia but I have no idea if she speaks Italian. If she speaks as badly as Roseland did, I'm going to be in trouble. Feel like coming along?'

I followed him to Roseland's house, which was barely three minutes away. The whole place was illuminated, and two police cars were parked outside. Virgilio managed to squeeze in between them and the little sports car, and all I could do was leave my car blocking the drive behind them. We knocked on the door and it was opened by Innocenti.

'She's in the lounge and she's understandably very upset.'

Roseland's wife, now widow, came as something of a surprise – at least to me. It turned out that the tall woman that I had seen in running gear that first morning at the club and then in Roseland's garden hadn't been his daughter as I had thought, but his wife. She was a very attractive woman, maybe in her late thirties, and she looked fit. She was sitting on the sofa with a tissue in one hand, red-eyed, and clearly very upset. Alongside her was a female officer.

'Signora Roseland, my condolences. I'm Inspector Pisano from Florence.' Virgilio sat down opposite her while I stayed in the background with Innocenti.

I was just about to offer an English translation in case her Italian was as poor as her husband's, but before I could speak she answered, and her Tuscan accent indicated that she wasn't going to need my help.

'Thank you, Inspector. It certainly was a shock.'

'What time were you expecting your husband home this evening?'

'We normally eat at eight. He's often late so I didn't really start worrying until half past. I tried calling him then but there was no reply.'

'Did you hear his phone ring?'

'No, it just came up with a message saying it hadn't been possible to connect. There are a number of places around here without good phone coverage. I was going to try again, but a few minutes later I got the call from one of your officers telling me about the accident.'

'About that: I'm afraid I have to inform you that it's looking very much as though it wasn't an accident.'

Her eyes opened wide. 'You mean somebody...?'

Virgilio nodded. 'Yes, I'm afraid it's very likely that your husband has been murdered.'

Silvia Roseland sat there in stunned silence for some time before tears began pouring down her cheeks. Either she was an outstanding actress, or this had come as a real shock to her. Virgilio gave her time to collect herself before pressing on with his questions.

'Signora Roseland, can you think of anybody who might have wanted to kill your husband? Did he have any enemies?'

'No, none at all... at least, not the sort of enemies who would have wanted to kill him. He was in business so I expect there were a few disgruntled customers, but nobody who would want to *kill* him.'

Virgilio leant forward and lowered his voice to soften the blow. 'I'm sorry to have to ask you this, but this is a murder investigation, and we need to get to the bottom of whoever did this to your husband. I can't help noticing that you're considerably younger than your husband. Might there be a jealous lover involved?'

She just stared blankly at him for a few moments before react-

ing. 'You mean, do I have a lover who might have killed William?'
Her expression changed from surprise to anger. 'I most certainly
do not. I loved my husband, Inspector, and I would never have
dreamt of doing anything like that to him.' She sounded
outraged, but I had a feeling there was something about her
response that didn't quite ring true to me, but maybe I'd just
become too cynical in my old age.

Virgilio was quick to attempt to defuse the situation. 'Thank
you, Signora Roseland. Like I said, I was obliged to ask the question and I wouldn't want you to interpret it as any kind of slight. I
just have a couple more questions and then we won't bother you
again. Could I ask how long you were married?'

She blew her nose and settled back against the cushions.
'William and I've been married a year and a half. We got married
in January of last year.'

'Were either of you married before?'

'Yes, both of us. I divorced my first husband three years ago
and William divorced his wife two years ago.'

'And when did you and your husband meet?'

'About three years ago, not long after I divorced my first
husband.' She looked up. 'I worked at the factory... you know,
his ceramics factory in Montespertoli. I'm an artist and
sculptor by profession and I used to paint the pots and plates
before firing. It's still a hobby of mine now, even though I no
longer work at the factory. I have my own studio in the
garden.'

So Roseland had traded in his first wife for a newer model:
younger, firmer, and fitter. I could well imagine the effect this
could have had on his ex-wife. It might be worth speaking to her.
Evidently Virgilio was thinking the very same thing.

'Do you have an address for his first wife?'

Silvia Roseland shook her head. 'I'm afraid she died of cancer last year. It was very sad.' Again, she managed to sound very convincing.

'And did you or your husband have children?'

'No, I'm afraid not.'

'Finally, I'm obliged to ask, is there anybody who can confirm that you were here between six and eight this evening?'

'I'm sorry, but no. I was here on my own, getting dinner ready.'

I slipped in a question of my own and saw surprise on both faces. 'And what was on the menu for tonight?'

'Um, *pasta con aglio e olio*. William likes... liked his pasta. Followed by steak. We have a gas barbecue.'

I gave her a little smile. 'Sounds wonderful, thank you.'

Virgilio took over again. 'Would you mind if we take a look around? Maybe see his bedroom?'

'Go wherever you like. His room's the first on the right. Mine's the one after.'

'You had separate bedrooms?'

Her cheeks flushed. 'If you must know, it's because of his snoring. I just couldn't sleep in the same bed as him.'

As Virgilio and I went upstairs to check out the bedroom, he glanced across at me and murmured, 'Love's young dream...'

We started in Roseland's room but found no sign of his phone. I checked the pockets of his jacket and trousers hanging on the back of a chair as well as looking in the drawer of the bedside table. 'Maybe he left it downstairs.'

But he hadn't. We scoured the house but there was no sign of the phone. I went out into the garden and checked inside the little stone construction housing his wife's studio, but there was no sign of anything except a new-looking kiln and some rather nice pots and sculptures. Silvia Roseland had talent. In the meantime, Virgilio got the victim's phone number from her and told Innocenti to get the phone company onto checking calls made and received in the course of the day. Finally we said goodnight to Silvia Roseland and left the house. Outside in the parking area, I checked my watch. It was midnight. I looked across at Virgilio.

'Fancy a drink at my place?'

Virgilio shook his head. 'No, thanks. I'd better get back to my wife. By the way, there's something I want to show you. Do you feel like coming down to Florence tomorrow? Bring Oscar, by all means. It'll concern him as well.'

My curiosity tickled, I arranged that Oscar and I would come to Virgilio's office at eleven next day to see whatever it was he wanted to show us.

15

THURSDAY MORNING

On the way down to Florence next morning, I was still thinking about the three big events of the previous day: Roseland's death, the email from Helen, and the wonderful news from Suzanne in London about the publishing contract. It was unprofessional of me but, of the three, the death of the fat man was the last thing on my mind. Overnight, I had come to terms with what I had already known: namely that my relationship with my ex-wife was well and truly over. What this meant as far as my future life was concerned remained to be seen. For a start, there was now no reason why I shouldn't seriously consider Virgilio's suggestion of setting myself up as a private investigator. Or was there? One impediment had removed itself, but another might just have materialised in its place. Had my ex-wife been replaced by my literary career? Would it be sensible to take on a contract to write more books at the same time as launching into a new career as a private detective?

I was still turning all this over in my head when Oscar and I arrived at police headquarters. The officers on the front desk knew me by now and made no objection to my four-legged companion coming with me up the stairs to Virgilio's office overlooking the mighty Fortezza da Basso, whose sixteenth-century brick and stone walls dominated the piazza in front of the police station. Virgilio was standing by his whiteboard on which the names of all the suspects in the country-club case had been written beneath photos of Rex Hunter's body lying in the bunker. Over to one side of the board was the name William Roseland, and a black cross alongside the name indicating that he had died. Next to him was the name of his widow, Silvia Roseland, and Virgilio had drawn a red question mark alongside her name. He gave me a little wave and bent down to pat Oscar.

'*Ciao* Dan. Did you manage to get some sleep after our late night?'

'I slept fine, thanks. Anything new?'

'I've just had the pathologist's report on Roseland. He actually died of a heart attack, but it was brought on by suffocation. But, more importantly, Gianni confirms your theory that somebody hit him with something hard, probably something made of metal, and there's no trace of a blow like that having been inflicted by anything on the inside of the car. Seeing as the driver's side window was open, Gianni agrees with you that the victim was probably leaning out to look at something or to speak to somebody when he was struck. That knocked him out and he was still unconscious when he suffocated to death. It was definitely murder.'

'So who would want to murder him? Surely it must have something to do with the Rex Hunter murder, or do we think this is unrelated? If so, could it have been the wife? Was Roseland killed because he knew too much, saw something he shouldn't have seen, or was his young wife's lover trying to get him out of the way to get their hands on his fortune?'

'I share your cynical opinion of the young woman marrying

an old man for his money, but she looked really upset, and in my experience not too many murderers weep for their victims.'

'I know what you mean, but there was something about her reaction that didn't ring true. I can't put my finger on it, but I don't like the fact that she has no alibi for the time of the murder. Let's face it: preparing a plate of pasta with oil and garlic and a steak on the barbecue doesn't take a whole lot of preparation. If I'd walked into the house to find a lingering aroma of bouillabaisse or ratatouille, I would have believed her more willingly.'

He shot me a little grin. 'Bouillabaisse and ratatouille? We're in Italy here, not France.'

'Well, a rich rabbit stew or some frying onions, then. But I smelt nothing.'

'So you think she might have slipped out and killed her husband?'

'It's a possibility, and she didn't even need to use her car. Maybe she walked along to the scene of the crime. It's not far away and it wouldn't have taken her long. From what I've seen of her, she keeps herself fit so she could have run down and back in no time at all. Or maybe she wasn't acting alone. Maybe she was the bait standing at the side of the road while her lover lay in wait with an iron bar.' I shook my head in frustration. 'I agree that she looked upset, and bursting into tears like that seems to indicate genuine grief, so maybe it's just me, but I don't think we should rule her out quite yet. After all, it might not have just been for the money. Maybe Roseland was killed because he'd found out that she had a lover and was on the warpath. The lover murdered him to silence him. Could it be the murderer was married and afraid of the trouble this would cause?'

'Anything's possible and if she had a lover, who was it? Somebody we know? Somebody at the club?'

'Assuming she chose somebody closer to her age than her

husband, that gives us Adam Hunter, Peter Nelson, or the golf pro. Adam and Dario have both got partners, but I think I remember Nelson saying he lives alone. Of course, it might be somebody completely different.' I paused for a few moments, my brain churning. 'It's just a thought, but I suppose Silvia Roseland's lover doesn't necessarily need to be a man. What about Elizabeth McGregor, the assistant manager? What if all that talk about her deep and burning love for Rex Hunter was nothing but a smoke-screen? Maybe Elizabeth was Silvia Roseland's mystery lover.'

'Anything's possible, but of course the murder of Roseland might have nothing to do with his wife at all. It might not even have anything to do with the Hunter case, although, like you, I reckon it would be a hell of a coincidence if it wasn't. My feeling is that it has to be linked to Rex Hunter's murder, but how?'

'If we assume it probably *is* linked to Hunter's murder, my money would be on Peter Nelson. What if he killed Rex Hunter up on the golf course last week and Roseland witnessed it, but for whatever reason promised to stay schtum? All was going well until our little bit of play-acting last night freaked Roseland into feeling he should confess, and Nelson knew he had to kill him to keep him quiet. What do you think?'

'He could have done it, but we're short of a motive. Yes, Nelson didn't like his boss a lot, but he'd learnt to live with him. I confess that I don't like the *questore* very much, but I'm hardly going to go out and murder him. Besides, why would Nelson suddenly react now? What happened to provoke him into doing something so radical? Still, we'd better check the CCTV at the club. It's feasible that Nelson left before Roseland last night and arranged the ambush on what he knew was likely to be a very quiet bit of road. Proving it isn't going to be easy though.'

'And then there's Luigi Signese. Maybe we could apply the same logic to him. He slipped through the fence and killed

Hunter last week, but he was seen by Roseland. For some reason or other, Roseland agreed to keep quiet about what he'd seen, but then had a change of heart last night and so Luigi knew he had to be killed.'

Virgilio gave a frustrated snort and dropped the marker pen back on his desk. 'Anyway, I told you there's something I want to show you. Fancy a short walk?'

Oscar recognised the magic word immediately – he was fluent in both languages when it was a question of food or walks – and headed for the door. Virgilio led the way out of police headquarters and three blocks along to the right. Turning into a narrow road lined with parked cars, we walked a few hundred yards along it before we came to an arched entrance set in an anonymous façade. We were well into the *centro storico* here, and I knew that many of the buildings dated back to the Renaissance. As somebody with a keen interest in the history of that period, I followed Virgilio through the archway with considerable anticipation. We walked into a flagstone-paved courtyard and turned right onto a wide stone stairway leading upwards. As we climbed, I admired little reminders of the antiquity of the *palazzo* – statues in niches, sculpted stone window frames and vaulted ceilings – until we stopped at a doorway on the first floor. Virgilio produced a key and opened the fine old carved wooden door. He ushered me and my dog inside and gave an expansive wave of the hand and an even more expansive grin.

'Well, what do you think, Dan?'

I looked around. We were in a little antechamber, separated from the room beyond by another fine door, this one with a glass panel set into it. Through this I could see that the floor inside was bare, the place apparently empty, except for a massive old wooden desk standing by the window. I went on in and looked around. The first thing that struck me was the fresco that occupied most of the left-hand wall. It was clearly very old and it portrayed a rural scene with men in pantaloons with swords at their sides riding after a pack of hounds on the heels of an unfortunate stag. There were two doors in the wall on the far side. Both were open and I could see that one led to a small kitchen and the other to a bathroom. Intrigued, I turned to see Virgilio looking on benevolently, still with a broad smile on his face.

'Welcome to the office of Dan Armstrong, Private Investigator. What do you think of it?'

For a moment I didn't know what to say and Virgilio took advantage of my silence to outline his plan. 'I reckon you should set yourself up with an office here and a nice brass plate on the wall outside. No need to spend a fortune on advertising; that's what the Internet's for. I'll spread the word and you just wait and see. There are hundreds, thousands of English speakers here in Florence alone, plus thousands more dotted all over Tuscany and goodness knows how many in the rest of Italy. You bet your life there'll be those who need help with more delicate matters that they wouldn't come to the police about. And there are always cases that we can't handle. I could see you making a very good living out of chasing runaways, checking up on unfaithful spouses, locating family heirlooms, and maybe even...' he glanced down at Oscar and grinned '...finding missing pets. Well, what do you say?'

By this time, I had got over my initial surprise. 'It's a fascinating thought. Ever since you suggested it, I've been thinking along those lines but there's one big problem for a start: ever since the divorce, my pension's having to stretch a long way. I couldn't possibly afford to pay the rent on somewhere bang in the city centre like this. It's in a great position, not far from the train station, the *duomo*, your office. I know it won't be cheap.'

His grin widened. 'Now, that's where you'd be wrong. You see, up until very recently, this office has been used by my uncle for his little business. He exported Tuscan ceramics all over the world from here and did rather well out of it. He's just hit seventy-five and he finally gave in to my aunt's badgering and retired a week ago. I bumped into him yesterday and he told me that twenty-two years ago he committed to a thirty-year lease at a very reasonable rate. If you want it, you can have this place for the next eight years at a quarter of today's going rate.'

This was sounding very appealing. I walked over to the window to the rear and saw that it looked out over the charming courtyard, which was larger than I had first thought. There was even a little garden over to the left with wisteria growing up the walls and rose bushes in full bloom around a little statue of what looked from here like Venus. Two cars were parked down there outside what looked like a workshop of some kind. Oscar, ever curious, trotted over with me and stood up on his hind legs, resting his paws on the windowsill as he, too, peered out, nostrils flared as he savoured the new scents. I looked down at him and ruffled his ears.

'What do you think, Doctor Watson? Are we interested?'

He licked my hand, and I took that as an endorsement. I turned back to Virgilio. 'I'm going to need to do some serious thinking. When does your uncle need to know?'

'What day is it today?' He pretended to do a bit of calculation. 'Thursday, isn't it? Take your time and let me know by the weekend.'

'The weekend? That starts tomorrow night.'

The grin was still there. 'How about I tell him you'll let him know by Sunday night? As you can imagine, he's got a queue of people who'd love to get their hands on this place, but I've told him you're a close friend of mine and I've always been his favourite nephew. I know he'll wait till then.'

'So that gives me just three days to decide on my whole future... wow.'

Any further discussion was interrupted by Virgilio's phone. It was a brief call and when he came off the line, he was looking surprised, 'Adam Hunter's just turned up in my office and he wants to talk to me. Feel like coming along?'

We hurried back to the police headquarters and found Adam and an older woman waiting for us. The moment I set eyes on her, I felt sure I knew who she was. Virgilio ushered them into his office and Adam made the introductions in English.

'This is my mother, June Hunter. She's just flown over from Australia.'

His mother was quick to correct him. 'June Holman now. I decided to revert to my maiden name.'

She was a grim-faced woman, but as she had presumably just stepped off a twenty-four-hour flight, that wasn't so surprising. She was probably nudging my age, give or take a year or two, but she had aged a whole lot better than I had. With her no doubt dyed blonde hair and remarkably wrinkle-free skin, she was still a very good-looking woman with the marked resemblance to her daughter, Jennifer, that had immediately struck me. Adam Hunter introduced me as 'Inspector Armstrong' and we all shook hands before Virgilio waved the two of them to seats. I stood by the window with my dog while Virgilio sat down behind his desk.

'To what do I owe this visit, Signor Hunter?' Remembering what we had been told about Adam's mother's dislike of Italy and the language, Virgilio stuck to English.

'I told my mother that Jennifer's been arrested, and she's come over to see Jen. Is that going to be possible?'

Virgilio transferred his attention to Adam's mother. 'I see no reason why not. I just got a report on your daughter this morning and you'll be pleased to hear that now that she's back on her tranquillisers, she's behaving a lot more rationally, although she'll have to remain in custody.' He hesitated. 'I imagine you know that she's admitted attempting to murder Natalie Hunter. Can I presume that you've heard about your ex-husband's other daughter?'

The reply was laced with acid. 'I always suspected Rex of having bastard children spread around the globe. Now that this one's come floating to the surface, I wonder how many more of them there are out there.' Attractive she might be, but June Holman had a bitterly sharp tongue. 'I understand Rex has left everything to her, rather than to his real children. It's a disgrace.'

Virgilio allowed a soothing tone to enter his voice. 'I couldn't comment on the terms of the will, but, if you like, I can make a call and see if you can visit your daughter later today.'

'Yes... thank you.' I could see that she was making a conscious effort to calm herself down. She looked even more like her daughter when she snarled, and it was easy to see how the toxic cocktail of this woman and the equally poisonous Rex Hunter had contributed to making Jennifer the way she was. It was a wonder that her brother hadn't turned out the same way. Or had he? We only had the word of his partner that he hadn't been out on the course that Monday evening. Maybe beneath his façade of geniality, there beat a far darker heart. After all, if he had been standing at the roadside last night, I'm sure Roseland would have stopped. I watched him closely as Virgilio continued.

'While I have you here, Signora Holman, could I ask you if you can think of any enemies your husband might have had, maybe even going back years?'

She gave a dismissive toss of the head. 'How long have you got? The list of people he screwed – and I mean in all senses of the word – goes on forever. To me, it's a wonder somebody didn't murder him sooner. I'll be honest, Inspector, if I could have thought of a way of doing it and getting away with it, I would probably have done it myself.'

Or maybe, I thought to myself, getting her son or somebody else to do it while she had the cast-iron alibi of being on the other side of the world had been the solution she had finally chosen. Virgilio gave a disapproving grunt.

'I'll pretend I didn't hear that.' He transferred his attention to Adam. 'Tell me, was there anybody over here in Italy with a particular grudge against him?'

I saw Adam hesitate, mulling it over in his head. 'You know he was engaged in a lawsuit for possession of a strip of land alongside the golf course, don't you? From what I heard, the owner of the land wasn't best pleased.'

'Mr Luigi Signese, yes, we know about him. Do you know him?'

'I've seen him in the fields a few times, but we've never spoken. The lawsuit was something my father initiated, and he alone dealt with Signese.'

'Anybody else? Think carefully, please, both of you.' When they shook their heads, Virgilio adopted his most tactful tone. 'Signora Holman, I understand that your husband divorced you because you admitted to having committed adultery. Is that correct?'

'Inspector, for God's sake! Is this sort of questioning necessary?' There was a harder edge to Adam's voice now.

'This is a murder investigation. It definitely *is* necessary.' Virgilio returned his attention to Adam's mother. 'I'm afraid I need an answer.'

'It's true that I admitted it. In fact, I threw it in Rex's face at a dinner party, but the truth of the matter is that the only person in our marriage who was being unfaithful was Rex.'

'So why confess to something you didn't do?'

'Because I'd been asking him for a divorce for two long years and he just kept on prevaricating. Money was everything to Rex and I knew that if I gave him the chance to get away without having to pay me everything I was owed, it would spur him into action. I even chose my moment carefully so that Pirandello, Rex's lawyer, was there to hear me say it.'

Virgilio and I briefly exchanged glances. We had hypothesised about how the ex-wife's aggrieved lover might have been prepared to commit murder, although the fact that he had waited so long to do it had made it unlikely. Assuming Adam's mother was telling the truth and there had never been another man, this was another possible suspect we could scrub off our list.

Virgilio picked up the phone and called through to the custody department to arrange for the mother to visit her daughter. While he was talking, I asked a few questions of my own.

'How was your flight from Australia? It's a long way to come.'

'You can say that again. I was stuck in Singapore for five hours while they fixed a problem with the aircraft. I didn't arrive in Rome until yesterday afternoon, and I decided to overnight there. I only got to Florence an hour ago. I'm still exhausted now.'

So she had arrived in Italy before Natalie's meeting and Roseland's death. A coincidence? The high-speed *Frecciarossa* train covered the almost three hundred kilometres from Rome to Florence in just over an hour and a half so she could easily have travelled up here yesterday and killed Roseland. But the question was, why?

I continued with my questioning. 'Can I ask how long you're planning on staying over here?'

'As little time as possible. I just want to see that Jennifer's getting the treatment she needs and then I'll be off back to Aus.'

'I gather she's had similar trouble before.'

She nodded. 'I'm afraid she inherited all the bad bits from her father.' I noted that there was no question of any admission of responsibility on her part for the bad genes. 'The new drugs appeared to be working so well...'

'Until she crushed them up and used them to try to kill her half-sister.' I cut in and deliberately let my voice sound harsh so as to see how she would react, but it was Adam who reacted first.

'Deep down, Jen's not a bad person. It's just that her brain gets fogged.'

'Adam's right: you've got to understand that she isn't responsible for her actions.' I was mildly surprised to hear a softer note in his mother's voice. Maybe beneath the crusty exterior, she wasn't so bad after all.

'I'm sure she'll be given the right treatment. Where are you staying while you're here?'

Adam answered for his mother. 'With me.'

Virgilio put the phone down and announced that she could see her daughter at two o'clock and he explained where they should go. After this, the two of them stood up and thanked him remarkably politely for his time before leaving.

With the door firmly closed behind them, Virgilio stood up and came over to the window beside me. I told him what Adam's mother had said about her arrival in Italy the previous day and how it could have been possible for her to have got here last night, and we both stood and stared in silence at the piazza below, deep in thought. It was a while before he glanced across at me.

'Tell me something, Dan: do you think Rex Hunter and William Roseland were killed by the same person?'

'I've been wondering the same thing. I suppose on balance it seems likely or, at least, if not the same killer, my gut feeling is that the two deaths are almost certainly linked.'

'And you said your money was on Peter Nelson, the accountant?'

'Yes, although he's lacking a motive. Are you sure there's nothing suspicious in the accounts?'

He walked back to his desk and handed me a thin file. 'Here's the report from the analysts. They couldn't find anything wrong.'

I let my eyes flit across the figures on the printouts. Everything did indeed look transparent and above board. The salaries of the staff at the club were there and I saw that Nelson himself was being paid a generous amount. Looking back over the past year, I spotted a regular monthly transfer of five thousand euros to an Australian bank, presumably Jennifer's allowance, and double the amount in previous years when Natalie's mother had still been alive. From time to time, as Nelson had told us, large sums were transferred across to Rex Hunter's private account as repayment of his initial investment. At the bottom of the page it was clear that the club was doing well and was definitely profitable. As for any grey areas, I couldn't see any. The experts who had pored over the accounts were right: it looked as though Peter Nelson hadn't been cooking the books. I glanced back up at Virgilio.

'Well, if it wasn't Nelson, maybe it was Roseland himself who's our murderer and Nelson, for whatever reason, decided to turn a blind eye and provide him with a fictitious alibi by saying that they had left the course together.'

'The question is why he should agree to perjure himself like that. I think I'm going to go up to the club and have another talk to Mr Nelson. What are you doing today? Back home to your writing?'

'On that subject, I have some great news.' I went on to tell him about the email from Suzanne at the publishers and he looked delighted for me.

'Good for you, Dan. Yes, I can just imagine you, typing away in your office just around the corner from here, when suddenly there's a knock on the door and a mysterious woman dressed all in black comes into your office. She asks for your help in solving a mystery – maybe finding hidden treasure or something like that – and that then subsequently ends up the plot of your next book. You might need a bigger brass plaque outside: Dan Armstrong, Private Investigator *and Novelist*.'

I made no response, but it did sound rather good.

He clapped me on the back. 'Anyway, I was wondering if you felt like a game of tennis some time. We haven't played for a couple of weeks, and I want to see if those lessons did anything for your backhand.'

'Sounds good to me. Why don't you book a court at the country club for when you finish interviewing Nelson? Text me and I'll come and join you.'

16

THURSDAY AFTERNOON

We played tennis from three to four that afternoon and it was ridiculously hot on the court. In fact, we were the only people playing. Wisely, Virgilio had only booked for an hour, and we were both quite happy to stop when the end of the session came along. I was also happy because my backhand had held up and I'd managed to beat him for a change.

We sat on a bench in the last of the shade and he gave me a brief summary of his talk with the accountant. As far as last night was concerned, Nelson claimed to have left Natalie's meeting and walked back down to the club with Roseland. They had both left their cars down there in the car park. Roseland had turned left for his home while Nelson said he had driven straight back to his apartment in Florence, although since he lived alone nobody could confirm the truth of this. A check of footage from the CCTV camera at the entrance to the club confirmed his story, showing the two cars leaving together and Nelson turning right for Florence rather than left towards Roseland's house, but of course he could have doubled back along another road. Even so, it was such a short journey from the club to Roseland's home that it would have been very hard for Nelson to have reached the site of the 'accident' before the victim.

As for the evening of Rex Hunter's murder, Nelson remained adamant that neither he nor Roseland had been involved. They had left Rex out on the course at eight-thirty and walked back to the club, stopping from time to time to talk business en route. CCTV in the club car park showed them getting into their cars and driving off at just before nine – once more Roseland to the left and Nelson to the right. There were no cameras out on the course to confirm their statements and now that Roseland was dead, there was nobody to confirm or discredit Nelson's description of events. When asked why he had bought a new golf glove, he had reached into the bin beside his desk and pulled out a battered old glove with a jagged tear in it, telling Virgilio he had had it for almost ten years but the time had come to replace it.

All very credible.

Innocenti had been sent to interview Luigi Signese again, who claimed to have left Natalie's party and gone straight back to his home where he had spent the evening with his relatives, who all vouched for him – including his police officer son. If he had killed Roseland, it meant that a lot of people were prepared to perjure themselves to protect him. Neither Virgilio nor I could see him as a killer so, for now, there was little else we could do.

We were heading back to the clubhouse after our game of tennis when we ran into a couple of people standing in the car park, chatting. Both were familiar faces but seeing them together came as a surprise. They were Dario, the golf pro, and Silvia Roseland, the grieving widow. She was still looking sombre, but, considering her husband had just been murdered, she didn't look that grief-stricken. I imagined she was on her way to the fitness centre as she was dressed in figure-hugging, spandex shorts and a tight crop top revealing impressive abs. There was no doubt about it: she certainly looked after her body, a lot better than I did mine. As for her lack of reaction to her husband's murder, maybe she was just one of those lucky people who managed to put bad news behind them and move on with their lives.

Or maybe she wasn't.

As we passed, she greeted us politely and Dario gave us a little wave. Virgilio waited until they were out of earshot before making the obvious observation.

'Two of our potential suspects and they know each other. That's interesting.'

'I agree. Not necessarily suspicious, but definitely interesting. I wonder how well she knows him. He's a good-looking guy. Could he be her mystery lover?'

'Even though he and your tennis coach claim to be an item.' Virgilio rolled his eyes theatrically. 'I'm beginning to think that there must be something in the water here in Acquarossa that gets everybody at it like rabbits. If the pharmaceutical companies could bottle it, they'd make a fortune.'

'You might be onto something there.'

When I emerged from the changing rooms after a refreshing, cool shower, I spotted Elizabeth McGregor behind the reception desk and stopped to chat. She had already heard of Roseland's death, and she expressed regret. Asked whether she had known him well, she shook her head.

'I saw him around here often enough, but I never mixed with him socially. His wife and June, Rex's ex-wife, often went to the fitness centre together and were friends. Rex told me to keep away as he didn't want either of them to find out about our relationship.'

This was fascinating. Not only did Silvia Roseland know the golf pro, but she and Hunter's ex-wife had been friends – and June Holman had just arrived here from Australia. Had they been such good friends that they had banded together last night to kill Silvia Roseland's husband for whatever reason? I struggled to see a man of Roseland's age and physical condition being caught in the middle of a love triangle and I couldn't think of any way June would have benefited from his death. Maybe this friendship – assuming that the assistant manager was telling the truth and it existed – meant nothing, but it did add a little handful of mud to the already murky waters of this case.

I gave Elizabeth a searching look. 'You don't think his wife knew about you and Rex?' Ines the gardener had made no bones about it being an open secret.

'If she did, she never said anything. Mind you, I stayed out of her way and rarely saw her.'

I decided to ask Hunter's ex-wife next time I ran into her. And that wasn't the only question I had for her. I waited until Virgilio emerged from the changing rooms and followed him outside before asking him what he intended to do next.

He glanced at his watch. 'Four-thirty. Seeing as we're here, I'm going up to Hunter's villa to have a talk to the cook and the butler. They are still potentially suspects in Hunter's death, although we haven't found a motive and, to be honest, I just can't see either of them doing it,. But we need to be thorough and they might be able to tell us more about Hunter's ex-wife. Feel like coming?'

I nodded in agreement. 'Good idea. And after that, I'd quite like to go across to Adam's bungalow. Hopefully his mother will have come back from visiting Jennifer by now. Ever since seeing her this morning, I've been wondering about her. Was she telling us the truth when she said her affair with some anonymous man was fictitious or was there really somebody? And, if so, who?'

We drove up to the villa in both of our cars and parked outside. Predictably, Battista must have heard us and was waiting at the door in his impeccable dark livery.

'Gentlemen, good afternoon. You've come to see Signora Natalie?'

'No, Battista, we've come to have a little chat to you and your wife. I'd like to ask you about Signor Hunter's ex-wife.'

Battista was an excellent butler but even he couldn't hide a momentary flash of what looked very much like compassion cross his august features. 'Certainly, sir. My wife's in the kitchen. Please come this way.'

We followed him through to the kitchen where we found a scene of serious culinary activity. The table was covered in glass jars – those big ones with a metal clip to close them and a thick rubber ring as a seal – and a wonderful smell of tomatoes and garlic filled the air. Mariarosa was making salsa for the pasta and after just a sandwich for lunch and a strenuous game of tennis, I felt my nostrils and my digestive juices stir. She was standing at the huge range cooker, gently stirring a pan the size of a small dustbin. At Virgilio's request, she turned down the gas and we all sat around the table. Virgilio launched into a series of questions.

'I'm sorry to disturb you and I promise I won't take too much of your time. I'd hate to be responsible for ruining your salsa, which smells wonderful. I just wanted to ask what you both thought of Rex Hunter's ex-wife, June.'

Battista replied first in cautious tones. 'She was a good woman... underneath, but her husband led her a very difficult life.'

'Because of his womanising?'

Battista nodded gravely. 'I know we shouldn't speak ill of the dead, but you're right; Signor Hunter behaved scandalously towards Signora June.'

'When you say she was a good woman *underneath*, could you elaborate for us?'

This time it was Mariarosa who answered. 'She had a nasty

temper on her, like her daughter. She could fly into a rage over nothing.'

Battista added, 'In fairness, she only took it out on us when her husband had driven her crazy about something.'

Mariarosa nodded. 'You're right; all her troubles came from her husband.'

'And I understand she developed a drink problem? Elizabeth McGregor at the club told us all about it. Apparently June Hunter hated life in Italy so much she turned to drink.'

Both faces looked blank. Battista answered for both of them. 'I don't know why Signora McGregor said that, Inspector, but I never saw Signora Hunter drink more than a small glass of wine with her meals. Signor Hunter, on the other hand, drank to excess on many occasions.'

Virgilio and I exchanged looks. This version of affairs differed radically from what Elizabeth McGregor had told us. Who was telling the truth? If this was correct, had the assistant manager been deliberately lying to us or had her lover lied to her about his wife's alcohol consumption?

'I've also been told that she blurted out that she'd been unfaithful to her husband and that's what led to the divorce. Is that correct?'

Battista nodded. 'Yes, at a dinner party in front of a dozen guests. I was serving and I heard it all.' That same expression of compassion crossed his face again. 'To be honest, Inspector, she told Mariarosa and me in advance that she was going to say it.'

'She told you she was having an affair?'

'She told us she'd had a... dalliance with another man.' He used the Italian word *avventura*, which sounded more exciting than the English translation.

'And by dalliance, what do you think she meant?'

I swear I saw two red spots of embarrassment appear on

Battista's cheeks for a second or two before he passed the buck. 'She spoke to Mariarosa about it.'

Mariarosa's cheeks were now the colour of her salsa. 'She revealed to me that she had... um... misbehaved with a man, one of her husband's friends. She said it only happened the once and she regretted it immediately, but the man, on the other hand, apparently became serious. She said she told her husband that evening partly in order to speed up getting the divorce she so longed for, and partly before the man went and did something silly like speaking to her husband.'

'And did she reveal the identity of this man?'

'That evening, to the dinner-party guests, no.'

'And to you? Did she tell either of you?'

There was a brief hiatus while the couple exchanged looks before Battista nodded. 'She told Mariarosa it was Signor Nelson, the accountant.'

Virgilio and I exchanged glances again. Had the butler and his wife just provided a possible motive for murder for one of our prime suspects? Had Hunter been killed by his wife's jealous lover? Was this finally a ray of light in an increasingly obscure case? Maybe my hunch that Nelson was our killer was going to be proved right.

Virgilio wound up the interview after that. On the way out, Battista accompanied us to the lounge, where we found Natalie looking much brighter. At her side was a red-haired woman with a face full of freckles. Natalie even smiled as she saw us. 'Hello, come and meet my best friend, Polly. She arrived from Australia this morning and it's so great to have her here.' We exchanged handshakes and then left them to it. Outside in the car park the conversation naturally led straight to the accountant.

'Well, that saves us the trouble of asking Hunter's ex-wife who the man was. Suddenly, Nelson is looking a lot more interesting.'

'Absolutely. Assuming Battista and his wife are telling the truth, it's looking more and more likely that you were right in your hunch, Dan. We've been struggling for a motive for him and now we have one. How's this for a scenario? Nelson's been simmering with anger ever since June went back to Australia, finding himself separated from the woman he loved by thousands of kilometres. When Rex Hunter appears with his new young wife and a big smile on his face, Nelson snaps and kills him out of spite.'

'It's possible.' I leant back against the bonnet of my car and immediately regretted it. Left standing out here in the afternoon sun, it was now scalding hot. Leaping away from it, I added a few thoughts. 'You're going to need more than that to convince a judge. If only we could pin something else on Nelson, like fiddling the accounts, for example.'

'It's not looking hopeful. My guys tell me that the accounts look perfect, right down to the last euro.'

'The last euro?' Suddenly an idea flashed into my head. 'Hang on a minute, maybe he *was* cooking the books. Do you remember Jennifer saying that she got an allowance of five thousand Australian dollars a month?' Virgilio nodded. 'And didn't Natalie say her mum got the same amount? But, as far as I can remember, when I looked through the club accounts, I saw an amount of five thousand *euros* being sent across to a Sydney bank every month for Jennifer and another five until Natalie's mother died. What's the Aussie dollar worth these days?'

As I asked the question I was already pulling out my phone to check, and the answer was illuminating. 'One Australian dollar is barely two thirds of a euro, so the five thousand dollars were only costing three and a half thousand euros. What I want to know is what happened to the euros that were left over every month.'

Virgilio clapped me on the shoulder. 'That's it, Dan, well

done. Of course! I'll get right on it, but I bet you're right. If Nelson was salting away fifteen hundred euros a month for each of them over the years he's worked here...' I could see him doing mental arithmetic a lot faster than I could have done. 'That works out to thirty-six thousand a year and multiplied by seven years that adds up to a quarter of a million euros – and that isn't a small amount.'

'Why not get your people to contact the bank in Australia and check what happens to the outstanding balance each month? I'd be ready to bet that there's an account there in the name of Peter Nelson. It's a near perfect crime. Hunter wasn't talking to his daughter or to the mother of his illegitimate child, so he had no way of knowing he was being screwed by Nelson.'

Virgilio leapt in. 'Until the bank contacted him to inform him of the death of Natalie's mother nine months ago and he went over to meet the daughter he'd never seen. Presumably at some point, Natalie must have told him how much her mum had been getting and it was then that it all came out. Hunter must have told Nelson he was going to report him to the police for embezzlement and Nelson killed him to shut him up.'

'Sounds good to me. What are you going to do? Arrest him now or wait until you get confirmation from the bank in Australia?'

'If we send an email through to the bank this evening, we should have the reply by the morning. Let's wait until then before we confront him. He has no reason to believe we're onto him, so I don't think he'll make a run for it.' He leant over and patted my cheeks triumphantly. 'That's it, I think you've cracked it. We knew he had means and opportunity, now we know he had motive.'

'For both murders. Roseland must have seen Nelson murder Hunter but then he started getting cold feet and was thinking of confessing to us, so presumably Nelson somehow found a shortcut to get himself back onto the road to Roseland's house so he could flag him down. That way he could kill the only witness to the murder.'

'And that would explain why Roseland's car window was open and there were no signs of skidding. He must have seen Nelson and stopped to see what he wanted.'

Later on, as the temperature began to drop a bit, I took Oscar for a walk. This time I thought I would check out the woods around the scene of Roseland's death. I tried convincing myself that this was just idle curiosity, rather than mistrust of Virgilio's men's ability to find the phone, but my subconscious treated that with the disdain it deserved. I've always been a believer in dotting the I's and crossing the T's. I drove over there and slowed as we reached the dried-up riverbed. The Mercedes had already been hauled away and all traces of the police presence had disappeared. Presumably the search of the surrounding area had been completed and I felt pretty sure Virgilio would have called me if they'd found anything of note.

All that was left was the flattened No Hunting sign and some trampled undergrowth. I parked at the side of the road and Oscar and I headed into the woods. This was an eclectic mixture of tree varieties ranging from tall cypresses to stunted thorn bushes and even a few gnarled olive trees, either remnants of an abandoned olive grove or trees that had sprung up all by themselves. A thick carpet of dead leaves and pine needles underfoot made walking tricky as they hid what was underneath. I discovered this to my cost when I almost turned my ankle over in an animal hole of some kind.

As usual, Oscar kept running up to me with sticks, pine cones, and other less salubrious objects for me to throw for him. When it came to retrieving random objects, Oscar wasn't choosy. I opted to throw him the pieces of wood he brought me rather than the spent shotgun cartridges, plastic bottles, or empty beer cans. It was as we were coming back to the road again after making a broad loop around that my dog presented me with something exceptional. He came crashing through the dry grass and scrub to emerge with a small object in his mouth that he proudly laid at my feet and stood there, panting expectantly.

It was a mobile phone with a cracked screen. I picked it up with the aid of a tissue and studied it closely. I'd never seen Roseland's phone, but it struck me as a hell of a coincidence to find one here, barely metres from the crime scene. I didn't really blame the officers who had searched the area. Looking for such a small object amid all the dry leaves was an almost impossible task – unless you were a Labrador with an all-consuming retrieval instinct.

Although the screen was broken, the phone looked relatively new and the little apple on the rear indicated that it hadn't been cheap. It was also clear it hadn't been out here during the rainstorm earlier in the week. At my feet, the Labrador gave a familiar little yelp to remind me that he was waiting for me to throw it for him, but I shook my head, picked up a stick, and threw that instead. I slipped the phone into another of Oscar's poo bags and put it safely into my pocket before taking a few photos so as to locate the area where Oscar had found it. Then we set off back to the car.

I called Virgilio to tell him about the phone and we arranged to meet up for the handover at a little bar we both knew well on the outskirts of Florence, on the hill not far from Piazzale Michelangelo. The view from up here was spectacular over the red-tiled roofs of Florence punctuated by domes, spires, and towers and with the massive bulk of the *duomo* in the centre, rising high above all other buildings around it. I got there first and took a seat in the shade of a faded parasol advertising Coca-Cola, with my dog sprawled happily under the table at my feet. I stared down at the iconic cityscape before me and, now that it looked as though we had solved the murder case, I tried to get my head around my plans for the future.

Dan Armstrong, Private Investigator, had considerable appeal, but so did Dan Armstrong, Bestselling Novelist. Of course, I told myself, the chances of one of my books ever becoming a best-seller were next to non-existent. Yes, miracles did happen, but in my experience they were few and far between. At the same time there was no guarantee that my new investigative venture would fare any better than my books. While I waited for Virgilio, I checked the Internet on my phone and wasn't surprised to find no fewer than three investigation agencies already listed under Florence. From their websites, I noticed that they all appeared to have an authorisation number provided by the Prefecture of Police. That sounded complicated but hopefully my friendship with Virgilio would stand me in good stead if I decided to go for it. At that moment, the man himself appeared.

'*Ciao*, Dan. Sorry to keep you waiting. Well done for finding the phone.'

'Thanks go to the Hound of the Baskervilles.'

'*Bravo*, Oscar!' He bent down to ruffle the Labrador's ears.

I handed the phone to him and told him the exact location of the spot where we had found it. He nodded and told me he would get a team with metal detectors out there next morning in case the killer had disposed of the murder weapon in the same area.

By this time, Oscar was climbing all over his Italian buddy. The waitress came over and Virgilio ordered a pair of cold beers for us and managed to persuade her to find a biscuit for Oscar as a thank you. The biscuit when it came turned out to be a handful of those fan-shaped biscuits you find in dishes of ice cream, and they were devoured with relish by the ever-hungry Labrador. After a mouthful or two of beer, Virgilio told me why he was late.

'I've been having another talk to Jennifer Hunter. Whether it was as a result of seeing her mother this afternoon or the effect of the medication, she was a lot more reasonable, and I believe she genuinely tried to answer my questions. One thing emerged in conversation. You remember she said she'd seen her father standing by the sand trap that evening? Well, she remarked on something that I should have picked up on before. She says he waved to her but, seeing as she'd been avoiding him like the plague ever since arriving from Australia, she didn't wave back. There was no love lost between them, so she couldn't understand why he wasted time waving at her in the first place.'

The penny dropped. 'Of course... because it wasn't him.'

Virgilio nodded emphatically. 'Because it wasn't him. The more I think about it, the more convinced I am that when she rode past on her brother's motorbike, her father was already dead, lying in the sand, unseen from the track. She says she didn't see the face of the man who waved to her very clearly in the evening shadows, but she recognised him by the silhouette of his body and his leather sunhat.'

'Have you still got the hat?'

'Yes, and I've sent it off to the lab to see if they can lift any prints off it. We should know in the morning.'

'Well, one thing's for sure: it can't have been Roseland; his silhouette is very different from Rex Hunter's.' I looked up from my beer. 'But Peter Nelson and Rex Hunter were both tall and fairly slim. It could have been Nelson, as we thought.'

'And if it was, does that mean that Roseland was an accomplice, or did he just agree to provide an alibi while Nelson did the deed?'

'If he was up there with Nelson, the only way he could have avoided being recognised by Jennifer would have been by throwing himself flat in the bunker when he heard the motorbike approaching. The lip was high enough to hide him from the track. Of course, that's why the sand had been so immaculately raked all over, not just around the body.'

'It's looking more and more likely that the perpetrator was Nelson, either watched by or aided by Roseland. He had the means, he had the opportunity, but what was his motive for murder? Was it because he feared his boss had worked out he'd been stealing money and he acted to silence Hunter before he could be accused? Was it because of the way Hunter had treated the woman Nelson had loved? Was it a combination of both of those things, or was it for some other reason that we don't yet know? Hopefully we'll find out tomorrow.'

17

FRIDAY

I got a call from Virgilio just after nine-thirty on Friday morning to say that the Australian bank had replied to confirm our suspicions: the balance left over every month from the ten thousand euros had for years been paid direct into a savings account in the name Peter Nelson, which now contained a six-figure sum. Even more damning, however, was the fact that forensics had been able to lift fingerprints off Rex Hunter's leather hat and had confirmed that these belonged to Nelson. No doubt he had been the figure Jennifer had seen that evening and had assumed to be her father. On the strength of this, Virgilio was already on his way up to the country club with Innocenti and a couple of uniformed officers to make the arrest. Would I like to come along?

Of course I would.

I arrived in the club car park barely a minute before the blue and white police car. We parked on either side of Nelson's silver BMW and Virgilio and I walked into the lobby together while Innocenti and the uniformed officers spread out and circled the building just in case the suspect decided to make a break for it. We went through the main lobby and down the corridor towards the changing rooms until we reached Nelson's door. Virgilio walked straight in without knocking and I followed, wondering if Nelson might be armed and whether Virgilio had brought a weapon. Nelson was sitting in his chair behind his desk with one hand on a coffee cup, just staring down at it. He made no attempt to look up or say anything. Out of the corner of my eye, I spotted Innocenti outside the half-open French windows and I was reassured to see a pistol in his hand.

'Peter Nelson, I'm arresting you for the murder of...'

Virgilio's voice tailed off as we both realised at the same moment that Peter Nelson was past being arrested. He was dead. Just in case we had been in any doubt, his body slowly tipped forward until his forehead made contact with the cup, his head ending up balanced on it like a golf ball on a tee. Sticking diagonally upwards out of the middle of his shoulder blades, like a teaspoon in a cup, was the handle of a knife. I turned towards Virgilio, who was looking as stunned and bamboozled as I felt.

'Well, I wasn't expecting this.'

'You can say that again.' Virgilio already had his phone in his hand. He called police headquarters to report what had happened and to ask for the pathologist and the scene of crime team to come out here without delay. While he did this, I walked around to the other side of the desk and let my fingers press against Nelson's neck. The skin was still warm, but there was no pulse. I caught Virgilio's eye and shook my head.

'He's dead, but he can't have been dead long. At a guess, a matter of minutes, certainly no more than an hour.' I checked my watch: six minutes past ten.

Virgilio and I wandered around Nelson's office, being careful not to touch anything. When Innocenti reappeared, Virgilio sent him with the two other officers to stop anybody from entering or leaving the building. He then asked Raffaello in Reception to key up this morning's footage from the security cameras outside on the drive and in the car park, as well as here in the entrance lobby. Fifteen minutes later, sirens announced the arrival of two police motorcycles, followed over the next half-hour by a series of vehicles from Florence, including the pathologist.

While Gianni and his forensic team got to work, Virgilio and I checked out the CCTV footage and made an interesting discovery. It turned out that fate had decreed that almost all of our remaining suspects happened to be here at the club this morning. The outside cameras showed the arrival at eight o'clock of the golf pro hand-in-hand with Abigail and they headed off in the direction of the pro shop. Half an hour later, we saw Elizabeth McGregor appear on the screen. The camera in the entrance hall showed her walking into her office behind the reception desk, which we knew had a French window leading out into the garden.

At a quarter to nine, Nelson himself arrived and headed straight for his office. Ten minutes later, Adam Hunter's car drove up and he came into the building, stopping to chat and shake hands with several people before disappearing into his office, which we knew also boasted a pair of glass doors leading out onto the grass. Potentially significant was the fact that Adam's mother arrived along with her son and went into the fitness centre. Minutes later, we were both surprised to see none other than Natalie arrive on foot from the villa and walk in through the lobby. But equally interesting was the fact that she was followed, almost immediately afterwards, by Silvia, the widow of William Roseland.

The cameras didn't extend to the corridors or the offices, so it was impossible to tell if everybody who worked here had stayed in their rooms. Similarly, although there was a camera in the fitness centre, it only showed part of the room where the exercise bikes and rowing machines were. Although both Silvia and June appeared on tape from time to time, there was no way of knowing if they might have left for a brief period. Annoyingly, the sliding glass doors opening from the gym into the rear garden were also open. Virgilio sat back and gave a snort of frustration.

'Back to square one! I don't believe it. I thought we had Nelson over a barrel and now look at us! And with all our suspects here! There's no way we can see if one of them slipped out into the garden to commit the murder. Any one of them could have done it.' He then produced a few delightfully colourful Tuscan expletives, most of which would have scandalised the local priest. I listened in silent appreciation for a minute, committing a couple of the more inventive ones to memory, before gently returning him to the matter in hand.

'Not quite all the suspects. No sign of our farmer friend, Luigi Signese.'

'True, but it's less than a couple of hundred yards from his farm so it's possible he could have sneaked in and out again through one of these open doors.'

'Working on the basis that all the other suspects are still here, why don't we start interviewing them? If you like, I can speak to Natalie and Hunter's ex-wife in English while you and Innocenti tackle the Italian speakers.'

'Sounds good, thanks. Uniform can question everybody else so we have an idea of who was where this morning.'

I glanced at the CCTV screen and saw that June Holman was currently sitting in the café in the main atrium, so I decided to start with her. I walked through to the café and went across to where she was sitting by the windows that looked out over the first tee. She glanced up as my shadow fell across her.

'Come for a chat, Inspector?'

'It's *former* Inspector, to be honest. I'm a writer now and I just help Inspector Pisano out with a bit of translation from time to time.'

She gave me a sceptical look. 'From what Adam tells me, you've been doing a lot more than that.'

'The inspector has asked me to find out where you've been between eight a.m. and now.'

'I was at home with Adam and Emily until eight forty-five or so and then he drove me down here. He went off to his office and I went into the fitness centre. After such a long journey getting here from Australia, I needed a good workout. I was in the shower when your officer came running in to tell us we were all confined to the premises. I gave him a piece of my mind and he ran out again.'

'Can anybody vouch for the fact that you were in the fitness centre all the time?'

'Bobo, the instructor, was there, and then Silvia came and joined me – you know, Silvia Roseland.'

'And you never left the gym?'

She shook her head, so I continued.

'Can I ask you something? Last time we met, the inspector asked you about your admission of infidelity that led to your divorce. You told him it was a made-up story, but I believe that wasn't true. I know it must have been hard for you to talk about this sort of thing in front of your son, but there are just the two of us now and this is a murder investigation, and we need to know. Was there a man involved, even if it was only the briefest of affairs?' I decided not to mention that I already knew his name, waiting to see how much information she was prepared to divulge.

To my surprise she replied almost immediately. 'It wasn't an affair. It was just me feeling sorry for myself and finding a sympathetic shoulder to cry on... well, a bit more than that. I knew as soon as we'd done it that it was a mistake and I made sure we never did it again.'

'What about him? Did he want the relationship to continue?'

'As far as I was concerned, it wasn't worthy of the name "relationship" but yes, he wanted it to continue. He even told me he loved me, but I did my best to push him away.'

'I see. I presume you've heard that there's been another murder here this morning.'

She looked surprised. 'Murder? I guessed something serious had happened, but I didn't know it was murder. Who was it? I know it wasn't Silvia and it can't have been Adam because I saw him walking past a little while ago.'

I watched her face very closely. 'I'm afraid it was Peter Nelson, the accountant.'

'Peter's dead?' Her hand shot to her mouth, and she looked genuinely stunned. 'But who... how?'

'He's been stabbed, and the police are still looking for the killer. Am I right in thinking that the man you've just been talking about was Peter Nelson?' I hardly needed to ask. The expression on her face said it all.

She nodded mutely and I had to wait almost a minute before she responded. 'Poor Peter. Fancy somebody killing him!' She looked up. 'If Rex were still alive, he might have done it, but seeing as he's dead too, I don't know who else it might have been.' She looked and sounded completely stunned.

'Why do you say that about your ex-husband? Do you think he'd got wind of your relationship with Nelson?'

'No, I'm sure he hadn't a clue. The reason I said that is because I'm pretty sure Rex thought Peter was on the make, stealing from him. He'd been suspicious for well over a year, but he couldn't find any proof.'

'And was Nelson cooking the books?'

'I've no idea, but I suppose he might have been.'

'And you're sure Rex didn't know about you and Peter Nelson?'

She gave a decisive shake of the head. 'I'm sure he didn't. If he'd known, he would have sacked Peter on the spot and probably broken his nose for him into the bargain. Rex could be violent when he felt like it. That's why I never revealed the name of the man to him. I knew what my husband... my ex-husband, was capable of.'

'What about Nelson? Do you think he was the person who killed your ex-husband?'

'It hardly seems to matter now, does it?' She gave a rueful shake of the head. 'I honestly don't know. Love does funny things to people, but if it was Peter, why did he wait so long to do it? Surely if he was going to kill Rex, he would have done it months ago.'

'There's one final question I have for you: were you aware that your ex-husband was having an affair?'

'*An* affair? If it had boobs and a smile, he chased it.' Her tone was more disdainful than angry.

'And did you know there was one woman with whom he'd been having a *prolonged* affair?' I hesitated to mention Elizabeth McGregor's name. June was going back to Australia soon, but in the meantime this was a close community. I soon discovered that I needn't have worried.

'What, apart from that Elizabeth woman in Reception? It wouldn't surprise me.' She looked up again. 'My ex-husband was a pig, Inspector. Write that down.'

After the conversation ended, I tracked Natalie down in the squash courts. She was all on her own, sitting by the water fountain with a paper cup in her hand, and she gave me a little smile when she saw me.

'Dan, hi, can you tell me what's going on? I was taking a look around the club and a policeman suddenly appeared and indicated I had to stay put. What's happened?'

I pulled up a stool and sat down near her. 'I'm afraid there's been another murder. It was—'

'Another murder?' She looked aghast.

'Yes, this time it was the club accountant, Peter Nelson.'

To my surprise she then went on to say almost exactly the same thing that Hunter's ex-wife had just said to me. 'If my father had been alive, he might even have done it.' Seeing my expression, she elaborated. 'I've been going through my father's things and in particular the club accounts. In my previous job, I was in the accounts department. I qualified as an accountant. I think that impressed my father more than if I'd got myself a PhD in nuclear physics. Business was everything to him.'

'Did you find some irregularities in the accounts?'

'Yes, I'm afraid I did. In fact I was intending telling you and the inspector about what I've discovered. Nelson covered his tracks well, but I've spotted that he had two different scams running and the first involved ripping off my mum.' She sounded understandably bitter.

'We just found out about that. He was playing off euros against dollars and creaming off the profit.'

'Exactly. But on top of that, he's been making payments to fake suppliers here at the club for things that never existed. It was when I saw that he had paid out for twenty golf buggies and Dario confirmed that there have only ever been ten that I realised the scale of the fraud. Do you know how much those things cost?'

'And your father never found out?'

'I think he must have done, but only very recently. There were lots of little scraps of paper covered in his scribbles lying around and from what I could decipher of them, he was onto Nelson.'

She looked up. 'Do you think Nelson killed him to protect himself?'

'If you'd asked me that two hours ago, I'd have said yes, but his murder throws all that back up into the air again. It was certainly a motive for him to kill your father, but I don't understand who had anything to gain by killing Nelson.' As I said it, it occurred to me that there might well be somebody here with a grudge against Nelson and it wasn't the woman sitting alongside me. I needed to check this idea out but first I wanted to ask Natalie something else.

'Can I ask you why you came down here this morning?'

'I came down to see Adam. I want to bury the hatchet between us. We *are* blood relatives, after all. I've had a long talk with him, and I get the feeling things are going to work out. He's going to carry on working here and I'm going to share out the money left to me by our father between the three of us: him, me and Jennifer. It's only fair.'

'That seems more than fair. You stand to lose a lot of money.'

'It's only money.' She looked up with a little smile. 'I know that's not the sort of thing an accountant should say, but a year ago I was living in Australia, earning a modest salary and I thought I was an only child. Now I suddenly find myself here in Tuscany. I have two siblings and far more money than I need. Surely it makes sense to split it equably, particularly if that helps to heal this broken family.'

I told her she was now free to go and as I watched her set off all alone back up the track towards the villa, I found myself with mixed emotions. On the one hand, there was a feeling of pity for this woman who had just discovered her long-lost father, only for him to be brutally removed from her life. The other side of the coin, however, was that in spite of her fine words and her generous offer towards her siblings, there was no doubt that because of the terms of the will, she was the one person here who had gained the most from the death of Rex Hunter. Could it be that beneath this demure, innocent exterior, there lurked the heart of a killer?

When I met up with Virgilio again, he had just received the pathologist's preliminary report. The cause of death had not been in doubt, but it was interesting to hear that, upon removal of the murder weapon, Gianni had discovered that it was not a knife but a viciously sharp chisel. The blade was seventeen centimetres long and a centimetre wide and it had been rammed in right up to the handle with considerable force. Death would have been instantaneous. From the angle of the blow, it had been delivered by somebody standing behind Nelson while he was seated at his desk. It came as no surprise to hear that the handle of the chisel had been wiped clean.

'This is just a thought, but the choice of weapon might be significant. Who's likely to have tools?'

'A farmer?'

I saw him nod. 'I was thinking that. Maybe another visit to Luigi Signese might be in order. Let's ask him where he was this morning.'

'Of course, it could well be that Beppe, the groundsman, might have tools over in his shed. I think I might just pop over there in a minute and take a look, see if any are missing.'

We were wandering through the clubhouse looking for anything that could break the impasse and give us a clue as to who Nelson's murderer might be. Virgilio had given the order to clear the building so that scene of crime officers could dust for prints, particularly on the open doors and windows leading to the garden. It would have been all too easy for the murderer to slip out of any of these, enter Nelson's office to kill him, and then slip back again to where they had come from. For now, the clubhouse was empty. Everybody had been allowed to leave and the main doors had been locked.

We reached the reception desk and I stopped. 'It occurred to me when I was talking to Natalie that if Nelson killed Rex Hunter, it's unlikely that any members of Hunter's family would have considered taking revenge – very much the opposite – so I can't really see any of them stabbing Nelson. The same applies to almost all the people working here, but with one exception.' I pointed to the door of Elizabeth McGregor's office. 'Except her. She's only just found out that Rex Hunter, the love of her life, didn't after all go off and marry another woman. It was all a charade. As a result, McGregor now realises that there might have been a chance of getting her happy ever after with Hunter after all, and that must have made her very angry indeed. What if she somehow discovered that it was Nelson who killed her beloved Rex? Her office is less than twenty metres from his. She could have sneaked out through the garden, killed him, and sneaked back in a matter of a minute or so. Did you get any joy out of her when you interviewed her?'

Virgilio nodded. 'The same thought had occurred to me. I put it to her when I saw her a few minutes ago and I did it as confrontationally as possible, in the hope that she would fold. The result: she started bawling like a baby and she looked and sounded inconsolable. I don't think an Oscar winner could have done better. Certainly there was no question of a confession of guilt and I have to say that I'm tempted to believe her.'

'It's interesting that Natalie is down here this morning. She told me she had a meeting with Adam, but then she went for a walk around on her own. I know she looks and sounds as though butter wouldn't melt in her mouth, but what if she's a devious little minx underneath?'

'I agree that appearances can be deceptive, but why would she want to kill Nelson?'

'Maybe she helped him kill her father and now she wanted to get rid of the evidence?'

'Anything's possible. And don't forget that we still need a perpetrator for Roseland's death. Are we looking for one killer who's struck three times, or two or even three separate murderers?' He wiped his hand wearily across his forehead. 'I give up. Do you think anybody would mind if we helped ourselves to a couple of drinks? I'll settle up when we let everybody back in.'

I went over to the bar with him and we raided the fridge for two low-alcohol beers. As we drank them, we carried on with our tour. When we got to the fitness centre, we made a discovery. This actually consisted of two rooms, side by side, with a broad opening linking them together. This meant that somebody on, for example one of the cross-trainers, would not have been able to see people lifting weights in the next room and people on the rowing machines would have had their backs to the rest of the gym all the time. It would have been risky, but far from impossible, for somebody to have slipped out unnoticed and killed Nelson. The finger of suspicion therefore had to remain pointed at Rex's ex-wife or the recent widow of William Roseland, who had both been in there between nine and ten.

I left an increasingly frustrated Virgilio to check out the last of the rooms while I went out and crossed the car park to the groundsman's shed to see if Beppe was missing a chisel. Inside the workshop I found four people sitting drinking coffee. These were Beppe himself, Alfredo his young helper, Ines the gardener and, to my considerable surprise, none other than Luigi Signese from the farm next door. Beppe gave me a wave and reached for a cup.

'Like a coffee? It's freshly made.'

'Thanks, Beppe, I'd love one.' Not least as it would hide the beer – albeit low alcohol – on my breath. I sat down on a sack of grass seed and looked around. They all looked relaxed and I hadn't detected any nervousness at my arrival. Beyond them was a sturdy bench and hanging behind it was an array of tools. I resolved to check the chisels out before leaving.

'Here, try this.' Beppe finished pouring coffee from a Thermos and picked up an anonymous bottle of clear liquid. 'A little drop of grappa in your coffee?'

I shook my head and thanked him. He gave me a look that indicated I was making a big mistake before adding a splash to his cup and passing it across to Luigi, who did the same.

I gave the farmer a little smile. 'What brings you here, Luigi? Come to sell these guys some of your wine?'

He pointed a finger towards Beppe. 'I dropped by earlier to check that my cousin can still give me a hand at the Montevolpone fair tomorrow afternoon. A second pair of hands on the stall means that I sell more wine. He told me he's been having trouble with the irrigation system and that's a bit of a speciality of mine, so I stayed on to give him a hand.'

'You and Beppe are cousins?' This was news, potentially significant news. 'I thought you and the country club were sworn enemies.'

'I have nothing against the club. I did very well out of selling them some of my land and I even toyed with the idea of trying my hand at golf at first, but I just couldn't find the time. It was only after Hunter decided to try and steal some more of my land that things turned sour.' He took a mouthful of coffee, smacked his lips appreciatively and grinned at me. 'Now there's nothing to stop me coming to give my cousin a hand.'

'You think your troubles are over? What if the new owner carries on where her father left off?'

He picked up an envelope lying on the trestle table in front of him and passed it across to me. 'I just received this in the post this morning.'

I pulled out a letter and scanned quickly through it. It was from Avvocato Pirandello, Rex Hunter's lawyer, informing Mr Signese that all proceedings had been stopped and acknowledging his right to the disputed land. I was pleased for him – and for Natalie doing the decent thing. I folded the letter and handed it back.

'That's great news. So there's no doubt that Rex Hunter's death did you a favour.' I caught his eye and raised an eyebrow, but all I got in return was another grin.

'God moves in mysterious ways.'

I drank my surprisingly good coffee – even without the grappa – and we chatted. There was a warm, friendly atmosphere in here and it was hard to imagine any of these country folk being involved in a murder. Finally, I told them why I had come over.

'You may already have heard, but Peter Nelson, the club accountant, has been murdered.' They all looked shocked, and Beppe reacted first.

'When did it happen?'

'An hour or two ago. The clubhouse is out of bounds at the moment. Didn't you know?'

'To be honest, we've been busy over here since seven-thirty. Why Nelson? He was a nice enough guy.'

'That's what we're trying to find out. Presumably none of you have any ideas as to why he should have been killed or by whom?'

They all shook their heads, and I couldn't spot any signs of guilt on any of the faces.

'He was stabbed in the back with a chisel. Beppe, the reason I came over was because I was wondering if you have any chisels here, and if there might be one missing by any chance.'

Beppe jumped to his feet remarkably nimbly and went over to the workbench. A quick check gave him the answer and he turned towards me and shook his head. 'No, all still here. I have four of them in different sizes. They're still hanging there. Look.' He pointed to four plastic-handled chisels hanging from nails. Sure enough, there were no empty nails.

But nails can easily be removed or replacement tools added. I thanked him for the coffee and left.

18

SATURDAY

The *festa del paese* in my home town of Montevolpone turned out to be eventful. Oscar and I walked down at five o'clock to find the main square full of people and a band tuning up in preparation for the procession through the narrow streets of the *centro storico*. All around the piazza were stalls selling local produce like porcini mushrooms in olive oil, focaccia and other breads, cakes and biscuits, cheeses, and artisan salami, as well as home-made items ranging from jewellery to knitwear. Needless to say, right in the centre of them were at least a dozen stalls selling wine. We were in the middle of Chianti, after all. Among these I spotted Luigi, with Beppe alongside him. I led my excited dog over to see how things were going.

'Hi gentlemen, how's business?'

'Lots of tourists eager to taste my Chianti and we've been selling well. Here.' Luigi thrust a paper cup into my hand. 'See if it tastes different out of a paper cup.'

It tasted excellent as usual. I stood with them for a few minutes, scanning the faces of the crowds, who all looked as though they were having a good time. The streets had been hung with bunting, and balconies decked with flowers. Green, white, and red Italian flags and the white Tuscan flags with their red stripes and silver image of Pegasus in the centre fluttered from the lampposts. There was a joyous feel to the little town today and I enjoyed the sensation of beginning to belong to the community. Yes, my decision to leave London last year and settle down over here in Tuscany had proved to be one of the best of my life.

A trumpet sounded and the massive wooden doors of the church were hauled open. Six men emerged, bearing the statue of Saint James on their shoulders. The statue itself had been firmly bolted onto a solid wooden base and it looked heavy. Luckily the eight bearers looked up to the task. As they descended the steps to the piazza, I could see why Tommaso and the others had been so insistent on ensuring it was firmly secured, as the statue of the saint swayed precariously with every step. Safely at ground level, they made their way across to where the others were waiting, and the procession started off.

I finished my wine and went over with Oscar to watch. First there were schoolchildren carrying flowers, in particular a magnificent arrangement of gladioli in a basket. Behind them came Don Carlo, the local parish priest, and a collection of fellow clergymen followed by a surprising number of nuns in dark habits. I'd never seen nuns in Montevolpone before and I wondered where they had been hiding. They were singing a hymn I didn't recognise but it suited the formal, traditional feel of the scene. The men carrying the statue slotted in behind the party of clerics and after them came a collection of local dignitaries comprising the mayor of Montevolpone wearing his green, white, and red sash of office, along with a motley selection of mayors of neighbouring towns and villages, local notables

including doctors, lawyers, teachers, and the chief of the town
police in his full dress uniform.

The marching band followed on behind and struck up a
rousing march as soon as the nuns disappeared from sight
around the corner. I wondered whether this had been pre-
arranged or whether the bandmaster had deliberately chosen to
drown the nuns out. The band itself was made up of men and
women playing highly polished brass instruments and at least a
dozen drummers, who produced a deafening racket that almost
loosened the fillings in my teeth. They were all clad in medieval
costume with brightly coloured tunics and pantaloons. At my
feet, Oscar was enthralled by everything that was going on and I
hoped the long walk we had had this afternoon and now this
excitement would serve to tire him out and calm him down
before he – and I – would venture out into the spotlight for the
pet show.

Once the procession had circled the town centre and the saint
had been safely returned to his place of honour behind the altar
in the church, the mood became less sober. The bars did a
roaring trade and it looked as though all the food and wine stalls
were doing good business as well. I would really have preferred a
cold beer, but, as this was a traditional Chianti gathering, I settled
for a beaker of red wine and sipped it slowly. A ring of straw bales
had been set up in the middle of the piazza and the contestants in
the best fruit and vegetable competition were displaying their
produce. Oscar and I wandered about, marvelling at tomatoes
bigger than grapefruit and onions the size of melons. It was as I
was standing in silent awe in front of the biggest marrow I had
ever seen – displayed in the wheelbarrow in which it had been
brought along to the fair – that I spotted a couple of other
familiar faces. There in the crowd were Natalie and her best
friend, Polly.

I went over to say hello, and Oscar immediately recognised Natalie and stood up on his hind legs to be petted. She was definitely looking more relaxed, and she gave me a smile as she made a fuss of him.

'Hi, Dan. We couldn't resist coming down to see the fair. Mariarosa and Battista have been talking about it for days and they're around here somewhere.' She straightened up and a more serious expression appeared on her face. 'Any developments?'

It was a good question. Nelson's death had sparked more questions than answers. Although the recent deaths had reduced our list of suspects by killing some of them off, it hadn't thrown up any new evidence. I wondered whether Virgilio's men with metal detectors had found anything more around the scene of Roseland's death. Also there was the question of his phone. Maybe there might be fingerprints on that, assuming it had been smashed and thrown away by his killer. As for Nelson, we at least had proof in the shape of his fingerprints on Rex Hunter's hat that he'd been involved with that murder, but that didn't help to solve the other two murders. I gave Natalie a little shrug.

'No major developments. I think it's safe to say that Nelson was the person who killed your father, presumably as he was about to be unmasked by your father as a fraudster, but why Roseland provided an alibi for him and then the two of them were killed and by whom remains a mystery. Maybe Nelson did some work for Roseland – although I got the impression Roseland didn't trust him – so maybe Nelson knew something about his business and was blackmailing him to help out. Who knows? But as for who killed Nelson, we're still struggling. A number of people had the opportunity, but we still can't find a credible motive.'

Any further conversation was interrupted by the loudspeakers announcing the winner of the vegetable competition – a cour-

gette the size of a small torpedo – and asking all participants in
the pet show to present themselves to the judges. I gave the ladies
an apologetic look and led Oscar towards the ring. What
happened next will forever remain seared into my memory
banks.

The set-up for the pet show was quite simple. Proud owners
stood around in a circle, exhibiting their freshly scrubbed pets
while the judges slowly made their way around the ring, peering
at teeth, stroking fur coats and, in the case of an elderly tortoise,
picking it up and studying its underside. Finally, all animals were
paraded around the ring. Those that could walk were led by their
owners, while the others were carried in cages or just in their
owners' arms.

All went well at first. Oscar behaved himself in spite of the
temptation provided by the other dozen dogs and a few terrified
cats in cages. He didn't bat an eyelid when the fierce-looking
female judge lifted his tail and inspected his 'bits' and he even let
her open his mouth and peer inside. The trouble started when I
had to take him on his circuit around the ring, passing each of the
other animals one by one.

I could feel him tugging at the lead and getting more and
more excited by all the interesting sights, sounds, and smells, but
it was when he reached a very smartly trimmed poodle that
things took a turn for the worse. There had been no sign of Elizabeth McGregor and her allegedly slutty poodle, but this one
appeared to be cut from the same cloth. As we passed, she must
have shot some sort of canine come-hither look or olfactory
billet-doux at Oscar, and he didn't need to be asked twice.
Suddenly I found myself with thirty kilos of canine bone and
muscle doing its best to pull my arm out of its socket. All would
have been well except that my phone started ringing at the exact

same moment. As I swapped the lead from my right hand to my left so as to grab the phone in my pocket, I momentarily lost hold of the lead, and Oscar launched himself towards the poodle with lust in his eyes.

A roar of laughter went up from the crowd while the poodle's elderly owner could only look on in horror as my Labrador did his best to mount her dog. I raised the phone to turn it off but saw that it was Helen. Hastily, I held it up to my ear and pressed green. All I heard was a voice saying, 'Dan, I wanted to talk you about last weekend. I'm so sorry...'

Aware of what my dog was attempting to do, all I could do was to shout, 'I'm sorry, I'm in the middle of something. I'll call you back,' before stuffing the phone into my pocket and making a mad dash to regain control of my dog before I found myself facing a canine paternity suit.

Needless to say, Oscar didn't win a prize.

As for me, once I had managed to grab his lead and tug him away from the lady dog, all I wanted to do was to go somewhere and hide, so I headed for Tommaso's bar and dived inside. Making sure the disgruntled dog was securely moored to the leg of the table, I pulled out my phone and called my ex-wife back, but she didn't answer. I tried again but still no response. I could imagine the thoughts going through her head. From the sound of it, this call could have been an attempt to mend fences, but all she had received in return had been rejection. I tried three more times to call her, but to no avail. In the end all I could do was to send her a text message explaining the circumstances and apologising.

By this time, it was past seven and Tommaso advised me to go and bag a seat on one of the long tables for dinner. I protested that I'd promised to help out, but he shook his head and told me they had loads of volunteers. Besides, he said with a grin, 'After your recent experience in the ring, you look as if you need a good meal and a few glasses of wine.'

Advising my dog in no uncertain terms that I expected him to be on his very best behaviour, I went out and looked for somewhere to sit. I was still looking around when I heard somebody call my name and saw Beppe beckoning. Oscar and I went across to him and he lowered his voice and whispered in my ear.

'You remember you told me to let you know if I ever heard any interesting gossip? Well, let me introduce you to some friends of mine. You might enjoy talking to them.' He gave me a knowing wink and led me to the table where he introduced me to a gentleman called Signor Artimino and his wife. I noticed that he just introduced me as 'Dan who lives near here', not mentioning my involvement with policing. They were a friendly-looking elderly couple and they welcomed me and Oscar and invited me to sit with them.

Beppe sat down alongside me and I felt Oscar squeeze in between us. Fortunately there were no other dogs in the vicinity but I hooked the end of his lead under my shoe just in case. A minute or two later, we were joined by Luigi Signese and I hoped he wouldn't turn out to be our killer or I would look pretty silly for dining with him.

By this time the sun was low on the horizon and the shadows were lengthening. Canny country folk, Signor Artimino and his wife had already worked this out and had chosen seats in the shade provided by the bulk of the church. A little breeze had come up and the temperature was very comfortable – by Tuscan standards. If this had been Britain, everybody would have been complaining of extreme weather and impending heatstroke, but here it just felt right and I gradually began to relax after my ordeal by Labrador.

Teams of volunteers appeared carrying baskets of sliced bread that they deposited in heaps every couple of metres all along the length of the table. Health and Safety would have had a fit if this had been back in the UK but nobody here minded, least of all Oscar when I surreptitiously handed down a crusty piece for him to crunch up. Paper plates were then handed out, each carrying slices of the local cured ham, salami and melon, as well as assorted olives and button mushrooms in oil. In front of us on the table were bottles of red wine and water and I filled the glasses and toasted my companions.

'Thanks for the company. This is my first *festa del paese* here in Montevolpone, and I hope I'll have many more.'

In response to Signora Artimino's query, I told them how I had taken the decision to move over to Chianti last year and described where I was living. In return they told me where they lived, and it was then that things got interesting.

'We live about ten minutes along the road from the Acquarossa Country Club where Beppe works. We're just past Luigi Signese's farm, not far from where there was that horrible accident the other night.'

'When a Mercedes went off the road and a man was killed?' I did my best to sound only casually interested.

'Yes, our neighbour, the English pig.' Signor Artimino's face assumed an apologetic expression. 'I'm sorry, I don't wish to malign your fellow countrymen, but he wasn't a very nice neighbour.'

'Really, why was that?'

'When he was married to his first wife, they screamed at each other all the time and now that he's married that... young woman, it started up all over again after barely a few months.'

'They argued a lot?' And yet his widow had appeared prostrate with grief at his death. Something didn't smell right.

'They never stopped.'

I tried to keep my tone as mildly disinterested as I could, although my mind was racing. 'I suppose it must be nice and peaceful for you now that he's died.'

Signor Artimino smiled. 'May he rest in peace, but now so can we. It's so wonderfully quiet. I'm sure the new Signora Roseland is equally happy. He's gone and she's got the house to herself.'

I couldn't forget the way tears had come pouring down Silvia Roseland's cheeks when she had heard of her husband's demise. 'You don't think she was sad to see him go?'

'I imagine she was delighted.'

'Are you sure? I saw her the other day and she looked very upset.'

Signora Artimino joined in to explain. 'If she was upset, it's because she's been crying for almost two weeks now.'

'Why was that?' No sooner had I asked, than an explanation presented itself in my head and Signora Artimino went on to confirm it.

'Ever since the death of the Australian – you know, the man at the golf club.'

'You think she was crying for him?' I had a sudden flash-back to the first time I'd set eyes on Silvia Roseland jogging past me on my original visit to the club. At that time, I'd noticed what might well have been tears on her cheeks. Had they been for Rex Hunter and what did this mean for the investigation?

Her husband nodded. 'If he's the man with the big blue Range Rover that he used to park in the bushes just around the corner from our house, then yes.'

I pleaded ignorance. 'Why would he do that?'

There was a distinct twinkle in the old man's eye. 'Because he didn't want anybody to know he was visiting his girlfriend.'

'His girlfriend...?' I was getting quite good at this clueless act. 'You mean he and Signora Roseland were...?'

He nodded. 'Roseland travelled a lot, back and forth to England on business. Every time he went away, the Range Rover reappeared.'

'Well, well, well.' This opened a whole new can of worms. If Silvia Roseland had been having an affair with Rex Hunter, might she have been involved in one or more of our murders? One thing was for sure: I needed to pass on this information to Virgilio as soon as possible. I wolfed down my antipasti and excused myself for a few minutes while I found a quiet spot in the corner of the piazza and made the call. Virgilio answered almost immediately.

'*Ciao*, Dan. I was just going to call you with the news.'

'What news?'

'The metal-detector team have found the murder weapon. It was buried deep inside a huge ants' nest. It's a steel bar like you thought, the sort they use for lifting weights with one arm. It's on its way to forensics, but they say there are definitely traces of blood on it. We should have the results of fingerprints in a couple of hours.'

'Terrific.' I went on to relate what I had just heard, and I heard him grunt.

'Suddenly it's all beginning to make sense. There's just one problem: we don't have prints for Silvia Roseland to compare them. If the prints they lift off the steel bar and the phone don't match anybody at the club, then we'll need to pay her a visit.'

I told him where I was and offered to help, but he turned down my offer. 'You enjoy yourself. I'll keep you posted.'

The rest of the meal was remarkably good, considering that the food was being prepared in the local school kitchens and ferried across to the piazza on handcarts. In true Tuscan tradition, there was a pasta course of *pappardelle alla lepre* – and the pasta and the rich gamey sauce were miraculously still hot when they reached us – and this was followed by cold chicken with a mixed salad of tomatoes, peppers, onions, and local pecorino cheese. Finally there were slices of traditional *Castagnaccio* tart, made with chestnut flour, raisins, and pine nuts and flavoured with rosemary. As if by magic, a flask appeared in Beppe's hand, and he poured a generous helping of grappa into my cup. I tasted it cautiously, well aware of the caustic properties of some types of grappa, but I found this to be extremely smooth and I told him so. He grinned.

'I'm glad you like it. I make it myself.'

'You distil your own liquor?' I almost asked him if that was legal but decided not to reinforce my background in law enforcement for tonight. He must have anticipated my question.

'Here in Italy, it's permitted to make grappa, but only for our own consumption, not for sale.'

'I see. So how much do you make each year for your own consumption?'

'Not a lot – about fifty litres a year.'

I was still wondering about the effect a litre of grappa each week could have on the human body when the meal came to an end and the tables were cleared for dancing. After the mayhem Oscar had created in the show ring, I decided not to risk him anywhere near a dance floor, so I thanked my dinner companions and walked back up the hill to home. It was when I got back there that I made a decision that my ex-wife would never have been able to understand or accept. I loaded Oscar into the car and drove the fifteen minutes to the scene of William Roseland's murder.

I drove past it and a minute or two later spotted the track leading off to one side that Signor Artimino had told me was where Rex Hunter used to hide his car when he went up to Roseland's villa for his trysts with Silvia. I pulled off the road and parked in among the strongly scented broom bushes. A glance back at the road through the bushes confirmed that Rex Hunter's choice of hiding place was pretty effective. Although it was almost dark now, there was still enough light for me to see that the track snaked up roughly in the direction of Roseland's villa, so I let Oscar out of the car and we set off up the hill.

As we walked, I debated what I was doing. At its simplest, I was just checking that this track led to the villa and provided a secure way for Hunter, or anybody else, to get to the house without running the gauntlet of being seen by Mr and Mrs Artimino or their neighbours. Of course this wasn't the only reason I had decided to come up here at ten o'clock on a Saturday night. I had also remembered that Silvia Roseland's studio in the garden contained not only pots, but also statues. And statues, whether made of clay, stone or wood, required the use of chisels. Could it be that the chisel sticking out of Peter Nelson's neck was one of hers?

It took barely ten minutes to walk up to the villa and it occurred to me that this could well have been the route Silvia had used if she had indeed decided to lure her husband to the side of the road and kill him twenty-four hours earlier. It was all falling into place, and I had to make a concerted effort to remind myself that I had been equally sure of Peter Nelson's guilt only this morning and look what had happened there. Doing my best to temper my expectations, I emerged from the bushes only a short distance from Silvia Roseland's villa and slipped in through a gate set in the wooden fence that surrounded it. This brought me out only a short distance from her studio and I made a beeline for it, hoping to find it unlocked.

Alas, I was to be thwarted. It was securely locked. I toyed with the idea of putting my shoulder to the door and trying to batter it

down, but it looked solid and, besides, the police would be
coming here soon. With Oscar trotting alongside me, I sneaked
around the side of the building so as to be able to peer in through
the window. Pulling out my phone, I switched on the torch and let
the light run around the room. As I did so, the phone started
ringing and I hurried to answer it before the noise gave me away.
It was Virgilio and from the metallic sound to his voice, he was in
the car.

'*Ciao*, Dan. I thought you'd like to know that forensics have
managed to get prints off Roseland's phone and the iron bar and,
guess what? They're from the same person. They belong to our
killer.'

'And they don't match any of the prints you've already got?'

'No. The more I think about it, the more I'm convinced that
we'll find they belong to his widow.'

'So we both agree that Silvia Roseland has to be our
murderer? I'm actually here...'

I didn't have a chance to complete the sentence as I was
startled by my dog giving a most uncharacteristic growl
followed by a loud woof that had me turning to shush him.
That turn probably saved my life as a figure materialised from
the shadows beside me and I felt a heavy blow skid down the
side of my head and land on my shoulder, sending stabs of pain
down my left arm and making me let go of the phone. If I
hadn't moved, that blow would have hit me square on my head.
The force of the impact dropped me to my knees, and I looked
up to see my assailant raising the club in her hands to strike
again but at that moment fate, in the shape of a previously
mild-mannered, friendly Labrador, intervened. Giving a
primeval snarl, Oscar threw himself at my assailant and sank
his fine set of gleaming white teeth – recently inspected by the
judge at the fair – into her leg. She screamed and transferred

her attention to the dog and I heard a blow, followed by a yelp of pain.

Ignoring the stabbing pain in my arm, I jumped to my feet and caught hold of her club arm with my good hand, spinning her towards me. I then did something I've never done before or since. Without any hesitation I released my grip on her, pulled back my fist, and punched her square in the face as hard as I could. The force of the contact hurt my knuckles and sent an even more vicious wave of pain shooting through my other shoulder, but I was gratified to see her fall backwards and sprawl onto the grass where she lay still. I dropped down to my knees again, retrieved what felt like an axe handle from her hand and threw it into the bushes before turning my attention to my dog. He was lying on his side, emitting little whining sounds. I reached out and stroked his face, before running my fingers softly over his back and ribs.

'You'll be okay, Oscar. Just lie still. You'll be okay.'

I rested there for a few moments, trying to work out how badly hurt he was and how badly hurt I was. My left arm was hanging useless at my side, and I could feel the warm sensation of blood running from my ear. I suddenly felt very tired, and it occurred to me that this sort of thing probably wasn't what a middle-aged man should be doing. A sudden image of Helen at my shoulder saying, 'I told you so,' was interrupted by sounds coming from the prone figure behind me. I pulled myself to my feet and staggered over to see Silvia Roseland beginning to come around. Without handcuffs and with one arm out of action I knew there was no way I'd be able to tie her up while waiting for the police to arrive so, rather than giving her another punch in the face, I straddled her and pinned her arms to the ground with my knees. In what little light was left, I could see that she was looking decidedly groggy and there was blood on her face, but I wasn't taking any chances. We stayed like that for some minutes before she looked up at me in the gloom.

'I'm glad I killed them, you know.' Her voice was weak but a punch in the face can do that, not least as I had drawn on my ten years of amateur boxing for the force when I'd hit her. It hadn't felt good to hit a woman but nobody hits my dog and gets away with it.

'You mean your husband and Nelson?'

'They killed him, you see. I had to kill them. It was only right.'

'How did you find out that they'd killed Rex Hunter?'

'William told me. He came home drunk a few nights ago and boasted to me that they'd battered to death the only man I've ever loved. He boasted about it!' The disgust and unbridled hatred in her voice reminded me all too closely of Hunter's elder daughter.

'But why kill them yourself? All you had to do was to tell the police and both of them would have been convicted and put away for years and years.'

She lay there in silence for a few moments. 'When they killed Rex, they didn't only kill him. They destroyed my whole life, my future.' There was a long pause before she asked me an unexpected question. 'Have you ever been in love? I mean really in love?'

It was a good question, which under other circumstances I might have been prepared to debate with her, but not here and now. I limited myself to shrugging my shoulders, which was a mistake as another stab of pain shot down my arm, almost making me faint. She took the shrug as a no.

'What I had with Rex was special. I loved him and I trusted him, and we told each other everything. I told him how unhappy I was with William and how I realised what a terrible mistake I'd made in marrying him. He told me how unhappy he was with that crazy woman he married.'

'I thought June and you were friends.'

'I knew her, but we weren't friends. She's a vicious, evil woman. Just look at the way her daughter turned out. That wasn't Rex's fault, that was June's.'

My father always used to tell me that there are two sides to every story, and, from what I'd learnt of Rex Hunter, trying to lay all the blame on his ex-wife was disingenuous in the extreme. I was feeling decidedly sick by this time so I gave no response, but she carried on anyway.

'He told me about Natalie and how he was going to pretend to be married to her so that he could put Adam and Jennifer to the test. That's what he said, "to the test". They were too like their mother, you see, and he needed to prove it to himself, if not to her.'

'So you weren't jealous of Natalie?' I could hear myself starting to slur my words.

'Not at all. I knew it was just a charade.'

'And do you think he intended to marry you?' I could feel an overwhelming sense of weariness descending on me.

'Just as soon as I'd divorced William. But then Rex was killed and part of me died with him that day.'

I was still trying to think of how to follow that when I became aware of the headlights and flashing blue lights of two police cars racing up the drive. Virgilio had arrived. I gave them a shout and was greatly relieved to see the powerful shape of Innocenti come running across towards me. Behind him was Virgilio and a brace of uniformed officers. Innocenti helped me to my feet and then two uniformed officers took charge of Silvia Roseland and led her away. As Innocenti turned the beam back onto me and my dog, Virgilio stepped forward and took in the scene.

'You okay, Dan?'

'Sore arm but I'm okay.' My voice sounded as though it belonged to somebody else. 'I'm worried about Oscar.'

Then, to my eternal relief, I saw the Labrador move as he gingerly got to his feet and limped slowly across to lick my hand. I was vaguely aware of Virgilio's voice coming at me out of a cloud.

'He's a tough old dog, Dan. Now, let's take a look at you and see how tough an old dog you are.'

EPILOGUE

A FEW DAYS LATER

'Do you want me to cut your steak for you, Signor Dan?'

Mariarosa ignored my protests as she reached over my shoulder. Efficiently, she sliced the meat into bite-sized chunks and straightened up again. I thanked her and tried a piece of steak with the fork in my good hand. It was predictably excellent, and I was quick to compliment her on her cooking. She waved the compliment away and spooned a heap of little roast potatoes onto my plate. As the smell of the meat permeated down to my feet, I felt a movement and glanced down to see my dog now resting his nose on my knee, a doleful expression in his eyes, pretending that he hadn't eaten all week.

'Don't you go giving him meat from your plate, Signor Dan. I'll make sure he gets the bone when Mariarosa's finished serving.' Battista appeared at my injured shoulder and refilled my glass with wine. Still, as he moved on, I did give Oscar a little piece of meat and it disappeared like magic. As they say in the adverts: he's worth it.

'What did the vet say about Oscar?' I could see that Natalie had developed considerable affection for my dog.

'He's got a badly bruised shoulder, but he's fine. Certainly he has no trouble going for walks and his appetite remains undiminished.'

'So you've both got sore shoulders. What about you? How long will you have to keep your arm in a sling?'

'Another few weeks apparently. They tell me broken collarbones usually mend themselves, but it can take time. Still, thanks to my four-legged friend, it turned out a lot better than it could have been.'

We were sitting outside Rex Hunter's villa in the shade of a magnificent umbrella pine. Natalie had invited her half-brother and his partner and Virgilio and me for dinner together with her best friend from Australia now that the dust had finally settled on the investigation. Rex Hunter's very low-key funeral had taken place earlier in the day and I hadn't been able to shake the conviction that if he'd been a better human being, none of this would have happened. Now the sun was setting and the temperature had dropped to a perfect level. I felt at one with the world – apart from a nagging regret that I had heard nothing more from my ex-wife and it had been almost a week now.

'So just who exactly killed my father?' Adam glanced across the table to his new half-sister. '*Our* father?'

Virgilio provided the explanation. 'According to Silvia Roseland, it was a joint effort by her husband and Peter Nelson. Nelson wanted your father dead to protect himself because he was about to be accused of serious fraud, and William Roseland wanted to kill him out of pure old-fashioned jealousy. He'd found out about his wife's long-running affair with your father, and he wanted revenge.'

'So they *both* killed him?'

'Yes, that explains why there were so many blows to your father's head. I'm afraid they must have taken it in turns. Then

they heard Jennifer approaching on your motorbike and Roseland lay down and hid in the bunker while Nelson put on your
father's hat and did his best to impersonate him.'

'And so Jennifer had nothing to do with it?' Adam looked
relieved.

'No, she has maintained her innocence of her father's murder
all along and Silvia Roseland has confirmed it.'

'So what's going to happen to Jen?'

Virgilio answered for Natalie. 'Natalie has asked for leniency
and it looks as though your sister will be sent to a secure unit to
receive treatment, initially here in Italy but in all probability she'll
soon be sent back to Australia to complete her recovery.'

'And when Silvia Roseland found out what her husband and
Nelson had done, she killed both men?' It was clear that Adam's
birdlike partner, Emily, was still struggling to come to terms with
what had happened. I had spoken to her today at the funeral for
the very first time and I had taken a liking to her. For somebody
connected with the weirdly dysfunctional Hunter family, she
struck me as being particularly grounded, and I felt sure she was
a benign influence on Adam. 'She killed her own husband?'

'Read your Shakespeare; love's a powerful motivator.' As I said
it, I found myself thinking yet again about my own failed
marriage. I felt confident that neither Helen nor I would have
resorted to murder, but there was no doubt that strong feelings
had been aroused towards the end of our relationship. 'William
Roseland made the mistake of boasting to his wife about what he
and Nelson had done, and because she'd been head over heels in
love with Rex Hunter, she freaked out and took revenge on both
men. She's a fit, strong woman and she was well able to smash an
iron bar into her husband's face and then to jam a six-inch chisel
into Nelson's back.'

Virgilio nodded. 'And she's a very good actress. When we

announced that her husband had been murdered, she turned on the tears like opening a tap. We interpreted this as grief at her husband's death, but we now know it was indeed grief, but for another man. She must have been deeply in love with Rex Hunter, and his death caused her to lose all control and set her on the road to revenge. She was a very dangerous woman.'

'You're lucky she didn't kill you too, Dan.' Natalie sounded genuinely concerned for me, which was nice.

'Saved by my faithful hound.' I glanced down again and saw that my faithful hound had now started to drool on my foot, so I hastily passed down a piece of bread before returning my attention to our hostess. 'And what are you going to do now that all the excitement's over? Are you planning on staying in Chianti or going back to Australia?'

'I'm going to stay over here. Now my mum's gone, I have no family to speak of back in Aus and here I've discovered a family I didn't know I had.' She shot Adam a gentle smile. 'Together with my brother, I plan on making the Acquarossa Country Club an even greater success – and there's a vacancy for an accountant and that'll suit me fine. But what about you, Dan? The inspector will go back to work, but you're a free agent, aren't you? Won't you be bored?'

I was about to tell her about my recent offer from the publishers when Virgilio revealed the big decision I had taken on Sunday evening. 'Dan's about to embark on a whole new career. Meet Dan Armstrong, Private Investigator.'

'You're setting up your own detective agency?' Adam's eyes crinkled into a smile. 'You can't give it up, can you?'

'You sound like my ex-wife, but yes, there's something about being a detective.'

'And will you have help?'

I pointed towards the dark shape at my feet. 'Oscar will help me sniff out the truth.'

There was a movement at my feet and a big black nose appeared and rested on my lap. A pair of big brown eyes looked up at me and, for a moment, I swear he winked.

ACKNOWLEDGMENTS

Warmest thanks to my lovely editor Emily Ruston and all the team at Boldwood books, and to the most aptly named proof-reader in the business: Emily Reader.

Special thanks also to my Italian friends, the Lupieri family, for helping me understand the different forces that make up the Italian police system.

MORE FROM T.A. WILLIAMS

We hope you enjoyed reading *Murder In Chianti*. If you did, please leave a review.

If you'd like to gift a copy, this book is also available as an ebook, digital audio download and audiobook CD.

Sign up to T.A. Williams' mailing list for news, competitions and updates on future books.

https://bit.ly/TAWilliamsNewss

Murder in Tuscany, the first in this series, is available now.

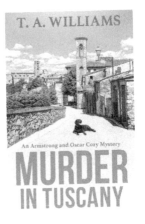

ABOUT THE AUTHOR

T. A. Williams is the author of over twenty bestselling romances for HQ and Canelo and is now turning his hand to cosy crime, set in his beloved Italy, for Boldwood. The series introduces us to to DCI Armstrong and his labrador Oscar. Trevor lives in Devon with his Italian wife.

Visit T. A. Williams' website:

http://www.tawilliamsbooks.com

Follow T. A. Williams' on social media:

twitter.com/TAWilliamsBooks

facebook.com/TrevorWilliamsBooks

Boldw∞d

Boldwood Books is an award-winning fiction publishing company seeking out the best stories from around the world.

Find out more at www.boldwoodbooks.com

Join our reader community for brilliant books, competitions and offers!

Follow us
@BoldwoodBooks
@BookandTonic

Sign up to our weekly deals newsletter

https://bit.ly/BoldwoodBNewsletter

Poison
& Pens

POISON & PENS IS THE HOME OF
COZY MYSTERIES SO POUR YOURSELF
A CUP OF TEA & GET SLEUTHING!

DISCOVER PAGE-TURNING NOVELS FROM
YOUR FAVOURITE AUTHORS &
MEET NEW FRIENDS

JOIN OUR
FACEBOOK GROUP

BIT.LYPOISONANDPENSFB

SIGN UP TO OUR
NEWSLETTER

BIT.LY/POISONANDPENSNEWS

Made in the USA
Middletown, DE
31 August 2024